Mistletoe Magic

Christmas is always a magical time when special things can happen. This year our heroes and heroines weave an emotional and romantic spell over the whole proceedings.

Prepare to be enchanted! For Theodosia, Christmas brings the kind of man that she can only dream about. Be swept away to Christmas in the Australian Outback, where a husband and wife are reunited to discover that they really do have a marriage worth keeping. Experience all the special warmth of the season, and keep a handkerchief nearby, as two people find love in rescuing a little girl who has never heard of Christmas.

Wishing you all a magical Christmas, with seasons greetings from

Betty Neels   *Margaret Way*
Rebecca Winters

Betty Neels spent her childhood and youth in Devonshire before training as a nurse and midwife. She was an army nursing sister during the war, married a Dutchman and subsequently lived in Holland for fourteen years. She lives with her husband in Dorset, and has a daughter and grandson. Her hobbies are reading, animals, old buildings and writing. Betty started to write on retirement from nursing, incited by a lady in a library bemoaning the lack of romantic novels.

Margaret Way takes great pleasure in her work and works hard at her pleasure. She enjoys tearing off to the beach with her family on weekends, loves haunting galleries and auctions and is completely enamoured of French champagne "for every possible joyous occasion." Her home, perched high on a hill overlooking Brisbane, Australia, is her haven. She started writing when her son was a baby, and now she finds there is no better way to spend her time.

Rebecca Winters, an American writer and mother of four, is a graduate of the University of Utah. She has also studied at schools in Switzerland and France, including the Sorbonne. Rebecca recently gave up teaching French and Spanish to junior high school students in order to write novels full-time. She's already researching the background for her next romance!

BETTY NEELS
MARGARET WAY
REBECCA WINTERS

Mistletoe
Magic

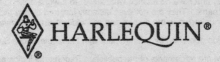

HARLEQUIN®

TORONTO • NEW YORK • LONDON
AMSTERDAM • PARIS • SYDNEY • HAMBURG
STOCKHOLM • ATHENS • TOKYO • MILAN • MADRID
PRAGUE • WARSAW • BUDAPEST • AUCKLAND

ISBN 0-373-83440-3

MISTLETOE MAGIC

Copyright © 2000 by Harlequin Books S.A.

The publisher acknowledges the copyright holders of the individual works as follows:

A CHRISTMAS ROMANCE
Copyright © 1999 by Betty Neels

OUTBACK CHRISTMAS
Copyright © 1999 by Margaret Way

SARAH'S FIRST CHRISTMAS
Copyright © 1999 by Rebecca Winters

This edition published by arrangement with Harlequin Books S.A.

® and TM are trademarks of the publisher. Trademarks indicated with ® are registered in the United States Patent and Trademark Office, the Canadian Trade Marks Office and in other countries.

Visit us at www.eHarlequin.com

Printed in U.S.A.

CONTENTS

CONTENTS

A Christmas Romance
Betty Neels

Dear Reader,

Christmas once again. A time of goodwill, family gatherings and all the excitement of giving and receiving gifts, singing carols and the midnight service on Christmas Eve. And a perfect time for romance and falling in love, just as Theodosia does in London.

But it doesn't need to be London. Romance is everywhere, even if, like Theodosia, one may not know it. Who knows what is just around the next corner?

A very happy Christmas to you all.

Betty Neels

CHAPTER ONE

THEODOSIA CHAPMAN, climbing the first of the four flights which led to her bed-sitter—or, as her landlady called it, her studio flat—reviewed her day with a jaundiced eye. Miss Prescott, the senior dietician at St Alwyn's hospital, an acidulated spinster of an uncertain age, had found fault with everyone and everything. As Theodosia, working in a temporary capacity as her personal assistant, had been with her for most of the day, she'd had more than her share of grumbles. And it was only Monday; there was a whole week before Saturday and Sunday...

She reached the narrow landing at the top of the house, unlocked her door and closed it behind her with a sigh of contentment. The room was quite large with a sloping ceiling and a small window opening onto the flat roof of the room below hers. There was a small gas stove in one corner with shelves and a cupboard and a gas fire against the wall opposite the window.

The table and chairs were shabby but there were bright cushions, plants in pots and some pleasant pictures on the walls. There was a divan along the end wall, with a bright cover, and a small bedside table close by with a pretty lamp. Sitting upright in the centre of the divan was a large and handsome ginger cat. He got down as Theodosia went in, trotted to meet her and she picked him up to perch him on her shoulder.

'I've had a beastly day, Gustavus. We must make up for it—we'll have supper early. You go for a breath of air while I open a tin.'

She took him to the window and he slipped out onto the roof to prowl among the tubs and pots she had arranged there. She watched him pottering for a moment. It was dark and cold, only to be expected since it was a mere five weeks to Christmas, but the lamplight was cheerful. As soon as he came in she would close the window and the curtains and light the gas fire.

She took off her coat and hung it on the hook behind the curtain where she kept her clothes and peered at her face in the small square mirror over the chest of drawers. Her reflection stared back at her—not pretty, perhaps, but almost so, for she had large, long-lashed eyes, which were grey and not at all to her taste, but they went well with her ginger hair, which was straight and long and worn in a neat topknot. Her mouth was too large but its corners turned up and her nose was just a nose, although it had a tilt at its tip.

She turned away, a girl of middle height with a pretty figure and nice legs and a lack of conceit about her person. Moreover, she was possessed of a practical nature which allowed her to accept her rather dull life at least with tolerance, interlarded with a strong desire to change it if she saw the opportunity to do so. And that for the moment didn't seem very likely.

She had no special qualifications; she could type and take shorthand, cope adequately with a word processor and a computer and could be relied upon, but none of these added up to much. Really, it was just as well that Miss Prescott used her for most of the day to run errands, answer the phone and act as go-between for that lady and any member of the medical or nursing staff who dared to query her decisions about a diet.

Once Mrs Taylor returned from sick leave then Theodosia supposed that she would return to the typing pool. She didn't like that very much either but, as she reminded herself with her usual good sense, beggars couldn't be choosers. She managed on her salary although the last few days of the month were always dicey and there was very little chance to save.

Her mother and father had died within a few weeks of each other, victims of flu, several years ago. She had been nineteen, on the point of starting to train as a physiotherapist, but there hadn't been enough money to see her through the training. She had taken a business course and their doctor had heard of a job in the typing pool at St Alwyn's. It had been a lifeline, but unless she could acquire more skills she knew that she had little chance of leaving the job. She would be twenty-five on her next birthday...

She had friends, girls like herself, and from time to time she had been out with one or other of the young doctors, but she encountered them so seldom that friendships died for lack of meetings. She had family, too—two great-aunts, her father's aunts—who lived in a comfortable red-brick cottage at Finchingfield. She spent her Christmases with them, and an occasional weekend, but although they were kind to her she sensed that she interfered with their lives and was only asked to stay from a sense of duty.

She would be going there for Christmas, she had received their invitation that morning, written in the fine spiky writing of their youth.

Gustavus came in then and she shut the window and drew the curtains against the dark outside and set about getting their suppers. That done and eaten, the pair of them curled up in the largest of the two shabby chairs by the gas fire and while Gustavus dozed Theodosia read her library book. The music on the radio was soothing and the room with its pink lampshades looked cosy. She glanced round her.

'At least we have a very nice home,' she told Gustavus, who twitched a sleepy whisker in reply.

Perhaps Miss Prescott would be in a more cheerful mood, thought Theodosia, trotting along the wet pavements to work in the morning. At least she didn't have to catch a bus; her bed-sitter might not be fashionable but it was handy...

The hospital loomed large before her, red-brick with a great many Victorian embellishments. It had a grand entrance, rows and rows of windows and a modern section built onto one side where the Emergency and Casualty departments were housed.

Miss Prescott had her office on the top floor, a large room lined with shelves piled high with reference books, diet sheets and files. She sat at an important-looking desk, with a computer, two telephones and a large open notebook filled with the lore of her profession, and she looked as important as her desk. She was a big woman with commanding features and a formidable bosom—a combination of attributes which aided her to triumph over any person daring to have a difference of opinion with her.

Theodosia had a much smaller desk in a kind of cubby-hole with its door open so that Miss Prescott could demand her services at a moment's notice. Which one must admit were very frequent. Theodosia might not do anything important—like making out diet sheets for several hundreds of people, many of them different—but she did her share, typing endless lists, menus, diet sheets, and rude letters to ward sisters if they complained. In a word, Miss Prescott held the hospital's stomach in the hollow of her hand.

She was at her desk as Theodosia reached her office.

'You're late.'

'Two minutes, Miss Prescott,' said Theodosia cheerfully. 'The lift's not working and I had five flights of stairs to climb.'

'At your age that should be an easy matter. Get the post opened, if you please.' Miss Prescott drew a deep indignant breath which made her corsets creak. 'I am having trouble with the Women's Medical ward sister. She has the impertinence to disagree with the diet I have formulated for that patient with diabetes and kidney failure. I have spoken to her on the telephone and when I have rewritten the diet sheet you will take it down to her. She is to keep to my instructions on it. You may tell her that.'

Theodosia began to open the post, viewing without relish the prospect of being the bearer of unwelcome news. Miss Prescott, she had quickly learned, seldom confronted any of those who had the temerity to disagree with her. Accordingly, some half an hour later she took the diet sheet and began her journey to Women's Medical on the other side of the hospital and two floors down.

Sister was in her office, a tall, slender, good-looking woman in her early thirties. She looked up and smiled as Theodosia knocked.

'Don't tell me, that woman's sent you down with another diet sheet. We had words...!'

'Yes, she mentioned that, Sister. Shall I wait should you want to write a reply?'

'Did she give you a message as well?'

'Well, yes, but I don't think I need to give it to you. I mean, I think she's already said it all...'

Sister laughed. 'Let's see what she says this time...'

She was reading it when the door opened and

she glanced up and got to her feet. 'Oh, sir, you're early…'

The man who entered was very large and very tall so that Sister's office became half its size. His hair was a pale brown, greying at the temples, and he was handsome, with heavy-lidded eyes and a high-bridged nose upon which was perched a pair of half glasses. All of which Theodosia noticed with an interested eye. She would have taken a longer look only she caught his eye—blue and rather cold—and looked the other way.

He wished Sister good morning and raised one eyebrow at Theodosia. 'I'm interrupting something?' he asked pleasantly.

'No, no, sir. Miss Prescott and I are at odds about Mrs Bennett's diet. They sent Theodosia down with the diet sheet she insists is the right one…'

He held out a hand and took the paper from her and read it.

'You do right to query it, Sister. I think that I had better have a word with Miss Prescott. I will do so now and return here in a short while.'

He looked at Theodosia and opened the door. 'Miss—er—Theodosia shall return with me and see fair play.'

She went with him since it was expected of her,

though she wasn't sure about the fair play; Miss Prescott usually made mincemeat of anyone disagreeing with her, but she fancied that this man, whoever he was, might not take kindly to such treatment.

Theodosia, skipping along beside him to keep up, glanced up at his impassive face. 'You work here too?' she asked, wanting only to be friendly. 'This is such a big place I hardly ever meet the same person twice, if you see what I mean. I expect you're a doctor—well, a senior doctor, I suppose. I expect you've met Miss Prescott before?'

There were climbing the stairs at a great rate. 'You'll have to slow down,' said Theodosia, 'if you want me to be there at the same time as you.'

He paused to look down at her. 'My apologies, young lady, but I have no time to waste loitering on a staircase.'

Which she considered was a rather unkind remark. She said tartly, 'Well, I haven't any time to waste either.'

They reached Miss Prescott's office in silence and he opened the door for her. Miss Prescott didn't look up.

'You took your time. I shall be glad when Mrs Taylor returns. What had Sister to say this time?'

She looked up then and went slowly red. 'Oh—you need my advice, sir?'

He walked up to her desk, tore the diet sheet he held into several pieces and laid them on the blotter before her. He said quietly, 'Miss Prescott, I have no time to waste with people who go against my orders. The diet is to be exactly as I have asked for. You are a dietician, but you have no powers to overrule the medical staff's requests for a special diet. Be so good as to remember that.'

He went quietly out of the room, leaving Miss Prescott gobbling with silent rage. Theodosia studied her alarmingly puce complexion. 'Shall I make a cup of tea?'

'No—yes. I'm upset. That man...'

'I thought he was rather nice,' said Theodosia, 'and he was very polite.'

Miss Prescott ground her teeth. 'Do you know who he is?'

Theodosia, putting teabags into the teapot, said that no, she didn't.

'Professor Bendinck. He's senior consultant on the medical side, is on the board of governers, has an enormous private practice and is an authority on most medical conditions.'

'Quite a lad!' said Theodosia cheerfully. 'Don't you like him?'

Miss Prescott snorted. 'Like him? Why should I like him? He could get me the sack today if he wanted to.' She snapped her mouth shut; she had said too much already.

'I shouldn't worry,' said Theodosia quietly. She didn't like Miss Prescott, but it was obvious that she had had a nasty shock. 'I'm sure he's not mean enough to do that.'

'You don't know anything about him,' snapped Miss Prescott, and took the proffered cup of tea without saying thank you. Theodosia, pouring herself a cup, reflected that she would rather like to know more about him...

The day was rather worse than Monday had been, and, letting herself into her bed-sitter that evening, she heaved a sigh of relief. A quiet evening with Gustavus for company...

There was another letter from her aunts. She was invited to spend the following weekend with them. They had read in their newspaper that the air in London had become very polluted—a day or two in the country air would be good for her. She was expected for lunch on Saturday. It was more of a command than an invitation and Theodosia, although she didn't particulary want to go, knew that she would, for the aunts were all the family she had now.

The week, which had begun badly, showed no signs of improving; Miss Prescott, taking a jaundiced view of life, made sure that everyone around her should feel the same. As the weekend approached Theodosia wished that she could have spent it quietly getting up late and eating when she felt like it, lolling around with the papers. A weekend with the great-aunts was hardly restful. Gustavus hated it—the indignity of the basket, the tiresome journey by bus and train and then another bus; and, when they did arrive, he was only too aware that he wasn't really welcome, only Theodosia had made it plain that if she spent her weekends with her great-aunts then he must go too...

It was Friday morning when, racing round the hospital collecting diet sheets from the wards, Theodosia ran full tilt into the professor, or rather his waistcoat. He fielded her neatly, collected the shower of diet sheets and handed them back to her.

'So sorry,' said Theodosia. 'Wasn't looking where I was going, was I?'

Her ginger head caught fire from a stray shaft of winter sunshine and the professor admired it silently. She was like a spring morning in the middle of winter, he reflected, and frowned at the nonsensical thought.

'Such a rush,' said Theodosia chattily. 'It's always the same on a Friday.'

The professor adjusted the spectacles on his nose and asked, 'Why is that?'

'Oh, the weekend, you know, patients going home and Sister's weekend, too, on a lot of the wards.'

'Oh, yes, I see.' The professor didn't see at all, but he had a wish to stay talking to this friendly girl who treated him like a human being and not like the important man he was. He asked casually, 'And you, miss...er... Do you also go home for the weekend?'

'Well, not exactly. What I mean is, I do have the weekend off, but I haven't got a home with a family, if that's what you mean. I've got quite a nice bed-sitter.'

'No family?'

'Two great-aunts; they have me for weekends sometimes. I'm going there tomorrow.'

'And where is "there"?' He had a quiet, rather deliberate voice, the kind of voice one felt compelled to answer.

'Finchingfield. That's in Essex.'

'You drive yourself there?'

Theodosia laughed. 'Me? Drive? Though I can ride a bike, I haven't a car. But it's quite easy—

bus to the station, train to Braintree and then the local bus. I quite enjoy it, only Gustavus hates it.'

'Gustavus?'

'My cat. He dislikes buses and trains. Well, of course, he would, wouldn't he?'

The professor agreed gravely. He said slowly, 'It so happens that I am going to Braintree tomorrow. I'd be glad to give you and Gustavus a lift.'

'You are? Well, what a coincidence; that would be…' She stopped and blushed vividly. 'I didn't mean to cadge a lift off you. You're very kind to offer but I think I'd better not.'

'I'm quite safe,' said the professor mildly, 'and since you didn't know that I would be going to Braintree in the morning you could hardly be accused of cadging.'

'Well, if you don't mind—I would be grateful…'

'Good.' He smiled then and walked away and she, remembering the rest of the diet sheets, raced off to the men's ward… It was only as she handed over the rest of the diet sheets to Miss Prescott that she remembered that he hadn't asked her where she lived nor had he said at what time he would pick her up. So that's that, reflected Theodosia, scarcely listening to Miss Prescott's cross voice.

If she had hoped for a message from him during

the day she was to be disappointed. Five o'clock came and half an hour later—for, of course, Miss Prescott always found something else for her to do just as she was leaving—Theodosia raced through the hospital, intent on getting home, and was brought up short by the head porter hailing her from his lodge in the entrance hall.

'Message for you, miss. You're to be ready by ten o'clock. You'll be fetched from where you live.'

He peered at her over his spectacles. 'That's what Professor Bendinck said.'

Theodosia had slithered to a halt. 'Oh, thank you, Bowden,' she said, and added, 'He's giving me a lift.'

The head porter liked her. She was always cheerful and friendly. 'And very nice too, miss,' he said. 'Better than them trains and buses.'

Theodosia, explaining to Gustavus that they would be travelling in comfort instead of by the public transport he so disliked, wondered what kind of car the professor would have. Something rather staid, suitable for his dignified calling, she supposed. She packed her overnight bag, washed her hair and polished her shoes. Her winter coat was by no means new but it had been good when she had bought it and she consoled herself with the thought that winter coats didn't change their style too much. It would have to be the green jersey dress...

At ten o'clock the next morning she went down to the front door with Gustavus in his basket and her overnight bag over her shoulder. She would give him ten minutes, she had decided, and if he didn't turn up she would get a bus to Liverpool Street Station.

He was on the doorstep, talking to Mrs Towzer, who had a head crammed with pink plastic curlers and a feather duster in one hand. When she saw Theodosia she said, 'There you are, ducks; I was just telling your gentleman friend here that you was a good tenant. A real lady—don't leave the landing lights on all night and leaves the bath clean...'

Theodosia tried to think of something clever to say. She would have been grateful if the floor had opened and swallowed her. She said, 'Good morning, Mrs Towzer—Professor.'

'Professor, are you?' asked the irrepressible Mrs Towzer. 'Well, I never...'

Theodosia had to admire the way he handled Mrs Towzer with a grave courtesy which left that lady preening herself and allowed him to stuff Theodosia into the car, put her bag in the boot,

settle Gustavus on the back seat with a speed
which took her breath and then drive off with a
wave of the hand to her landlady.

Theodosia said tartly, 'It would have been much
better if I had gone to the hospital and met you
there.'

He said gently, 'You are ashamed of your landlady?'

'Heavens, no! She's kind-hearted and good-
natured, only there really wasn't any need to tell
you about turning off the lights…'

'And cleaning the bath!' To his credit the professor adopted a matter-of-fact manner. 'I believe
she was paying you a compliment.'

Theodosia laughed, then said, 'Perhaps you are
right. This is a very comfortable car.'

It was a Bentley, dark grey, with its leather up-
holstery a shade lighter.

'I expect you need a comfortable car,' she went
on chattily. 'I mean, you can't have much time to
catch buses and things.'

'A car is a necessity for my job. You're warm
enough? I thought we might stop for coffee presently. At what time do your great-aunts expect
you?'

'If I don't miss the bus at Braintree I'm there in

time for lunch. But I'll catch it today; I don't expect it takes long to drive there.'

He was driving north-east out of the city. 'If you will direct me I will take you to Finchingfield; it is only a few miles out of my way.'

She looked at his calm profile uncertainly; without his specs he was really very handsome... 'You're very kind but I'm putting you out.'

'If that were the case I would not have suggested it,' he told her. A remark which she felt had put her in her place. She said meekly, 'Thank you,' and didn't see him smile.

Clear out of the city at last, he drove to Bishop's Stortford and turned off for Great Dunmow, and stopped there for coffee. They had made good time and Theodosia, enjoying his company, wished that their journey were not almost at an end. Finchingfield was only a few miles away and all too soon he stopped in front of the great-aunts' house.

It stood a little way from the centre of the village, in a narrow lane with no other houses nearby; it was a red-brick house, too large to be called a cottage, with a plain face and a narrow brick path leading from the gate to its front door. The professor got out, opened Theodosia's door, collected her bag and Gustavus in his basket and opened the gate and followed her up the path. He put the bag and the basket down. 'I'll call for you at about half past six tomorrow, if that isn't too early for you?'

'You'll drive me back? You're sure it's not disturbing your weekend?'

'Quite sure. I hope you enjoy your visit, Theodosia.'

He went back to the car and got in, and sat waiting until she had banged the door knocker and the door was opened. And then he had gone.

Mrs Trickey, the aunt's daily housekeeper, opened the door. She was a tall, thin woman, middle-aged, with a weather-beaten face, wearing an old-fashioned pinny and a battered hat.

'You're early.' She craned her neck around Theodosia and watched the tail-end of the car disappear down the lane. ''Oo's that, then?'

Mrs Trickey had been looking after the aunts for as long as Theodosia could remember and considered herself one of the household. Theodosia said cheerfully, 'Hello, Mrs Trickey; how nice to see you. I was given a lift by someone from the hospital.'

The housekeeper stood aside to let her enter and then went ahead of her down the narrow, rather dark hall. She opened a door at its end, saying, 'Go on in; your aunts are expecting you.'

The room was quite large, with a big window

overlooking the garden at the back of the house. It was lofty-ceilinged, with a rather hideous wallpaper, and the furniture was mostly heavy and dark, mid-Victorian, and there was far too much of it. Rather surprisingly, here and there, were delicate Regency pieces, very beautiful and quite out of place.

The two old ladies got up from their places as Theodosia went in. They were tall and thin with ramrod backs and white-haired, but there the resemblance ended.

Great-Aunt Jessica was the elder, a once handsome woman with a sweet smile, her hair arranged in what looked like a bird's nest and wearing a high-necked blouse under a cardigan and a skirt which would have been fashionable at the turn of the century. It was of good material and well made and Theodosia couldn't imagine her aunt wearing anything else.

Great-Aunt Mary bore little resemblance to her elder sister; her hair was drawn back from her face into a neat coil on top of her head and although she must have been pretty when she was young her narrow face, with its thin nose and thin mouth, held little warmth.

Theodosia kissed their proffered cheeks, explained that she had been driven from London by

an acquaintance at the hospital and would be called
for on the following evening, and then enquired
about the old ladies' health.

They were well, they told her, and who exactly
was this acquaintance?

Theodosia explained a little more, just enough
to satisfy them and nip any idea that Mrs Trickey
might have had in the bud. The fact that the professor was a professor helped; her aunts had had a
brother, be-whiskered and stern, who had been a
professor of something or other and it was obvious
that the title conferred respectability onto anyone
who possessed it. She was sent away to go to her
room and tidy herself and Gustavus was settled in
the kitchen in his basket. He didn't like the aunts'
house; no one was unkind to him but no one talked
to him except Theodosia. Only at night, when
everyone was in bed, she crept down and carried
him back to spend the night with her.

Lunch was eaten in the dining room, smaller
than the drawing room and gloomy by nature of
the one small window shrouded in dark red curtains and the massive mahogany sideboard which
took up too much space. The old ladies still main-
tained the style of their youth; the table was covered with a starched white linen cloth, the silver
was old and well polished and the meal was served

on china which had belonged to their parents. The food didn't live up to the table appointments, however; the aunts didn't cook and Mrs Trickey's culinary skill was limited. Theodosia ate underdone beef, potatoes and cabbage, and Stilton cheese and biscuits, and answered her aunts' questions...

After lunch, sitting in the drawing room between them, she did her best to tell them of her days. Aunt Jessica's questions were always kind but Aunt Mary sometimes had a sharp tongue. She was fond of them both; they had always been kind although she felt that it was from a sense of duty. At length their questions came to an end and the subject of Christmas was introduced.

'Of course, you will spend it here with us, my dear,' said Great-Aunt Jessica. 'Mrs Trickey will prepare everything for us on Christmas Eve as she usually does and I have ordered the turkey from Mr Greenhorn. We shall make the puddings next week...'

'We are so fortunate,' observed Great-Aunt Mary. 'When one thinks of the many young girls who are forced to spend Christmas alone...' Which Theodosia rightly deduced was a remark intended to remind her how lucky she was to have the festive season in the bosom of her family.

At half past four exactly she helped Mrs Trickey

bring in the tea tray and the three of them sat at a small table and ate cake and drank tea from delicate china teacups. After the table had been cleared, they played three-handed whist, with an interval so that they could listen to the news. There was no television; the aunts did not approve of it.

After Mrs Trickey had gone home, Theodosia went into the kitchen and got supper. A cold supper, of course, since the aunts had no wish to cook, and once that was eaten she was told quite kindly that she should go to bed; she had had a long journey and needed her rest. It was chilly upstairs, and the bathroom, converted years ago from one of the bedrooms, was far too large, with a bath in the middle of the room. The water wasn't quite hot so she didn't waste time there but jumped into bed, reminding herself that when she came at Christmas she must bring her hot-water bottle with her...

She lay awake for a while, listening to the old ladies going to their beds and thinking about the professor. What was he doing? she wondered. Did he live somewhere near Finchingfield? Did he have a wife and children with whom he would spend Christmas? She enlarged upon the idea; he would have a pretty wife, always beautifully dressed, and two or three charming children. She nodded off as she added a dog and a couple of cats to his house-

hold and woke several hours later with cold feet
and thoughts of Gustavus, lonely in the kitchen.

She crept downstairs and found him sitting on
one of the kitchen chairs, looking resigned. He was
more than willing to return to her room with her
and curl up on the bed. He was better than a hot-
water bottle and she slept again until early morning, just in time to take him back downstairs before
she heard her aunts stirring.

Sunday formed a well-remembered pattern:
breakfast with Mrs Trickey, still in a hat, cooking
scrambled eggs, and then church. The aunts wore
beautifully tailored coats and skirts, made exactly
as they had been for the last fifty years or so, and
felt hats, identical in shape and colour, crowning
their heads. Theodosia was in her winter coat and
wearing the small velvet hat she kept especially for
her visits to Finchingfield.

The church was beautiful and the flowers decorating it scented the chilly air. Although the congregation wasn't large, it sang the hymns tunefully.
And after the service there was the slow progress
to the church porch, greeting neighbours and
friends and finally the rector, and then the walk
back to the house.

Lunch, with the exception of the boiled vegetables, was cold. Mrs Trickey went home after

breakfast on Sundays, and the afternoon was spent sitting in the drawing room reading the *Sunday Times* and commenting on the various activities in the village. Theodosia got the tea and presently cleared it away and washed the china in the great stone sink in the scullery, then laid the table for the aunts' supper. It was cold again so, unasked, she found a can of soup and put it ready to heat up.

She filled their hot-water bottles, too, and popped them into their beds. Neither of them approved of what they called the soft modern way of living—indeed, they seemed to enjoy their spartan way of living—but Theodosia's warm heart wished them to be warm at least.

The professor arrived at exactly half past six and Theodosia, admitting him, asked rather shyly if he would care to meet her aunts, and led the way to the drawing room.

Great-Aunt Jessica greeted him graciously and Great-Aunt Mary less so; there was no beard, though she could find no fault with his beautiful manners. He was offered refreshment, which he declined with the right amount of regret, then he assured the old ladies that he would drive carefully, expressed pleasure at having met them, picked up

Gustavus's basket and Theodosia's bag and took his leave, sweeping her effortlessly before him.

The aunts, in total approval of him, accompanied them to the door with the wish, given in Great-Aunt Jessica's rather commanding voice, that he might visit them again. 'You will be most welcome when you come again with Theodosia,' she told him.

Theodosia wished herself anywhere but where she was, sitting beside him in his car again. After a silence which lasted too long she said, 'My aunts are getting old. I did explain that I had accepted a lift from you, that I didn't actually know you, but that you are at the hospital...'

The professor had left the village behind, making for the main road. He said impassively, 'It is only natural that they should wish to know who I am. And who knows? I might have the occasion to come this way again.'

Which somehow made everything all right again. In any case she had discovered it was hard to feel shy or awkward with him. 'Did you enjoy your weekend?' she wanted to know.

'Very much. And you? A couple of quiet days away from the hospital can be just what one needs from time to time.'

Perhaps not quite as quiet as two days with the

great-aunts, reflected Theodosia, and felt ashamed
for thinking it for they must find her visits tiresome, upsetting their quiet lives.

'Shall we stop for a meal?' asked the professor.
'Unless you're anxious to get back? There is a
good place at Great Dunmow. I'll have to go
straight to the hospital and won't have time to eat.'

'You don't have to work on a Sunday evening?'
asked Theodosia, quite shocked.

'No, no, but I want to check on a patient—Mrs
Bennett. It will probably be late by the time I get
home.'

'Well, of course we must stop,' said Theodosia.
'You can't go without your meals, especially when
you work all hours.' She added honestly, 'I'm
quite hungry, too.'

'Splendid. I could hardly eat a steak while you
nibbled at a lettuce leaf.'

He stopped in the market place at Great
Dunmow and ushered her into the Starr restaurant.
It was a pleasing place, warm and very welcoming,
and the food was splendid. While the professor ate
his steak, Theodosia enjoyed a grilled sole, and
they both agreed that the bread and butter pudding
which followed was perfection. They lingered over
coffee until Theodosia said, 'We really ought to go
or you'll never get to bed tonight, not if you are

going to see your patient when we get back. It's after nine o'clock…'

The professor ignored the time for he was enjoying himself; Theodosia was good company. She was outspoken, which amused him, and, unlike other girls in his acquaintance, she was content with her lot and happy. And she made him laugh. It was a pity that once they got back to London he would probably not see her again; their paths were unlikely to cross.

The rest of their journey went too swiftly; he listened to Theodosia's cheerful voice giving her opinion on this, that and the other, and reflected that she hadn't once talked about herself. When they reached Mrs Towzer's house, he got out, opened her car door, collected Gustavus in his basket and her bag and followed her up the stairs to her attic. He didn't go in—she hadn't invited him anyway—but she offered a hand and thanked him for her supper and the journey. 'I enjoyed every minute of it,' she assured him, looking up at him with her gentle grey eyes. 'And I do hope you won't be too late going to bed. You need your rest.'

He smiled then, bade her a quiet goodnight, and went away, back down the stairs.

CHAPTER TWO

MONDAY morning again, and a cold one. Theodosia, going shivering to the bathroom on the floor below, envied Gustavus, curled up cosily on the divan. And there was a cold sleet falling as she went to work. A cheerful girl by nature, Theodosia was hard put to view the day ahead with any equanimity. But there was something to look forward to, she reminded herself; the hospital ball was to be held on Saturday and she was going with several of the clerical staff of the hospital.

She hadn't expected that she would be asked to go with any of the student doctors or the young men who worked in the wages department. She was on good terms with them all but there were any number of pretty girls from whom they could choose partners. All the same, when she had gone to earlier years' balls, she had had partners enough for she danced well.

She would need a new dress; she had worn the only one she had on three successive years. She pondered the problem during the day. She couldn't afford a new dress—that was quite out of the question—but someone had told her that the Oxfam shops in the more fashionable shopping streets quite often yielded treasures...

On Tuesday, she skipped her midday dinner, begged an extra hour of Miss Prescott and took a bus to Oxford Street.

The professor, caught in a traffic jam and inured to delays, passed the time glancing idly around him. There was plenty to catch his eye; shoppers thronged the pavement and the shop windows were brilliantly lighted. It was the sight of a gleaming ginger head of hair which caught his attention. There surely weren't two girls with hair that colour...?

The Oxfam lights were of the no-nonsense variety; the shopper could see what he or she was buying. Theodosia, plucking a dove-grey dress off the rails, took it to the window to inspect it better and he watched her as she examined it carefully—the label, the price tag, the seams... It was a pity that the traffic moved at last and he drove on, aware of an unexpected concern that she should be forced to buy someone else's dress.

Theodosia, happily unaware that she had been seen, took the dress home that evening, tried it on and nipped down to the bathroom where there was a full-length mirror. It would do; she would have to take it in here and there and the neck was too low. She brought out her work basket, found a needle and thread and set to. She was handy with her needle but it took a couple of evenings' work till she was satisfied that it would pass muster.

It wasn't as though she was going with a partner, she reminded herself. There would be a great many people there; no one would notice her. Miss Prescott would be going, of course, but any mention of the ball during working hours was sternly rebuked and when Theodosia had asked her what she would be wearing she'd been told not to be impertinent. Theodosia, who had meant it kindly, felt hurt.

She dressed carefully on Saturday evening. The grey dress, viewed in the bathroom looking-glass by the low-wattage bulb, looked all right. A pity she couldn't have afforded a pair of those strappy sandals. Her slippers were silver kid and out of date but at least they were comfortable. She gave Gustavus his supper, made sure that he was warm and comfortable on the divan, and walked to the hospital wrapped in her winter coat and, since it was drizzling, sheltered under her umbrella.

The hospital courtyard was packed with cars for this was an evening when the hospital Board of Governers and their wives, the local Mayor and his wife and those dignitaries who were in some way connected to St Alwyn's came to grace the occasion. Theodosia slipped in through a side door, found her friends, left her coat with theirs in a small room the cleaners used to store their buckets and brooms and went with them to the Assembly Hall where the ball was already under way.

It looked very festive, with paper chains and a Christmas tree in a corner of the stage where the orchestra was. There were balloons and holly and coloured lights and already there were a great many people dancing. Once there, one by one her friends were claimed and she herself was swept onto the dance floor by one of the technicians from the path lab. She didn't know him well and he was a shocking dancer but it was better than hovering on the fringe of the dancers, looking as though dancing was the last thing one wanted to do.

When the band stopped, one of the students with whom she had passed the time of day occasionally claimed her. It was a slow foxtrot and he had time to tell her about the post-mortem he had attended that morning. She listened carefully, feeling slightly sick, but aware that he was longing to talk about it to someone. There were several encores, so that it was possible for him to relate the very last of the horrid details. When the band stopped finally and he offered to fetch her a drink she accepted thankfully.

She had seen the professor at once, dancing with an elegantly dressed woman, and then again with the sister from Women's Medical and for a third time with the Mayor's wife.

And he had seen her, for there was no mistaking that gingery head of hair. When he had danced with all the ladies he was expected to dance with, he made his way round the dancers until he came upon her, eating an ice in the company of the hospital engineer.

He greeted them both pleasantly, and after a few moments of talk with the engineer swept her onto the dance floor.

'You should ask me first,' said Theodosia.

'You might have refused! Are you enjoying yourself?'

'Yes, thank you.' And she was, for he danced well and they were slow foxtrotting again. The hospital dignitaries wouldn't allow any modern dancing; there was no dignity in prancing around waving arms and flinging oneself about…but foxtrotting with a woman you liked was very satisfying, he reflected.

The professor, his eye trained to see details at a glance, had recognised the grey dress. It was pretty in a demure way but it wasn't her size. He could see the tucks she had taken on the shoulders to make a better fit and the neat seams she had taken in at the waist. It would be a pleasure to take her to a good dress shop and buy her clothes which fitted her person and which were new. He smiled at the absurd thought and asked her with impersonal kindness if she was looking forward to Christmas.

'Oh, yes, and it will be three days this year because of Sunday coming in between.' She sounded more enthusiastic than she felt; three days with the aunts wasn't a very thrilling prospect, but she reminded herself that that was ungrateful. She added, by way of apology for thinking unkindly of them, 'The great-aunts enjoy an old-fashioned Christmas.'

He could make what he liked of that; it conjured up pictures of a lighted Christmas tree, masses of food and lots of presents; with a party on Boxing Day...

She underestimated the professor's good sense; he had a very shrewd idea what her Christmas would be like. He glanced down at the ginger top-knot. It would be a mistake to pity her; she had no need of that. He had never met anyone so content with life and so willing to be happy as she, but he found himself wishing that her Christmas might be different.

He resisted the urge to dance with her for the rest of the evening, handed her back to the engineer and spent the next few moments in cheerful talk before leaving her there.

It was at the end of the evening that he went looking for her amongst the milling crowd making their way out of the hospital. She was on her way out of the entrance when he found her. He touched her arm lightly.

'Come along; the car's close by.'

'There's no need... It's only a short walk... I really don't...' She could have saved her breath; she was propelled gently along away from the crowded forecourt, stuffed tidily into the car and told to fasten her seat belt. It was only as he turned out of the forecourt into the street that she tried again. 'This is quite...'

'You're wasting your breath, Theodosia.' And he had nothing more to say until they reached Mrs Towzer's house. No lights were on, of course, and the rather shabby street looked a bit scary in the dark; walking back on her own wouldn't have been very nice...

He got out, opened her door and took the key she had ready in her hand from her, opened the door silently and switched on the dim light in the hall.

Theodosia held out a hand for the key and whispered, 'Thank you for the lift. Goodnight.' And took off her shoes.

The professor closed the door without a sound, picked up her shoes and trod silently behind her as she went upstairs. She was afraid that he might make a noise but he didn't and she had to confess that it was comforting to have him there. Mrs Towzer, with an eye to economy, had installed landing lights which switched off unless one was nippy between landings.

At her own door he took her key, opened the door and switched on the light, gave her back her key and stood aside for her to pass him.

'Thank you very much,' said Theodosia, still whispering. 'Do be careful going downstairs or you'll be left in the dark, and you will shut the street door?'

The professor assured her in a voice as quiet as her own that he would be careful, and bade her goodnight, pushed her gently into the room and closed the door. Back in his car he wondered why he hadn't kissed her; he had very much wanted to.

As for Theodosia, tumbling into bed presently, hugging a tolerant Gustavus, her sleepy head was full of a jumble of delightful thoughts, all of them concerning the professor.

Going for a brisk walk in Victoria Park the following afternoon, she told herself that he had just happened to be there and that common politeness had forced him to give her a lift back. She went home and had a good tea then went to evensong, to pray there for a happy week ahead!

She wasn't sure if it was an answer to her prayers when she received a letter from Great-Aunt Jessica in the morning. She was asked to go to Fortnum & Mason and purchase the items on the enclosed list. 'And you may bring them down next weekend,' wrote her aunt.

Theodosia studied the list: ham on the bone, Gentleman's Relish, smoked salmon, brandy butter, a Stilton cheese, Bath Oliver biscuits, *marrons glacés*, Earl Grey tea, coffee beans, peaches in brandy... Her week's wages would barely pay for them, not that she could afford to do that. She peered into the envelope in the forlorn hope of finding a cheque or at least a few bank notes but it was empty. She would have to go to the bank and draw out the small amount of money she had so painstakingly saved. If she skipped her midday dinner she would have time to go to the bank.

Great-Aunt Jessica would pay her at the weekend and she could put it back into her account.

It wasn't until Wednesday that she had the opportunity to miss her dinner. There was no time to spare, so she hurtled down to the entrance, intent on getting a bus.

The professor, on his way to his car, saw her almost running across the forecourt and cut her off neatly before she could reach the street. She stopped in full flight, unable to get past his massive person.

Theodosia said, 'Hello, Professor,' and then added, 'I can't stop…'

A futile remark with his hand holding her firmly. 'If you're in a hurry, I'll drive you. You can't run to wherever you're going like that.'

'Yes, I can…'

'Where to?'

She had no need to answer his question yet she did. 'The bank and then Fortnum & Mason.'

He turned her round and walked her over to his car. Once inside he said, 'Now tell me why you are in such a hurry to do this.'

He probably used that gentle, compelling voice on his patients, and Theodosia felt compelled once more to answer him. She did so in a rather disjointed manner. 'So, you see, if you don't mind I must catch a bus...'

'I do mind. What exactly do you have to buy?'

She gave him the list. 'You see, everything on it is rather expensive and, of course, Great-Aunt Jessica doesn't bother much about money. She'll pay me at the weekend. That's why I have to go to the bank.'

'That will take up too much time,' said the professor smoothly. 'We will go straight to Fortnum & Mason; I'll pay for these and your aunt can pay me. It just so happens,' he went on in a voice to convince a High Court judge, 'that I am going to Braintree again on Saturday. I'll give you a lift and deliver these things at the same time.'

Theodosia opened her mouth to speak, shut it again and then said, 'But isn't this your lunch hour?'

'Most fortunately, yes; now, let us get this shopping down.'

'Well, if you think it is all right?'

'Perfectly all right and sensible.'

Once there he ushered her in, handed her list over to a polite young man with the request to have the items packed up and ready within the next half an hour or so, and steered her to the restaurant.

'The food department will see to it all,' he told

her. 'So much quicker and in the meantime we can
have something to eat.'

Theodosia found her tongue. 'But ought I not to
choose everything?'

'No, no. Leave everything to the experts; that's
what they are here for. Now, what would you like?
We have about half an hour. An omelette with
French fries and a salad and a glass of white wine?'

It was a delicious meal and all the more delicious because it was unexpected. Theodosia, still
breathless from the speed with which the professor
had organised everything, and not sure if she
hadn't been reckless in allowing him to take over
in such a high-handed manner, decided to enjoy
herself. This was a treat, something which seldom
came her way.

So she ate her lunch, drank the wine and a cup
of coffee and followed him back to the food hall,
to find a box neatly packed and borne out to the
car by the doorman. She was ushered into the car,
too, and told to wait while the professor went back
to pay the bill and tip the doorman .

'How much was it?' asked Theodosia anxiously
as he got in beside her.

'Would it be a good idea,' suggested the professor carefully, 'if I kept this food at my house?

There's not any need to unpack it; everything on the list is there and I have the receipted bill.'

'But why should you do that? It may be a great nuisance for you or your wife…'

'I'm not married, and my housekeeper will stow it safely away until Saturday.'

'Well, if it's really no trouble. And how much was it?'

'I can't remember exactly, but your aunt must have a good idea of what the food costs and the bill seemed very reasonable to me. It's in the boot with the food or I would let you have it.'

'No, no. I'm sure it's all right. And thank you very much.'

He was driving back to the hospital, taking short cuts so that she had still five minutes of her dinner hour left by the time he stopped in the forecourt. She spent two of those thanking him in a muddled speech, smiling at him, full of her delightful lunch and his kindness and worry that she had taken up too much of his time.

'A pleasure,' said the professor, resisting a wish to kiss the tip of her nose. He got out of the car and opened her door and suggested that she had better run.

Despite Miss Prescott's sharp tongue and ill temper, the rest of her day was viewed through rose-coloured spectacles by Theodosia. She wasn't sure why she felt happy; of course, it had been marvellous getting her shopping done so easily and having lunch and the prospect of being driven to the aunts' at the weekend, but it was more than that; it was because the professor had been there. And because he wasn't married.

She saw nothing of him for the rest of the week but on Friday evening as she left the hospital there was a message for her. Would she be good enough to be ready at ten o'clock in the morning? She would be fetched as before. This time there was no mistaking the twinkle in the head porter's eye as he told her. Over the years he had passed on many similar messages but never before from the professor.

'We're going to the aunts' again,' Theodosia told Gustavus. 'In that lovely car. You'll like that, won't you?'

She spent a happy evening getting ready for the morning, washing her hair, examining her face anxiously for spots, doing her nails, and putting everything ready for breakfast in the morning. It would never do to keep the professor waiting.

She went down to the front door punctually in the morning to find him already there, leaning against Mrs Towzer's door, listening to that lady's detailed descriptions of her varicose veins with the same quiet attention he would have given any one of his private patients. Mrs Towzer, seeing Theodosia coming downstairs, paused. 'Well, I'll tell you the rest another time,' she suggested. 'You'll want to be on your way, the pair of you.'

She winked and nodded at him and Theodosia went pink as she wished them both a rather flustered good morning, trying not to see the professor's faint smile. But it was impossible to feel put out once she was sitting beside him as he drove off. Indeed she turned and waved to Mrs Towzer, for it seemed wrong to feel so happy while her landlady was left standing at her shabby front door with nothing but rows of similar shabby houses at which to look.

It was a gloomy morning and cold, with a leaden sky.

'Will it snow?' asked Theodosia.

'Probably, but not just yet. You'll be safely at your great-aunts' by then.'

He glanced at her. 'Will you be going to see them again before Christmas?'

'No, this is an unexpected visit so that I could buy all those things.' In case he was thinking that she was angling for another lift she added, 'I expect you'll be at home for Christmas?'

He agreed pleasantly in a voice which didn't invite more questions so she fell silent. When the silence became rather too long, she began to talk about the weather, that great stand-by of British conversation.

But she couldn't talk about that for ever. She said, 'I won't talk any more; I expect you want to think. You must have a lot on your mind.'

The professor debated with himself whether he should tell her that he had her on his mind, increasingly so with every day that passed. But if he did he would frighten her away. Being friendly was one thing but he sensed that she would fight shy of anything more. He was only too well aware that he was considered by her to be living on a different plane and that their paths would never meet. She was friendly because she was a girl who would be friends with anyone. It was in her nature to be kind and helpful and to like those she met and worked with. Even the redoubtable Miss Prescott.

He said now, 'There is no need to make polite conversation with you, Theodosia; do you not feel the same?'

'Well, yes, I do. I mean, it's nice to be with someone and not have to worry about whether they were wishing you weren't there.'

His rather stern mouth twitched. 'Very well put,

Theodosia. Shall we have coffee at Great Dunmow?'

They sat a long while over coffee. The professor showed no signs of hurry. His questions were casual but her answers told him a great deal. She wouldn't admit to loneliness or worry about her future; her answers were cheerful and hopeful. She had no ambitions to be a career girl, only to have a steady job and security.

'You wouldn't wish to marry?'

'Oh, but I would—but not to anyone, you understand,' she assured him earnestly. 'But it would be nice to have a husband and a home; and children.'

'So many young women want a career—to be a lawyer, or a doctor, or a high-powered executive.'

She shook her head. 'Not me; I'm not clever to start with.'

'You don't need to be clever to marry?' He smiled a little.

'Not that sort of clever. But being married isn't just a job, is it? It's a way of life.'

'And I imagine a very pleasant one if one is happily married.'

He glanced at his watch. 'Perhaps we had better get on...'

At the great-aunts' house Mrs Trickey, in the

same hat, admitted them and ushered them into the drawing room. Aunt Jessica got up to greet them but Aunt Mary stayed in her chair, declaring in a rather vinegary voice that the cold weather had got into her poor old bones, causing her to be something of an invalid. Theodosia kissed her aunts, sympathised with Aunt Mary and hoped that she wasn't expecting to get free medical treatment from their visitor. She had no chance to say more for the moment since Aunt Jessica was asking Theodosia if she had brought the groceries with her.

The professor greeted the two ladies with just the right amount of polite pleasure, and now he offered to fetch the box of food into the house.

'The kitchen?' he wanted to know.

'No, no. We shall unpack it here; Mrs Trickey can put it all away once that is done. You have the receipted bill, Theodosia?'

'Well, actually, Professor Bendinck has it. He paid for everything. I hadn't enough money.' She could see that that wasn't enough to satisfy the aunts. 'We met going out of the hospital. I was trying to get to the bank to get some money. To save time, because it was my dinner hour, he kindly drove me to Fortnum & Mason and gave them your order and paid for it.'

Aunt Mary looked shocked. 'Really, Theodosia, a young girl should not take any money from a gentleman.'

But Aunt Jessica only smiled. 'Well, dear, we are grateful to Professor Bendinck for his help. I'll write a cheque…'

'Perhaps you would let Theodosia have it? She can let me have it later. I shall be calling for her tomorrow evening.'

Aunt Mary was still frowning. 'I suppose you had spent all your money on clothes—young women nowadays seem to think of nothing else.'

Theodosia would have liked to tell her that it wasn't new clothes, more's the pity. It was cat food, and milk, bread and cheese, tea and the cheaper cuts of meat, and all the other necessities one needed to keep body and soul together. But she didn't say a word.

It was the professor who said blandly, 'I don't imagine that Theodosia has a great deal of money to spare—our hospital salaries are hardly generous.'

He smiled, shook hands and took his leave. At the door to the drawing room he bent his great height and kissed Theodosia's cheek. 'Until tomorrow evening.' His smile included all three ladies as he followed Mrs Trickey to the front door.

Great-Aunt Jessica might not have moved with the times—in her young days gentlemen didn't kiss young ladies with such an air, as though they had a right to do so—but she was romantic at heart and now she smiled. It was Great-Aunt Mary who spoke, her thin voice disapproving.

'I am surprised, Theodosia, that you allow a gentleman to kiss you in that manner. Casual kissing is a regrettable aspect of modern life.'

Theodosia said reasonably, 'Well, I didn't allow him, did I? I'm just as surprised as you are, Aunt Mary, but I can assure you that nowadays a kiss doesn't meant anything—it's a social greeting—or a way of saying goodbye.'

And she had enjoyed it very much.

'Shall I unpack the things you wanted?' she asked, suddenly anxious not to talk about the professor.

It was a task which took some time and successfully diverted the old ladies' attention.

The weekend was like all the others, only there was more talk of Christmas now. 'We shall expect you on Christmas Eve,' said Aunt Jessica. 'Around teatime will suit us very nicely.'

That would suit Theodosia nicely, too. She would have to work in the morning; patients still had diets even at Christmas. There would be a tremendous rush getting the diets organised for the holiday period but with luck she would be able to get a late-afternoon train. She must remember to check the times...

In bed much later that night, with Gustavus curled up beside her, she allowed herself to think about the professor. It was, of course, perfectly all right for him to kiss her, she reassured herself, just as she had reassured her aunts: it was an accepted social greeting. Only it hadn't been necessary for him to do it. He was a very nice man, she thought sleepily, only nice wasn't quite the right word to describe him.

It was very cold in church the next morning and, as usual, lunch was cold—roast beef which was underdone, beetroot and boiled potatoes. The trifle which followed was cold, too, and her offer to make coffee afterwards was rejected by the aunts, who took their accustomed seats in the drawing room, impervious to the chill. Theodosia was glad when it was time for her to get the tea, but two cups of Earl Grey, taken without milk, did little to warm her.

She was relieved when the professor arrived; he spent a short time talking to her aunts and then suggested that they should leave. He hadn't kissed her; she hadn't expected him to, but he did give her a long, thoughtful look before bidding his fare-wells in the nicest possible manner and sweeping her out to the car.

It must have been the delightful warmth in the car which caused Theodosia to sneeze and then shiver.

'You look like a wet hen,' said the professor, driving away from the house. 'You've caught a cold.'

She sneezed again. 'I think perhaps I have. The church was cold, but the aunts don't seem to mind the cold. I'll be perfectly all right once I'm back at Mrs Towzer's.' She added, 'I'm sorry; I do hope I won't give it to you.'

'Most unlikely. We won't stop for a meal at Great Dunmow, I'll drive you straight back.'

'Thank you.'

It was the sensible thing to do, she told herself, but at the same time she felt overwhelming dis-appointment. Hot soup, a sizzling omelette, piping hot coffee—any of these would have been wel-come at Great Dunmow. Perhaps, despite his de-nial, he was anxious not to catch her cold. She muffled a sneeze and tried to blow her nose sound-lessly.

By the time they reached the outskirts of London she was feeling wretched; she had the beginnings of a headache, a running nose and icy shivers down her spine. The idea of getting a meal, seeing to Gustavus and crawling down to the bathroom was far from inviting. She sneezed again and he handed her a large, very white handkerchief.

'Oh, dear,' said Theodosia. She heaved a sigh of relief at his quiet, 'We're very nearly there.'

Only he seemed to be driving the wrong way. 'This is the Embankment,' she pointed out. 'You missed the way...'

'No. You are coming home with me. You're going to have a meal and something for that cold, then I'll drive you back.'

'But that's a lot of trouble and there's Gustavus...'

'No trouble, and Gustavus can have his supper with my housekeeper.'

He had turned into a narrow street, very quiet, lined with Regency houses, and stopped before the last one in the terrace.

Theodosia was still trying to think of a good reason for insisting on going back to Mrs Towzer's but she was given no chance to do so. She found herself out of the car and in through the handsome door and borne away by a little stout woman with grey hair and a round, cheerful face who evinced no surprise at her appearance but ushered her into a cloakroom at the back of the narrow hall, tut-tutting sympathetically as she did so.

'That's a nasty cold, miss, but the professor will have something for it and there'll be supper on the table in no time at all.'

So Theodosia washed her face and tidied her hair, feeling better already, and went back into the hall and was ushered through one of the doors there. The room was large and high-ceilinged with a bow window overlooking the street. It was furnished most comfortably, with armchairs drawn up on each side of the bright fire burning in the steel grate, a vast sofa facing it, more smaller chairs, a scattering of lamp tables and a mahogany rent table in the bow window. There were glass-fronted cabinets on either side of the fireplace and a long case clock by the door.

Theodosia was enchanted. 'Oh, what a lovely room,' she said, and smiled with delight at the professor.

'Yes, I think so, too. Come and sit down. A glass of sherry will make you feel easier; you'll feel better when you have had a meal. I'll give you some pills later; take two when you go to bed and two more in the morning. I'll give you enough for several days.'

She drank her sherry and the housekeeper came

presently to say that supper was on the table. 'And that nice cat of yours is sitting by the Aga as though he lived here, miss. Had his supper, too.'

Theodosia thanked her and the professor said, 'This is Meg, my housekeeper. She was my nanny a long time ago. Meg, this is Miss Theodosia Chapman; she works at the hospital.'

Meg smiled broadly. 'Well, now, isn't that nice?' And she shook the hand Theodosia offered.

Supper was everything she could have wished for—piping hot soup, an omelette as light as air, creamed potatoes, tiny brussels sprouts and little egg custards in brown china pots for pudding. She ate every morsel and the professor, watching the colour creep back into her cheeks, urged her to have a second cup of coffee and gave her a glass of brandy.

'I don't think I would like it...'

'Probably not. I'm giving it to you as a medicine so toss it off, but not too quickly.'

It made her choke and her eyes water, but it warmed her too, and when she had finished it he said, 'I'm going to take you back now. Go straight to bed and take your pills and I promise you that you will feel better in the morning.'

'You've been very kind; I'm very grateful. And it was a lovely supper...'

She bade Meg goodbye and thanked her, too, and with Gustavus stowed in the back of the car she was driven back to Mrs Towzer's.

The contrast was cruel as she got out of the car: the professor's house, so dignified and elegant, and Mrs Towzer's, so shabby and unwelcoming. But she wasn't a girl to whinge or complain. She had a roof over her head and a job and the added bonus of knowing the professor.

He took the key from her and went up the four flights of stairs, carrying her bag and Gustavus in his basket. Then he opened her door and switched on the light and went to light the gas fire. He put the pills on the table and then said, 'Go straight to bed, Theodosia.' He sounded like an uncle or a big brother.

She thanked him again and wished him goodnight and he went to the door. He turned round and came back to where she was standing, studying her face in a manner which disconcerted her. She knew that her nose was red and her eyes puffy; she must look a sight…

He bent and kissed her then, a gentle kiss on her mouth and quite unhurried. Then he was gone, the door shut quietly behind him.

'He'll catch my cold,' said Theodosia. 'Why

ever did he do that? I'll never forgive myself if he does; I should have stopped him.'

Only she hadn't wanted to. She took Gustavus out of his basket and gave him his bedtime snack, put on the kettle for her hot-water bottle and turned the divan into a bed, doing all these things without noticing what she was doing.

'I should like him to kiss me again,' said Theodosia loudly. 'I liked it. I like him—no, I'm in love with him, aren't I? Which is very silly of me. I expect it's because I don't see many men and somehow we seem to come across each other quite often. I must stop thinking about him and feeling happy when I see him.'

After which praiseworthy speech she took her pills and, warmed by Gustavus and the hot-water bottle, presently went to sleep—but not before she had had a little weep for what might have been if life had allowed her to tread the same path as the professor.

CHAPTER THREE

THEODOSIA felt better in the morning; she had a cold, but she no longer felt—or looked—like a wet hen. She took the pills she had been given, ate her breakfast, saw to Gustavus and went to work. Miss Prescott greeted her sourly, expressed the hope that she would take care not to pass her cold on to her and gave her enough work to keep her busy for the rest of the day. Which suited Theodosia very well for she had no time to think about the professor. Something, she told herself sternly, she must stop doing at once—which didn't prevent her from hoping that she might see him as she went around the hospital. But she didn't, nor was his car in the forecourt when she went home later that day.

He must have gone away; she had heard that he was frequently asked to other hospitals for consultations, and there was no reason why he should have told her. It was during the following morning, on her rounds, that she overhead the ward sister remark to her staff nurse that he would be back for his rounds at the end of the week. It seemed that he was in Austria.

Theodosia dropped her diet sheets deliberately and took a long time picking them up so that she could hear more.

'In Vienna,' said Sister, 'and probably Rome. Let's hope he gets back before Christmas.'

A wish Theodosia heartily endorsed; the idea of him spending Christmas anywhere but at his lovely home filled her with unease.

She was quite herself by the end of the week; happy to be free from Miss Prescott's iron hand, she did her shopping on Saturday and, since the weather was fine and cold, decided to go to Sunday's early-morning service and then go for a walk in one of the parks.

It was still not quite light when she left the house the next morning and there was a sparkle of frost on the walls and rooftops. The church was warm, though, and fragrant with the scent of chrysanthemums. There wasn't a large congregation and the simple service was soon over. She started to walk back, sorry to find that the early-morning sky was clouding over.

The streets were empty save for the occasional car and an old lady some way ahead of her. Theodosia, with ten minutes' brisk walk before her, walked faster, spurred on by the thought of breakfast.

She was still some way from the old lady when a car passed her, going much too fast and swerving from side to side of the street. The old lady hadn't a chance; the car mounted the kerb as it reached her, knocked her down and drove on.

Theodosia ran. There was no one about, the houses on either side of the street had their curtains tightly pulled over the windows, and the street was empty; she wanted to scream but she needed her breath.

The old lady lay half on the road, half on the pavement. She looked as though someone had picked her up and tossed her down and left her in a crumpled heap. One leg was crumpled up under her and although her skirt covered it Theodosia could see that there was blood oozing from under the cloth. She was conscious, though, turning faded blue eyes on her, full of bewilderment.

Theodosia whipped off her coat, tucked it gently under the elderly head and asked gently, 'Are you in pain? Don't move; I'm going to get help.'

'Can't feel nothing, dearie—a bit dizzy, like.'

There was a lot more blood now. Theodosia lifted the skirt gently and looked at the awful mess under it. She got to her feet, filling her lungs ready to bellow for help and at the same time starting towards the nearest door.

*   *   *

The professor, driving himself back from Heathrow after his flight from Rome, had decided to go first to the hospital, check his patients there and then go home for the rest of the day. He didn't hurry. It was pleasant to be back in England and London—even the shabbier streets of London—was quiet and empty. His peaceful thoughts were rudely shattered at the sight of Theodosia racing across the street, waving her arms like a maniac.

He stopped the car smoothly, swearing softly, something he seldom did, but he had been severely shaken…

'Oh, do hurry, she's bleeding badly,' said Theodosia. 'I was just going to shout for help for I'm so glad it's you…'

He said nothing; there would be time for words later. He got out of the car and crossed the street and bent over the old lady.

'Get my bag from the back of the car.' He had lifted the sodden skirt. When she had done that he said, 'There's a phone in the car. Get an ambulance. Say that it is urgent.'

She did as she was told and went back to find him on his haunches, a hand rummaging in his bag, while he applied pressure with his other hand to the severed artery.

'Find a forceps,' he told her. 'One with teeth.'

She did that too and held a second pair ready, trying not to look at the awful mess. 'Now put the bag where I can reach it and go and talk to her.' He didn't look up. 'You got the ambulance?'

'Yes, I told them where to come and that it was very urgent.'

She went and knelt by the old lady, who was still conscious but very pale.

'Bit of bad luck,' she said in a whisper. 'I was going to me daughter for Christmas…'

'Well, you will be well again by then,' said Theodosia. 'The doctor's here now and you're going to hospital in a few minutes.'

'Proper Christmas dinner, we was going ter 'ave. Turkey and the trimmings—I like a bit of turkey…'

'Oh, yes, so do I,' said Theodosia, her ears stretched for the ambulance. 'Cranberry sauce with it…'

'And a nice bit of stuffing.' The old lady's voice was very weak. 'And plenty of gravy. Sprouts and pertaters and a good bread sauce. Plenty of onion with it.'

'Your daughter makes her own puddings?' asked Theodosia, and thought what a strange conversation this was—like a nightmare only she was already awake.

'Is there something wrong with me leg?' The blue eyes looked anxious.

'You've cut it a bit; the doctor's seeing to it. Wasn't it lucky that he was passing?'

'Don't 'ave much ter say for 'imself, does 'e?'

'Well, he is busy putting a bandage on. Do you live near here?'

'Just round the corner—Holne Road, number six. Just popped out ter get the paper.' The elderly face crumpled. 'I don't feel all that good.'

'You'll be as bright as a button in no time,' said Theodosia, and heard the ambulance at last.

Things moved fast then. The old lady, drowsy with morphia now, was connected up to oxygen and plasma while the professor tied off the torn arteries, checked her heart and with the paramedics stowed her in the ambulance.

Theodosia, making herself small against someone's gate, watched the curious faces at windows and doors and wondered if she should go.

'Get into the car; I'll drop you off. I'm going to the hospital.'

He stared down at her unhappy face. 'Hello,' he said gently, and he smiled.

He had nothing more to say and Theodosia was feeling sick. He stopped at Mrs Towzer's just long enough for her to get out and drove off quickly.

She climbed the stairs and, once in her room, took off her dirty, blood-stained clothes and washed and dressed again, all the while telling Gustavus what had happened.

She supposed that she should have breakfast although she didn't really want it. She fed Gustavus and put on the kettle. A cup of tea would do.

When there was a knock on the door she called, 'Come in,' remembering too late that she shouldn't have done that before asking who was there.

The professor walked in. 'You should never open the door without checking,' he said. He turned off the gas under the kettle and the gas fire and then stowed Gustavus in his basket.

'What are you doing?' Theodosia wanted to know.

'Taking you back for breakfast—you and Gustavus. Get a coat—something warm.'

'My coat is a bit—that is, I shall have to take it to the cleaners. I've got a mac.' She should have been annoyed with him, walking in like that, but somehow she couldn't be bothered. Besides, he was badly in need of the dry cleaners, too. 'Is the old lady all right?'

'She is in theatre now, and hopefully she will recover. Now, hurry up, dear girl.'

She could refuse politely but Gustavus was already in his basket and breakfast would be very welcome. She got into her mac, pulled a woolly cap over her bright hair and accompanied him downstairs. There was no one about and the street was quiet; she got into the car when he opened the door for her, mulling over all the things she should have said if only she had had her wits about her.

As soon as they had had their breakfast she would tell him that she was having lunch with friends… She discarded the idea. To tell him fibs, even small, harmless ones, was something she found quite impossible. She supposed that was because she loved him. People who loved each other didn't have secrets. Only he didn't love her.

She glanced sideways at him. 'You've spoilt your suit.'

'And you your coat. I'm only thankful that it was you who were there. You've a sensible head under that bright hair; most people lose their wits at an accident. You were out early?'

'I'd been to church. I planned to go for a long walk. I often do on a Sunday.'

'Very sensible—especially after being cooped up in the hospital all week.'

Meg came to meet them as they went into the house. She took Theodosia's mac and cap and said firmly, 'Breakfast will be ready just as soon as you've got into some other clothes, sir. Miss Chapman can have a nice warm by the fire.'

She bustled Theodosia down the hall and into a small, cosy sitting room where there was a bright fire burning. Its window overlooked a narrow garden at the back and the round table by it was set for breakfast.

'Now just you sit quiet for a bit,' said Meg. 'I'll get Gustavus.'

The cat, freed from his basket, settled down before the fire as though he had lived there all his life.

The professor came presently in corduroys and a polo-necked sweater. Cashmere, decided Theodosia. Perhaps if she could save enough money she would buy one instead of spending a week next summer at a bed and breakfast farm.

Meg followed him in with a tray of covered dishes; Theodosia's breakfasts of cornflakes, toast and, sometimes, a boiled egg paled to oblivion beside this splendid array of bacon, eggs, tomatoes, mushrooms and kidneys.

He piled her plate. 'We must have a good breakfast if we are to go walking, too,' he observed.

She stared at him across the table. 'But it is me who is going walking...'

'You don't mind if I come, too? Besides, I need

your help. I'm going to Worthing to collect a dog; he'll need a good walk before we bring him back.'

'A dog?' said Theodosia. 'Why is he at Worthing? And you don't really need me with you.'

He didn't answer at once. He said easily, 'He's a golden Labrador, three years old. He belongs to a friend of mine who has gone to Australia. He's been in a dog's home for a week or so until I was free to take him over.'

'He must be unhappy. But not any more once he's living with you. If you think it would help to make him feel more at home if I were there, too, I'd like to go with you.' She frowned. 'I forgot, I can't. Gustavus...'

'He will be quite happy with Meg, who dotes on him.' He passed her the toast. 'So that's settled. It's a splendid day to be out of doors.'

They had left London behind them and were nearing Dorking when he said, 'Do you know this part of the country? We'll leave the main road and go through Billingshurst. We can get back onto the main road just north of Worthing.'

Even in the depths of winter, the country was beautiful, still sparkling from the night frost and the sun shining from a cold blue sky. Theodosia, snug in the warmth and comfort of the car, was in seventh heaven. She couldn't expect anything as delightful as this unexpected day out to happen again, of course. It had been a kindly quirk of fate which had caused them to meet again.

She said suddenly, 'That old lady—it seems so unfair that she should be hurt and in hospital while we're having this glorious ride—' She stopped then and added awkwardly, 'What I mean is, I'm having a glorious ride.'

The professor thought of several answers he would have liked to make to that. Instead he said casually, 'It's a perfect day, isn't it? I'm enjoying it, too. Shall we stop for a cup of coffee in Billingshurst?'

When they reached Worthing, he took her to one of the splendid hotels on the seafront where, the shabby raincoat hidden out of sight in the cloakroom, she enjoyed a splendid lunch with him, unconscious of the glances of the other people there, who were intrigued by the vivid ginger of her hair.

It was early afternoon when they reached the dog's home. He was ready and waiting for them, for he recognized the professor as a friend of his master and greeted him with a dignified bark or two and a good deal of tail-wagging. He was in a pen with a small dog of such mixed parentage that it was impossible to tell exactly what he might be.

He had a foxy face and bushy eyebrows, a rough coat, very short legs and a long thin tail. He sat and watched while George the Labrador was handed over and Theodosia said, 'That little dog, he looks so sad...'

The attendant laughed. 'He's been George's shadow ever since he came; can't bear to be parted from him. They eat and sleep together, too. Let's hope someone wants him. I doubt it—he came in off a rubbish dump.'

The professor was looking at Theodosia; he knew with resigned amusement that he was about to become the owner of the little dog. She wasn't going to ask, but the expression on her face was eloquent.

'Then perhaps we might have the little dog as well since they are such friends. Has he a name?'

He was rewarded by the happiness in her face. 'He may come, too?' She held out her arms for the little beast, who was shivering with excitement, and he stayed there until the professor had dealt with their payment, chosen a collar and lead for him and they had left the home.

'A brisk walk on the beach will do us all good,' said the professor. 'We must have a name,' he observed as the two dogs ran to and fro. They had got into the car without fuss and now they were savouring their freedom.

'Max,' said Theodosia promptly. 'He's such a little dog and I don't suppose he'll grow much more so he needs an important name. Maximilian—only perhaps you could call him Max?'

'I don't see why not,' agreed the professor. He turned her round and started to walk back to the car. He whistled to the dogs. 'George, Max…'

They came running and scrambled into the car looking anxious.

'It's all right, you're going home,' said Theodosia, 'and everyone will love you.' She remembered then. 'Gustavus—he's not used to dogs; he never sees them…'

'Then it will be a splendid opportunity for him to do so. We will put the three of them in the garden together.'

'We will? No, no, there's no need. If you'll give me time to pop him into his basket, I can take him with me.'

The professor was driving out of Worthing, this time taking the main road to Horsham and Dorking. The winter afternoon was already fading into dusk and Theodosia reflected on how quickly the hours flew by when one was happy.

He hadn't answered her; presumably he had

agreed with her. There would be buses, but she would have to change during the journey back to her bed-sitter. She reminded herself that on a Sunday evening with little traffic and the buses half empty she should have an easy journey.

They talked from time to time and every now and then she turned round to make sure the dogs were all right. They were sitting upright, close together, looking uncertain.

'Did you have a dog when you were a little girl?' asked the professor.

'Oh, yes, and a cat. I had a pony, too.'

'Your home was in the country?' he asked casually.

She told him about the nice old house in Wiltshire and the school she had gone to and how happy she had been, and then said suddenly, 'I'm sorry, I must be boring you. It's just that I don't get the chance to talk about it very often. Of course, I think about it whenever I like.' She glanced out of the window into the dark evening. 'Are we nearly there?'

'Yes, and you have no need to apologize; I have not been bored. I have wondered about your home before you came to London, for you are so obviously a square peg in a round hole.'

'Oh? Am I? I suppose I am, but I'm really very

lucky. I mean, I have the great-aunts and a job and I know lots of people at the hospital.'

'But perhaps you would like to do some other work?'

'Well, I don't think I'm the right person to have a career, if you mean the sort who wear those severe suits and carry briefcases...'

He laughed then, but all he said was, 'We're almost home.'

If only it were home—her home, thought Theodosia, and then told herself not to be a silly fool. She got out when he opened her door and waited while he took up the dogs' leads and ushered them to the door. When she hesitated he said, 'Come along, Theodosia. Meg will have tea waiting for us.'

Much later, lying in bed with Gustavus curled up beside her, Theodosia thought over her day, minute by minute. It had been like a lovely dream, only dreams were forgotten and she would never forget the hours she had spent with the professor. And the day had ended just as he had planned it beforehand; they had had tea by the fire with the two dogs sitting between them as though they had lived there all their lives. Although she had been a bit scared when the professor had fetched Gustavus and introduced him to the dogs, she had said nothing. After a good deal of spitting and gentle growling the three animals had settled down together.

She had said that she must go back after tea, but somehow he'd convinced her that it would be far better if she stayed for supper. 'So that Gustavus can get used to George and Max,' he had explained smoothly. She hated leaving his house and her bed-sitter was cold and uninviting.

The professor had lighted the gas fire for her, drawn the curtains over the window and turned on the table lamp, before going to the door, smiling at her muddled thanks and wishing her goodnight in a brisk manner.

There was no reason why he should have lingered, she told herself sleepily. Perhaps she would see him at the hospital—not to talk to, just to get a glimpse of him would do, so that she knew that he was still there.

In the morning, when she woke, she told herself that any foolish ideas about him must be squashed. She couldn't pretend that she wasn't in love with him, because she was and there was nothing she could do about that, but at least she would be sensible about it.

This was made easy for her since Miss Prescott was in a bad mood. Theodosia had no time at all to think about anything but the endless jobs her superior found for her to do, but in her dinner hour she went along to the women's surgical ward and asked if she might see the old lady.

She was sitting propped up in bed, looking surprisingly cheerful. True, she was attached to a number of tubes and she looked pale, but she remembered Theodosia at once.

'I'd have been dead if you hadn't come along, you and that nice doctor. Patched me up a treat, they have! My daughter's been to see me, too. Ever so grateful, we both are.'

'I'm glad I just happened to be there, and it was marvellous luck that Professor Bendinck should drive past...'

'Professor, is he? A very nice gentleman and ever so friendly. Came to see me this morning.'

Just to know that he had been there that morning made Theodosia feel happy. Perhaps she would see him too...

But there was no sign of him. The week slid slowly by with not so much as a glimpse of him. Friday came at last. She bade Miss Prescott a temporary and thankful goodbye and made her way through the hospital. It had been raining all day and it was cold as well. A quiet weekend, she promised herself, making for the entrance.

The professor was standing by the main door and she saw him too late to make for the side door. As she reached him she gave him a cool nod and was brought to a halt by his hand.

'There you are. I was afraid that I had missed you.'

'I've been here all this week,' said Theodosia, aware of the hand and filled with delight, yet at the same time peevish.

'Yes, so have I. I have a request to make. Would you be free on Sunday to take the dogs into the country? George is very biddable, but Max needs a personal attendant.' He added, most unfairly, 'And since you took such an interest in him...'

She felt guilty. 'Oh, dear. I should have thought... It was my fault, wasn't it? If I hadn't said anything... Ought he to go back to Worthing and find another owner?'

'Certainly not. It is merely a question of him settling down. He is so pleased to be with George that he gets carried away. They couldn't be separated.' He had walked her through the door. 'I'll drive you home...'

'There's no need.'

Which was a silly remark for it was pouring with rain, as well as dark and cold.

She allowed herself to be stowed in the car and

when they got to Mrs Towzer's house he got out with her. 'I'll be here at ten o'clock on Sunday,' he told her, and didn't wait for her answer.

'Really,' said Theodosia, climbing the stairs. 'He does take me for granted.'

But she knew that wasn't true. He merely arranged circumstances in such a way that he compelled her to agree to what he suggested.

She was up early on Sunday morning, getting breakfast for herself and Gustavus, explaining to him that she would have to leave him alone. 'But you shall have something nice for supper,' she promised him. The professor hadn't said how long they would be gone, or where. She frowned. He really did take her for granted; next time she would have a good excuse...

It was just before ten o'clock when he knocked on her door. He wished her good morning in a casual manner which gave her the feeling that they had known each other all their lives. 'We'll take Gustavus, if you like. He'll be happier in the car than sitting by himself all day.'

'Well, yes, perhaps—if George and Max won't mind and it's not too long.'

'No distance.' He was settling Gustavus in his basket. 'A breath of country air will do him good.'

Mrs Towzer wasn't in the hall but her door was

just a little open. As the professor opened the door he said, 'We shall be back this evening, Mrs Towzer,' just as her face appeared in the crack in the door.

'She's not being nosy,' said Theodosia as they drove away. 'She's just interested.'

She turned her head a little and found George and Max leaning against her seat, anxious to greet her and not in the least bothered by Gustavus in his basket. She was filled with happiness; it was a bright, cold morning and the winter sun shone, the car was warm and comfortable and she was sitting beside the man she loved. What more could a girl want? A great deal, of course, but Theodosia, being the girl she was, was content with what she had at the moment.

'Where are we going?' she asked presently. 'This is the way to Finchingfield.'

'Don't worry, we are not going to your great-aunts'. I have a little cottage a few miles from Saffron Walden; I thought we could go there, walk the dogs and have a picnic lunch. Meg has put something in a basket for us.'

He didn't take the motorway but turned off at Brentwood and took the secondary roads to Bishop's Stortford and after a few miles turned off again into a country road which led presently to a village. It was a small village, its narrow main street lined with small cottages before broadening into a village green ringed by larger cottages and several houses, all of them overshadowed by the church.

The professor turned into a narrow lane leading from the green and stopped, got out to open a gate in the hedge and then drove through it along a short paved driveway, with a hedge on one side of it and a fair-sized garden on the other, surrounding a reed-thatched, beetle-browed cottage with a porch and small latticed windows, its brick walls faded to a dusty pink. The same bricks had been used for the walls on either side of it which separated the front garden from the back of the house, pierced by small wooden doors.

The professor got out, opened Theodosia's door and then released the dogs.

'Gustavus…' began Theodosia.

'We will take him straight through to the garden at the back. There's a high wall, so he'll be quite safe there and he can get into the cottage.'

He unlocked one of the small doors and urged her through with the dogs weaving themselves to and fro and she could see that it was indeed so; the garden was large, sloping down to the fields and surrounded by a high brick wall. It was an old-fashioned garden with narrow brick paths between beds which were empty now, but she had no doubt they would be filled with rows of orderly vegetables later on. Beyond the beds was a lawn with fruit bushes to one side of it and apple trees.

'Oh, how lovely—even in winter it's perfect.'

He sat Gustavus's basket down, opened it and presently Gustavus poked out a cautious head and then sidled out.

'He's not used to being out of doors,' said Theodosia anxiously, 'only on the roof outside my window. At least, not since I've had him. He was living on the streets before that, but that's not the same as being free.'

She had bent to stroke the furry head and the professor said gently, 'Shall we leave him to get used to everything? The dogs won't hurt him and we can leave the kitchen door open.'

He unlocked the door behind him and stood aside for her to go inside. The kitchen was small, with a quarry-tiled floor, pale yellow walls and an old-fashioned dresser along one wall. There was an Aga, a stout wooden table and equally stout chairs and a deep stone sink. She revolved slowly, liking what she saw; she had no doubt that the kitchen lacked nothing a housewife would need, but it was a place to sit cosily over a cup of coffee, or to come down to in the morning and drink a cup of tea by the open door...

'Through here,' said the professor, and opened a door into the hall.

It was narrow, with a polished wooden floor and cream-painted walls. There were three doors and he opened the first one. The living room took up the whole of one side of the cottage, with little windows overlooking the front garden and French windows opening onto the garden at the back. It was a delightful room with easy chairs, tables here and there and a wide inglenook. The floor was wooden here, too, but there were rugs on it, their faded colours echoing the dull reds and blues of the curtains. There were pictures on the walls but she was given no chance to look at them.

'The dining room,' said the professor as she crossed the hall. It was a small room, simply furnished with a round table, chairs and a sideboard, and all of them, she noted, genuine pieces in dark oak.

'And this is my study.' She glimpsed a small room with a desk and chair and rows of bookshelves.

The stairs were small and narrow and led to a square landing. There were three bedrooms, one quite large and the others adequate, and a bathroom. The cottage might be old but no expense had been spared here. She looked at the shelves piled with towels and all the toiletries any woman could wish for.

'Fit for a queen,' said Theodosia.

'Or a wife…'

Which brought her down to earth again. 'Oh, are you thinking of getting married?'

'Indeed, I am.'

She swallowed down the unhappiness which was so painful that it was like a physical hurt. 'Has she seen this cottage? She must love it…'

'Yes, she has seen it and I think that she has found it very much to her taste.'

She must keep on talking. 'But you won't live here? You have your house in London.'

'We shall come here whenever we can.'

'The garden is lovely. I don't suppose you have much time to work in it yourself.'

'I make time and I have a splendid old man who comes regularly, as well as Mrs Trump who comes every day when I'm here and keeps an eye on the place when I'm not.'

'How nice,' said Theodosia inanely. 'Should I go and see if Gustavus is all right?'

He was sitting by his basket looking very composed, ignoring the two dogs who were cavorting around the garden.

'It's as though he's been here all his life,' said Theodosia. She looked at the professor. 'It's that kind of house, isn't it? Happy people have lived in it.'

'And will continue to do so. Wait here; I'll fetch the food.'

They sat at the kitchen table eating their lunch; there was soup in a Thermos; little crusty rolls filled with cream cheese and ham, miniature sausage rolls, tiny buttery croissants and piping hot coffee from another Thermos. There was food for the animals as well as a bottle of wine. Theodosia ate with the pleasure of a child, keeping up a rather feverish conversation. She was intent on being cool and casual, taking care to talk about safe subjects—the weather, Christmas, the lighter side of her work at the hospital. The professor made no effort to change the subject, listening with tender amusement to her efforts and wondering if this would be the right moment to tell her that he loved her. He decided it was not, but he hoped that she might begin to do more than like him. She was young; she might meet a younger man. A man of no conceit, he supposed that she thought of him as a man well past his first youth.

They went round the garden after lunch with Gustavus in Theodosia's arms, the dogs racing to and fro, and when the first signs of dusk showed they locked up the little house, stowed the animals in the car and began the drive back to London.

They had reached the outskirts when the professor's bleeper disturbed the comfortable silence. Whoever it was had a lot to say but at length he said, 'I'll be with you in half an hour.' Then he told Theodosia, 'I'll have to go to the hospital. I'll drop you off on the way. I'm sorry; I had hoped that you would have stayed for supper.'

'Thank you, but I think I would have refused; I have to get ready for work tomorrow—washing and ironing and so on.' She added vaguely, 'But it's kind of you to invite me. Thank you for a lovely day; we've enjoyed every minute of it!' Which wasn't quite true, for there had been no joy for her when he'd said that he was going to get married.

When they reached Mrs Towzer's she said, 'Don't get out; you mustn't waste a moment...'

He got out all the same without saying anything, opened the door for her, put Gustavus's basket in the hall and then drove away with a quick nod.

'And that is how it will be from now on,' muttered Theodosia, climbing the stairs and letting herself into her cold bed-sitter. 'He's not likely to ask me out again, but if he does I'll not go. I must let him see that we have nothing in common; it was just chance meetings and those have to stop!'

She got her supper—baked beans on toast and a pot of tea—fed a contented Gustavus and presently went to bed to cry in comfort until at last she fell asleep.

CHAPTER FOUR

THE week began badly. Theodosia overslept; Gustavus, usually so obedient, refused to come in from the roof; and the coil of ginger hair shed pins as fast as she stuck them in. She almost ran to work, to find Miss Prescott, despite the fact that it would be Christmas at the end of the week, in a worse temper than usual. And as a consequence Theodosia did nothing right. She dropped things, spilt things, muddled up diet sheets and because of that went late to her dinner.

It was cottage pie and Christmas pudding with a blindingly yellow custard—and on her way back she was to call in at Women's Medical and collect two diet sheets for the two emergencies which had been admitted. Because it was quicker, although forbidden, she took the lift to the medical floor and when it stopped peered out prudently before alighting; one never knew, a ward sister could be passing.

There was no ward sister but the professor was standing a few yards away, his arm around a woman. They had their backs to her and they were

91

laughing and as Theodosia looked the woman stretched up and kissed his cheek. She wasn't a young woman but she was good-looking and beautifully dressed.

Theodosia withdrew her head and prayed hard that they would go away. Which presently they did, his arm still around the woman's shoulders, and as she watched, craning her neck, Women's Medical ward door opened, Sister came out and the three of them stood talking and presently went into the ward.

Theodosia closed the lift door and was conveyed back to Miss Prescott's office.

'Well, let me have those diet sheets,' said that lady sharply.

'I didn't get them,' said Theodosia, quite beside herself, and, engulfed in feelings she hadn't known she possessed, she felt reckless. 'I went late to dinner and I should have had an hour instead of the forty minutes you left me. Someone else can fetch them. Why don't you go yourself, Miss Prescott?'

Miss Prescott went a dangerous plum colour. 'Theodosia, can I believe my ears? Do you realise to whom you speak? Go at once and get those diet sheets.'

Theodosia sat down at her desk. There were several letters to be typed, so she inserted paper into her machine and began to type. Miss Prescott hesitated. She longed to give the girl her notice on the spot but that was beyond her powers. Besides, with all the extra work Christmas entailed she had to have help in her office. There were others working in the department, of course, but Theodosia, lowly though her job was, got on with the work she was familiar with.

'I can only assume that you are not feeling yourself,' said Miss Prescott. 'I am prepared to overlook your rudeness but do not let it occur again.'

Theodosia wasn't listening; she typed the letters perfectly while a small corner of her brain went over and over her unexpected glimpse of the professor. With the woman he was going to marry, of course. He would have been showing her round the hospital, introducing her to the ward sisters and his colleagues, and then they would leave together in his car and go to his home...

As five o'clock struck she got up, tidied her desk, wished an astonished Miss Prescott good evening and went home. The bed-sitter was cold and gloomy; she switched on the lamps, turned on the fire, fed Gustavus and made herself a pot of tea. She was sad and unhappy but giving way to self-pity wasn't going to help. Besides, she had

known that he was going to marry; he had said so.
But she must avoid him at the hospital…

She cooked her supper and presently went to
bed. She had been happy, allowing her happiness
to take over from common sense. She had no doubt
that sooner or later she would be happy again; it
only needed a little determination.

So now, instead of hoping to meet him as she
went round the hospital, she did her rounds with
extreme caution. Which took longer than usual, of
course, and earned Miss Prescott's annoyance. It
was two days later, sharing a table with other late-
comers from the wards and offices, that the talk
became animated. It was a student nurse from
Women's Medical who started it, describing in de-
tail the companion Professor Bendinck had brought
to see the ward. 'She was gorgeous, not very
young, but then you wouldn't expect him to be
keen on a young girl, would you? He's quite
old…'

Theodosia was about to say that thirty-five
wasn't old—a fact she had learned from one of her
dancing partners at the ball—and even when he
was wearing his specs he still looked in his prime.
But she held her tongue and listened.

'She was wearing a cashmere coat and a little
hat which must have cost the earth, and her

boots…!' The nurse rolled expressive eyes. 'And they both looked so pleased with themselves. He called her "my dear Rosie", and smiled at her. You know, he doesn't smile much when he's on his rounds. He's always very polite, but sort of reserved, if you know what I mean. I suppose we'll be asked to fork out for a wedding present.'

A peevish voice from the other end of the table said, 'Those sort of people have everything; I bet he's loaded. I wonder where he lives?'

Theodosia wondered what they would say if she told them.

'Oh, well,' observed one of the ward clerks. 'I hope they'll be happy. He's nice, you know—opens doors for you and says good morning—and his patients love him.'

Someone noticed the time and they all got up and rushed back to their work.

Two more days and it would be Christmas Eve and she would be free. Her presents for the aunts were wrapped, her best dress brushed and ready on its hanger, her case already half packed with everything she would need for the weekend, Gustavus's favourite food in her shoulder bag. She should be able to catch a late-afternoon train, and if she missed it there was another one leaving a short while later. She would be at the aunts' well before bedtime.

She was almost at the hospital entrance on her way home that evening when she saw the professor. And he had seen her, for he said something to the house doctor he was talking to and began to walk towards her.

Help, thought Theodosia. She was so happy to see him that if he spoke to her she might lose all her good sense and fling herself at him.

And help there was. One of the path lab assistants, the one who had danced with her at the ball, was hurrying past her. She caught hold of his arm and brought him to a surprised halt.

'Say something,' hissed Theodosia. 'Look pleased to see me, as though you expected to meet me.'

'Whatever for? Of course I'm pleased to see you, but I've a train to catch...'

She was still holding his sleeve firmly. The professor was very close now, not hurrying, though; she could see him out of the corner of her eye. She smiled up at her surprised companion. She said very clearly, 'I'll meet you at eight o'clock; we could go to that Chinese place.' For good measure she kissed his cheek and, since the professor was now very close, wished him good evening. He returned her greeting in his usual pleasant manner and went out to his car.

'Whatever's come over you?' demanded the young man from the path lab. 'I mean, it's all very well, but I've no intention of taking you to a Chinese restaurant. For one thing my girl wouldn't stand for it and for another I'm a bit short of cash.' He goggled at her. 'And you kissed me!'

'Don't worry, it was an emergency. I was just pretending that we were keen on each other.'

He looked relieved. 'You mean it was a kind of joke?'

'That's right.' She looked over his shoulder and caught a glimpse of the Bentley turning out of the forecourt. 'Thanks for helping me out.'

'Glad I could help. A lot of nonsense, though.'

He hurried off and Theodosia walked back to her bed-sitter, then told Gustavus all about it. 'You see,' she explained, 'if he doesn't see me or speak to me, he'll forget all about me. I shan't forget him but that's neither here nor there. I daresay he'll have a holiday at Christmas and spend it with her. She's beautiful and elegant, you see, and they were laughing together...' Theodosia paused to give her nose a good blow. She wasn't going to cry about it. He would be home by now, sitting in his lovely drawing room, and Rosie would be sitting with him.

Which is exactly what he was doing, George and Max at his feet, his companion curled up on a sofa. They were both reading, he scanning his post, she leafing through a fashion magazine. Presently she closed it. 'You have no idea how delightful it is to have the whole day to myself. I've spent a small fortune shopping and I can get up late and eat food I haven't cooked myself. It's been heaven.'

The professor peered at her over his specs. 'And you're longing to see James and the children...'

'Yes, I am. It won't be too much for you having us all here? They'll give you no peace—it will be a houseful.' She added unexpectedly, 'There's something wrong, isn't there? You're usually so calm and contained, but it's as though something— or someone?—has stirred you up.'

'How perceptive of you, my dear. I am indeed stirred—by a pair of grey eyes and a head of ginger hair.'

'A girl. Is she pretty, young? One of your house doctors? A nurse?'

'A kind of girl Friday in the diet department. She's young—perhaps too young for me—perhaps not pretty but I think she is beautiful. And she is gentle and kind and a delight to be with.' He smiled. 'And her hair really is ginger; she wears it in a bunch on top of her head.'

His sister had sat up, the magazine on the floor. 'You'll marry her, Hugo?'

'Yes, if she will have me. She lives in a miserable attic room with a cat and is to spend Christmas with her only family—two great-aunts. I intend to drive her there and perhaps have a chance to talk…'

'But you'll be here for Christmas?'

'Of course. Perhaps I can persuade her to spend the last day of the holiday here.'

'I want to meet her. Pour me a drink, Hugo, and tell me all about her. How did you meet?'

The following day the professor did his ward rounds, took a morning clinic, saw his private patients in the afternoon and returned to the hospital just before five o'clock. He had made no attempt to look for Theodosia during the morning—he had been too busy—but now he went in search of her. He hadn't been unduly disturbed by the sight of her talking to the young fellow from the path lab. After all, she was on nodding terms with almost everyone in the hospital, excluding the very senior staff, of course. But he had heard her saying that she would meet him that evening; moreover, she had kissed him. He had to know if she had given her heart to the man; after all, he was young and good-looking and she had never shown anything other than friendliness with himself.

He reviewed the facts with a calm logic and made his way to the floor where Theodosia worked.

She came rushing through the door then slithered to a halt because, of course, he was standing in her way. Since he was a big man she had no way of edging round him.

'Oh, hello,' said Theodosia, and then tried again. 'Good evening, Professor.'

He bade her good evening, too, in a mild voice. 'You're looking forward to Christmas? I'll drive you to Finchingfield. The trains will be packed and running late. Could you manage seven o'clock?'

She had time to steady her breath; now she clutched at the first thing that entered her head. On no account must she go with him. He was being kind again. Probably he had told his fiancée that he intended to drive her and Rosie had agreed that it would be a kindness to take the poor girl to these aunts of hers. She shrank from kindly pity.

'That's very kind of you,' said Theodosia, 'but I'm getting a lift—he's going that way, staying

with friends only a few miles from Finchingfield.'
She was well away now. 'I'm going to a party
there—parties are such fun at Christmas, aren't
they?' She added for good measure, 'He'll bring
me back, too.'

She caught the professor's eye. 'He works in the
path lab...'

If she had hoped to see disappointment on his
face she was disappointed herself. He said pleasantly, 'Splendid. You're well organised, then.'

'Yes, I'm looking forward to it; such fun...' She
was babbling now. 'I must go—someone waiting.
I hope you have a very happy Christmas.'

She shot away, racing down the stairs. He made
no attempt to follow her. That he was bitterly disappointed was inevitable but he was puzzled, too.
Theodosia had been altogether too chatty and anxious to let him know what a splendid time she was
going to have. He could have sworn that she had
been making it up as she went along... On the
other hand, she might have been feeling embarrassed; she had never been more than friendly but
she could possibly be feeling awkward at not having mentioned the young man from the path lab.

He went back to his consulting rooms, saw his
patients there and presently went home, where his
manner was just as usual, asking after his sister's

day, discussing the preparations for Christmas, for
Rosie's husband and the two children would be
arriving the next morning. And she, although she
was longing to talk about Theodosia, said nothing,
for it was plain that he had no intention of men-
tioning her.

And nor did he make any attempt to seek her
out at the hospital during the following day. There
was a good deal of merriment; the wards looked
festive, the staff were cheerful—even those who
would be on duty—and those who were able to
left early. The professor, doing a late round,
glanced at his watch. Theodosia would have left
by now for it was almost six o'clock. He made his
way to the path lab and found the young man who
had been talking to Theodosia still there.

'Not gone yet?' he asked. 'You're not on duty
over the weekend, are you?'

'No, sir, just finishing a job.'

'You live close by?' asked the professor idly.

'Clapham Common. I'm meeting my girlfriend
and we'll go home together. I live at home but
she's spending Christmas with us.'

'Ah, yes. There's nothing like a family gathering. You're planning to marry.'

'Well, as soon as Dorothy's sold her flat—her
parents are dead. Once it's sold we shall put our

savings together and find something around Clapham.'

'Well, I wish you the best of luck and a happy Christmas!'

The professor went on his unhurried way, leaving the young man with the impression that he wasn't such a bad old stick after all, despite his frequent requests for tests at a moment's notice.

The professor went back to his office; ten minutes' work would clear up the last odds and ends of his work for the moment. He had no idea why Theodosia had spun such a wildly imaginative set of fibs but he intended to find out. Even if she had left at five o'clock she would hardly have had the time to change and pack her bag and see to Gustavus.

He was actually at the door when he was bleeped...

Theodosia hurried home. Miss Prescott, true to form, had kept her busy until the very last minute, which meant that catching the early train was an impossibility. She would phone the aunts and say that she would be on the later train. Once in her room she fed an impatient Gustavus, changed into her second-best dress, brushed her coat, found her hat and, since she had time to spare, put on the kettle for a cup of tea. It would probably be chilly on the train and there would be a lot of waiting round for buses once she got to Braintree.

She was sipping her tea when someone knocked on the door, the knock followed by Mrs Towzer's voice. Theodosia asked her in, explaining at the same time that she was just about to leave for her train.

'Won't keep you then, love. Forgot to give you this letter—came this morning—in with my post. Don't suppose it's important. 'Ave a nice time at your auntys'. 'Aving a bit of a party this evening; must get meself poshed up. The 'ouse'll be empty, everyone off 'ome.' They exchanged mutual good wishes and Mrs Towzer puffed her way down the stairs.

The letter was in Great-Aunt Mary's spidery hand. Surely not a last-minute request to shop for some forgotten article? Unless it was something she could buy at the station there was no time for anything else.

Theodosia sat down, one eye on the clock, and opened the letter.

She read it and then read it again. Old family friends, an archdeacon and his wife, had returned to England from South America, wrote Aunt Mary. Their families were in Scotland and they did not care to make such a long journey over the holiday period.

'Your aunt Jessica and I have discussed this at some length and we have agreed that it is our duty to give these old friends the hospitality which our Christian upbringing expects of us. Christmas is a time for giving and charity,' went on Aunt Mary, and Theodosia could almost hear her vinegary voice saying it. As Theodosia knew, continued her aunt, the accommodation at the cottage was limited, and since she had no lack of friends in London who would be only too glad to have her as a guest over Christmas they knew she would understand. 'We shall, of course, miss you...'

Theodosia sat quite still for a while, letting her thoughts tumble around inside her head, trying to adjust to surprise and an overwhelming feeling that she wasn't wanted. Of course she had friends, but who, on Christmas Eve itself, would invite themselves as a guest into a family gathering?

Presently she got up, counted the money in her purse, got her shopping bag from behind the door, assured Gustavus that she would be back presently and left the house. There was no one around; Mrs Towzer was behind closed doors getting ready for the party. She walked quickly to a neighbouring street where there was a row of small shops. There was a supermarket at its end but she ignored it; there the shops would stay open for another hour or so, catching the last-minute trade. Although she had the money she had saved for her train ticket she needed to spend it carefully.

Tea, sugar, butter and a carton of milk, cheese, food for Gustavus and a bag of pasta which she didn't really like but which was filling, baked beans and a can of soup. She moved on to the butcher, and since it was getting late and he wouldn't be open again for three days he let her have a turkey leg very cheap. She bought bacon, too, and eggs, and then went next door to the greengrocer for potatoes and some apples.

Lastly she went to the little corner shop at the end of the row, where one side was given over to the selling of bread, factory-baked in plastic bags, and lurid iced cakes, the other side packed with everything one would expect to find in a bazaar.

Theodosia bought a loaf and a miniature Christmas pudding and then turned her attention to the other side of the shop. She spent the last of her money on a miniature Christmas tree, which was plastic, with a few sprigs of holly, and very lastly a small box of chocolates.

Thus burdened she went back to Mrs Towzer's. The front door was open; there were guests for the party milling about in the hall. She passed them unnoticed and climbed the stairs.

'We are going to have a happy Christmas together,' she told Gustavus. 'You'll be glad, anyway, for you'll be warm here, and I've bought you a present and you've bought me one, too.'

She unpacked everything, stowed the food away and then set the Christmas tree on the table. She had no baubles for it but at least it looked festive. So did the holly and the Christmas cards when she had arranged them around the room.

Until now she hadn't allowed her thoughts to wander but now her unhappiness took over and she wept into the can of soup she had opened for her supper. It wasn't that she minded so very much being on her own; it was knowing that the great-aunts had discarded her in the name of charity. But surely charity began at home? And she could have slept on the sofa...

She ate her soup, unpacked the weekend bag she had packed with such pleasure, and decided that she might as well go to bed. And for once, since there was no one else to dispute her claim, she would have a leisurely bath...

It was half past eight before the professor left the hospital and now that he was free to think his own thoughts he gave them his full attention. Obviously he had nothing to fear from the lad in the path lab. For reasons best known to herself, Theodosia had embarked on some rigmarole of her own devising—a ploy to warn him off? She might not love him but she liked him. A man of no conceit, he was aware of that. And there was something wrong somewhere.

He drove himself home, warned his sister and brother-in-law that he might be late back, sought out Meg in the kitchen and told her to get a room ready for a guest he might be bringing back with him. Then he got into his car, this time with George and Max on the back seat, and drove away.

His sister, at the door to see him off, turned to see Meg standing beside her.

'It'll be that nice young lady with the gingery hair,' said Meg comfortably. 'Dear knows where she is but I've no doubt he'll bring her back here.'

'Oh, I do hope so, Meg; she sounds just right for him. Should we wait for dinner any longer?'

'No, ma'am, I'll serve it now. If they're not back by midnight I'll leave something warm in the Aga.'

Once he had left the centre of the city behind, the streets were almost empty. The professor reached

Bishop's Stortford in record time and turned off to Finchingfield.

There were lights shining from the windows of the great-aunt's house. He got out with a word to the dogs and thumped the knocker.

Mrs Trickey opened the door, still in her hat. She said, 'You're a bit late to come calling; I'm off home.'

The professor said in his calm way, 'I'd like to see Miss Theodosia.'

'So would I. She's not here, only that archdeacon and his wife wanting hot water and I don't know what—a fire in their bedroom, too. You'd best come in and speak to Miss Chapman.'

She opened the door into the drawing room. 'Here's a visitor for you, Miss Chapman, and I'll be off.'

Great-Aunt Jessica had risen from her chair. 'Professor, this is unexpected. May I introduce Archdeacon Worth and Mrs Worth, spending Christmas with us...?'

The professor's manners were beautiful even when he was holding back impatience. He said all the right things and then, 'I came to see Theodosia...'

It was Aunt Mary who answered him.

'These old family friends of ours are spending

Christmas with us. Having just returned from South America, they had no plans for themselves. We were delighted to be able to offer them hospitality over the festive season.'

'Theodosia?' He sounded placid.

'I wrote to her,' said Aunt Mary. 'A young gel with friends of her own age—I knew that she would understand and have no difficulty in spending Christmas with one or other of them.'

'I see. May I ask when she knew of this arrangement?'

'She would have had a letter—let me see, when did I post it? She must have had it some time today, certainly. We shall, of course, be delighted to see her—when something can be arranged.'

He said pleasantly, 'Yes, we must certainly do that once we are married. May I wish you all a happy Christmas.' He wasn't smiling. 'I'll see myself out.'

He had driven fast to Finchingfield, and now he drove back to London even faster. He was filled with a cold rage that anyone would dare to treat his Theodosia with such unkindness! He would make it up to her for the rest of her life; she should have everything she had ever wanted—clothes, jewels, and holidays in the sun... He laughed suddenly, knowing in his heart that all she would want would be a home and children and love. And he could give her those, too.

The house was quiet as Theodosia climbed the stairs from the bathroom on the floor below. All five occupants of the other bed-sitters had gone home or to friends for Christmas. Only Mrs Towzer was in her flat, entertaining friends for the evening. She could hear faint sounds of merriment as she unlocked her door.

The room looked welcoming and cheerful; the holly and the Christmas cards covered the almost bare walls and the Christmas tree, viewed from a distance, almost looked real. The cat food, wrapped in coloured paper, and the box of chocolates were arranged on each side of it and she had put the apples in a dish on the table.

'Quite festive,' said Theodosia to Gustavus, who was washing himself in front of the gas fire. 'Now I shall have a cup of cocoa and you shall have some milk, and we'll go to bed.'

She had the saucepan in her hand when there was a knock on the door. She remembered then that Mrs Towzer had invited her to her party if she wasn't going away for Christmas. She had refused, saying that she would be away, but Mrs Towzer must have seen her coming in with the shopping and come to renew her invitation.

How kind, thought Theodosia, and opened the door. The professor, closely followed by George and Max, walked in.

'Always enquire who it is before opening your door, Theodosia,' he observed. 'I might have been some thug in a Balaclava helmet.'

She stared up at his quiet face. And even like that, she thought, I would still love him... Since he had walked past her into the room there was nothing for it but to shut the door.

'I was just going to bed...' She watched as the two dogs sat down side by side before the fire, taking no notice of Gustavus.

'All in good time.' He was leaning against the table, smiling at her.

'How did you know I was here?' She was pleased to hear that her voice sounded almost normal, although breathing was a bit difficult.

'I went to see your aunts.'

'My aunts, this evening? Surely not...?'

'This evening. I've just come from them. They are entertaining an archdeacon and his wife.'

'Yes, I know. But why?'

'Ah, that is something that I will explain.'

He glanced around him, at the tree and the holly

and the cards and then at the tin of cocoa by the sink. Then he studied her silently. The shapeless woolly garment she was wearing did nothing to enhance her appearance but she looked, he considered, beautiful; her face was fresh from soap and water, her hair hanging around her shoulders in a tangled gingery mass.

He put his hands in his pockets and said briskly, 'Put a few things in a bag, dear girl, and get dressed.'

She goggled at him. 'Things in a bag? Why?'

'You are spending Christmas with me at home.'

'I'm not. I have no intention of going anywhere.' She remembered her manners. 'Thank you for asking me, but you know as well as I that it's not possible.'

'Why not—tell me?'

She said wildly, 'I saw you at the hospital. I wasn't spying or anything like that but I got out of the lift and saw you both standing there. You had your arm round her and she was laughing at you. How could you possibly suggest...?' She gave a great gulp. 'Oh, do go away,' she said, and then asked, 'Does she know you are here? Did she invite me, too?'

The professor managed not to smile. 'No, she

doesn't but she expects you. And Meg has a room ready for you...'

'It is most kind of you,' began Theodosia, and put a hand on his arm. This was a mistake, for he took it, turned it over and kissed the palm.

'Oh, no,' said Theodosia in a small voice as he wrapped his great arms round her.

She wriggled, quite uselessly, and he said gently, 'Keep still, my darling; I'm going to kiss you.'

Which he did at some length and very thoroughly. 'I have been wanting to do that for a long time. I've been in love with you ever since we first met. I love you and there will be no reason for anything I do unless you are with me.'

Somewhere a nearby church clock struck eleven. 'Now get some clothes on, my love, and we will go home.'

Theodosia dragged herself back from heaven. 'I can't— Oh, Hugo, you know I can't.'

He kissed her gently. 'You gave me no chance to explain; indeed you flung that lad from the path lab in my face, did you not? My sister, Rosie, and her husband and children are spending Christmas with me. It was she you saw at the hospital and you allowed yourself to concoct a lot of nonsense.'

'Yes, well...' She smiled at him. 'Do you really want to marry me?'

'More than anything in the world.'

'You haven't asked me yet.'

He laughed then and caught her close again. 'Will you marry me, Theodosia?

'Yes, yes, of course I will. I did not try to fall in love with you but I did.'

'Thank heaven for that. Now find a toothbrush and take off that woolly thing you are wearing and get dressed. You can have fifteen minutes. Gustavus and the dogs and I will doze together until you are ready.'

'I can't leave him.'

'Of course not; he is coming too.'

The professor settled in a chair and closed his eyes.

It was surprising how much one could do in a short time when one was happy and excited and without a care in the word. Theodosia was dressed, her overnight bag packed after a fashion, her hair swept into a topknot and the contents of her handbag checked in something like ten minutes. She said rather shyly, 'I'm ready...'

The professor got to his feet, put Gustavus into his basket, fastened the window, turned off the gas and went to look in the small fridge. He eyed the morsel of turkey and the Christmas pudding, but said merely, 'We'll turn everything off except the fridge. We can see to it in a few days; you won't be coming back here, of course.'

'But I've nowhere else—the aunts...'

'You will stay with me, and since you are an old-fashioned girl Meg shall chaperon you until I can get a special licence and we can be married.' He gave her a swift kiss. 'Now come along.'

He swept her downstairs and as they reached the hall Mrs Towzer came to see who it was.

'Going out, Miss Chapman? At this time of night?' She eyed the professor. 'You've been here before; you seemed a nice enough gent.' She stared at him severely. 'No 'anky-panky, I 'ope.'

The professor looked down his splendid nose at her. 'Madam, I am taking my future wife to spend Christmas at my home with my sister and her family. She will not be returning here, but I will call after Christmas and settle any outstanding expenses.'

'Oh, well, in that case... 'Appy Christmas to you both.' She looked at George and Max and Gustavus's whiskery face peering from his basket. 'And all them animals.'

Stuffed gently into the car, Theodosia said, 'You

sounded just like a professor, you know—a bit stern.'

'That is another aspect of me which you will discover, dear heart, although I promise I will never be stern with you.' He turned to look to her as he started the car. 'Or our children.'

She smiled and wanted to cry, too, for a moment. From happiness, she supposed. 'What a wonderful day to be in love and be loved. I'm so happy.'

As they reached his house, the first strokes of midnight sounded from the church close by, followed by other church bells ringing in Christmas Day. The professor ushered his small party out of the car and into his house. The hall was quiet and dimly lit and George and Max padded silently to the foot of the stairs where they sat like statues. He closed the door behind him, set Gustavus in his basket on the table and swept Theodosia into his arms. 'This is what I have wanted to do—to wish you a happy Christmas in my own home—your home, too, my dearest.'

Theodosia, after being kissed in a most satisfactory manner, found her breath. 'It's true, it's all true? Dearest Hugo, Happy Christmas.' She stretched up and kissed him and then kissed him again for good measure.

Outback Christmas
Margaret Way

Dear Reader,

Christmas has been special to me from my earliest memories of childhood. The thrill and honor of being allowed to stay up to attend Midnight Mass, a skyful of stars, holding tightly to my father's hand, always wearing one of the beautiful dresses my maternal grandmother, Margaret, used to bring me on her annual visit from Melbourne: a time of great excitement for all of us. Afterward such a supper! But we never did sleep in. Presents had to be opened.

Christmas has even managed to retain its healing magic through the sad times that are an inevitable part of life. Christmas is ritual and tradition, family and the annual renewing of the greatest gift we can offer one another—love. With this in mind, perhaps this Christmas we might commit ourselves to making this great family feast an occasion of paramount importance and show all our loved ones how deeply we care for them.

Marvelous Christmas dinners, a good many of them lovingly cooked by me, carefully chosen and beautifully wrapped presents are fine. They add to the joy and excitement. But in the end what makes us feel absolutely happy is the priceless gift of shared love and peace within the fold. If we've got that, we won't miss much else.

May I take this opportunity to wish you all my sincere good wishes for the upcoming holiday season with the hope that it will bring more joy and significance than ever before.

Margaret Way

CHAPTER ONE

THE convention hall was almost full when Ronnie arrived ten minutes late and almost out of breath. The Premier was there, along with the Minister for Primary Industries, a visiting Federal senator, representatives of the Cattleman's Union and a good many pastoralists who had flown in from all points of the vast Queensland outback to discuss what was happening within the beef industry. They were there to let the government know of their concerns and hopefully come up with some much needed strategies for the new millennium. As the biggest beef producer in the world, Australia like the other big beef-production countries, was suffering an industry downturn, and conventions like this were being given top priority.

As expected, the print and television media were there to cover the occasion. Ronnie knew all of them. These were her colleagues. Her eyes ranged swiftly over the large crowded room and struggled valiantly to get past a particular tall male figure who seemed to dominate the rest.

Finally she caught sight of two of her pals.

There was an empty seat between them almost as though they had been keeping it for her. As indeed they had. And very few people would wonder why. Rowena Warrender was making quite a name for herself in the world of television news. Not exactly a new talent, she had worked for Brisbane's top TV station a couple of years before her much publicised marriage to Kel Warrender. At that time, he was one of the most eligible bachelors in the country and son and heir to Sir Clive Warrender, easily the most colourful and controversial of the country's cattle kings.

Now when her ''splendid'' marriage was said to be on the rocks, she had returned to her old TV station and been taken on as part of their news team. She was smart, poised, a woman as opposed to the fresh-faced girl she had once been, and she had the excitement of the Warrender name.

As well, she was a good journalist and a skilled interviewer with a natural talent to connect with the people she spoke to. Best of all, she looked marvellous on camera, golden-haired and brown-eyed with a charming speaking voice full of expression. In short, she had the gift for drawing the audience in and, in the process, lifting those all-important ratings. To her bosses at Channel 8, Rowena Warrender was professional magic.

Several yards from her, waiting impatiently for proceedings to begin, was Owen Humphries, top political reporter from *The Courier*. He turned his big, genial head and caught sight of Ronnie, approaching nervously. Of course, the husband, Owen thought with a wave of empathy. He hadn't emerged from the breakdown of his own marriage unscathed. As one of the State's leading cattle barons, Warrender was bound to be here and not surprisingly listed as a speaker.

"Hey, Ronnie," he called, patting the seat between him and Josh Marshall, the well-known TV presenter, almost consolingly, "a seat here."

Poor girl looked like she was ready to fall into it. Everyone in the business knew Ronnie's sorrowful story. The failed marriage that had started out so brilliantly in a blaze of publicity. The little girl, Tessa, now five, apparently so traumatised by her parents' break-up it was said she had become a selective mute, talking only to her mother and, of all things, an imaginary friend. Not that the child wasn't highly intelligent. Owen had seen her with her mother on several occasions.

Tessa Warrender was a beautiful little girl, but like her mother, full of a hidden heartache. Owen knew of the vulnerable person hiding behind Ronnie's glamorous subterfuge.

As ever, she looked great. Every male in the room turned to look at her. Except Warrender. Owen didn't wonder why. The separation was said to be tearing both of them apart.

Guessing painfully at people's speculation, Ronnie moved in her friends' direction sweeping a few strands of her trademark shoulder-length hair from her face. It had been blowing madly outside—typical gusty September day—and she had been delayed overlong talking to Tessa's teacher, a lovely, sympathetic young woman, and the school psychologist, who was on the verge of throwing up her hands at Tessa's determination to remain silent. Everyone was trying so hard to help her little daughter. To no avail. No amount of dedicated efforts could trigger Tessa's voice.

Mercifully her little classmates in the first grade found Tessa's "differentness" exotic. They loved her and made no attempt to tease. Anyway, Tessa was at the top level of her class. She had even won a prize for her exceptional drawing—a beautiful big book with marvellous illustrations of fairies and elves and pixies in their realm of wonder. Tessa, too, lived in her own secret world and it was a source of much worry and anguish to her mother.

Josh was smiling at her, not making any attempt to shift—they both wanted her in the middle like the meat in a sandwich—so she had to struggle past Owen's well-padded knees even though he turned them to one side to accommodate her. Owen was something of a gourmand. Someone, it could even have been her, said he would never make fifty unless he lay off the great quantities of fine food and vintage wines he consumed. Josh, smooth-faced and handsome, was just the opposite, keeping his distance from the dinner table, a slave to staying in great shape and always looking good in front of the ruthless eye of the camera.

"I see your ex is here," Josh warned her, sympathetic and protective. He had been pursuing Ronnie with a passion since her return.

Ronnie squirmed, holding back her pain. "Not my *ex*, Josh, as you very well know."

Josh tightened his well-cut mouth. "It's just a matter of time. Tessa needs a father."

"She has a father, Josh." Ronnie gave him an ironic smile. "He's right over there."

"Hard to miss him," Owen grunted. "A superlative-looking guy. It must be wonderful to look like that and have all the money in the world. Better yet, he's got the kind of brains and energy this country needs. I have to confess I'm eager to hear him speak."

Ronnie smoothed the short skirt of her pinkish

beige power suit closer to her knees. "No one better," she said laconically. "One of Kel's great talents is igniting excitement." Kelvin Clive Warrender. One hell of a man and one it paid to keep her distance from. His skin was dark from his life in the blazing Outback sun, and his thick black hair had a deep wave to it. She had always loved it when it grew too long between haircuts. He had extraordinary light eyes that went from silver to slate, hard, high cheekbones, which gave him very definite features although there was a new severity to his commanding handsomeness. Then came the never-ending surprise of his beautiful smile. Like the sunshine coming out from behind a cloud. How many thousand times had he blinded her with that smile?

Even without the extraordinary glamour of his everyday cattleman's gear, the marvellous Akubras, worn at such a rakish angle, the denims, the brilliant bandannas knotted backwards around his neck, the fancy silver-buckled belts and the splendid handmade high boots, he looked incredibly dynamic. Kel was a complete original.

For the conference, he was suited like the rest but never so soberly. He was wearing a beautiful charcoal-grey suit, Australian merino, of that Ronnie was certain, an expensive white shirt with bold blue stripes and a pristine white collar, and an elegant ruby silk tie with some sort of a gold fleck. At six-three, he towered over the group that was standing with him hard in discussion. Every face was lifted to him with attention and respect. Apart from the strength, the acuteness of his intelligence, he was so stunning it was hard for most people to keep from staring. It was like being caught up in some gravitational force-field.

No safe place to hide.

Kelvin Clive Warrender was a man who sparked off passions. Who should know better than her? Once, her own passion for him had been all-consuming. Without boundaries. He had filled her life from day one with the sweetest, wildest joy and excitement. Lord, was it really seven years ago? She had already been launched on a career, a bundle of energy herself in those days, full of the intense curiosity that motivated a good reporter. It was her old boss, Hugh Denton, who had sent her along to try to inveigle an interview out of Sir Clive.

Sir Clive, like his son, always had an eye for a good-looking woman. Both of them, she had found, would use any means short of force to get their way. Not that they would need anything like force. Both the sweetest and, in the end, the most brutal of men, these were ones to steal and imprison a woman's heart.

Ronnie's father-in-law, like her husband, had had a complicated nature. Both of them had strayed. Too often, but maybe that was the fault of their passionate natures. In any event, she had loved both of them. To her cost. Kel had bought her and bound her body, heart and soul. Ronnie's beautiful melting brown eyes began to burn and she turned them away from the sight and the sound of her once adored husband. What was good about Kel, the most difficult of men, was that he loved his little daughter even if he didn't love his wife. What Ronnie had amounted to in the end was a possession.

Her mind went back to their final bitter confrontation when for the first time they had both shown their real feelings—a scene etched forever in her memory.

"Let's get something straight, Rowena," he had warned her in that quiet tone that was infinitely the more chilling for being so still and certain. "I will never, *ever* relinquish my claim to my daughter. She's a Warrender and she'll take her place in our world. I'll remind you, too, that you're my wife. Talk of a divorce means little to me. You're my *wife*. What I have, I hold."

She nodded in bitter amusement. "Why not, when possession is everything? Don't think I've forgotten you're the big cattle baron, and take your hands off me," she flashed, her body even then confused and reacting.

But his grip had only tightened. "Your decision to leave me is only doing injury to all of us, Rowena." The cold mask of control started to crack. "You're not thinking of Tessa. Are you emotionally blind? These past terrible months have affected her to the point she's withdrawing like a little animal into her shell."

That had turned her to maternal indignation. "You think I don't know that? You think I'm not filled with endless regret? But what's the alternative, Kel? Tell me that. I tolerate your rotten affairs?"

He showed her a face almost shadowed by grief. "My transgression, Rowena." He stared directly into her furious eyes, trying to exert his extraordinary power. "One bloody, loose night when my mood couldn't have been lower. I know it shocked you, but I've tried in every way I know how to make amends. You were giving me hell. You'd turned away from me for no good reason. Nothing was normal."

He tried to wrap her in his arms, but she broke

away. "So are you telling me you've got it all out of your system now. No way! You're just like your father." She worked herself up into a fine rage. "Any good-looking woman is fair game."

"Then why do I love *you*?" He grabbed her by the shoulder. "You're so beautiful, but one sanctimonious, judgemental, unforgiving ice goddess. Full of your own sense of righteousness. What happened to the passionate girl I married? Overflowing with love. Limitless, unconditional love. How the hell did you turn into someone else? Now you're so bloody cold you might as well be a nun."

"That's enough!" She fixed him with withering eyes. "Who are you to speak of love? You never loved me. All you ever had for me was *lust*."

He raised his hand then, almost as though he was going to strike her, but even while her heart fluttered, she knew he would never do that. Kel was a very stylish man. He had been raised to behave with perfect courtesy around women and children. Meticulously the gentleman. Anyway, it wasn't true what she said, but that was the extraordinarily bitter position she had reached.

Afterwards she did what Hilary, her sister-in-law, advised her. "Leave him for a bit, Ronnie. I know I would. Kel has always had everything his own way. Make him sit up and take notice. Leave.''

So she did. Flying out while Kel was away on business. For all she knew, meeting up with Sasha, the woman who had never really been out of his life. She couldn't even bring herself to leave a note. With betrayal raging through her, she had left her home and the husband she had adored. The harder one was hit, the heavier one fell.

He saw her the moment she walked in. You'd have to be blind to miss her. Rowena had always had a glow about her. The beautiful golden hair, full and swirling, the soft brilliance of her dark eyes, inherited from her Italian mother along with the fabulous olive skin, the graceful body that showed off her stylish clothes so well, those long, flashing slender legs. The whole spirit of her, so luminous it imbued her with a kind of radiance. Rowena Warrender. His wife.

She had been moving swiftly, engaged in getting a seat before the Premier opened the conference, but her body moved more slowly after she picked up on him.

"Go away. Leave me alone, Kel," it seemed to say. The truth of it was he would never leave her alone. She was part of his flesh, sunk deep into him, his self-sufficiency never to be regained. He followed her progress even when he appeared not to. She was joining Owen Humphries, one of the State's best-known and respected journalists, and that airhead, Josh Marshall.

He focused on Marshall hard, interested in his body language. No doubt about it. It didn't need a gut feeling to tell him Marshall was in love with his wife. The high priestess of sanctity. How unwise to have chosen Rowena. Rowena had been involved with no man since the terrible day she had left him. He kept himself apprised of such things. With Rowena, when you did a wrong, you did a wrong. Other women forgave their men. Rowena never would.

"You should never have married her in the first place, Kel," his stepsister, Hilary, had tried to console him in her unintentionally insensitive way. "Don't think I blame you. Ronnie is a very hard girl to pass by. I'm fond of her myself, but she sure knows how to hurt."

Hurt? There had to be another word. So far as he was concerned, he had stumbled into hell. Nights were the hardest. By day he could work himself to the bone. There was even a trancelike aspect to his life. Like now. Here he was holding court with the State's top pastoralists when his

mind was in pursuit of Rowena. She knew exactly
how to punish him. And what about Tessa, his little
princess, golden-haired like her mother but with
his grey eyes. Once, they had reflected such joy,
such serenity. ''Daddy, Daddy, can you make me
a tree house?''

To his beautiful little daughter, he had been a
magician. He could do anything, make anything,
cause wonderful things to happen. Their last
Christmas together as a family had been magic.
Now another Christmas was coming up.

He hadn't made things easy for Rowena. He had
won the right to have his daughter for periods of
time. The coming Christmas vacation would take
in seven weeks. He couldn't wait for it, though his
daughter caught in her trauma never spoke to him.
She kissed him, let him cuddle her, put her arms
around his neck, but she never spoke. Why? She
held him responsible for her strange new life.

It wasn't Rowena manipulating her. Rowena
would never do such a thing. She adored their child
as much as he did. In recent times, he had seen
Rowena cry her heart out when she was pushed
beyond endurance. But she had never allowed him
to share her grief. In sleeping with Sasha—hell,
had he really slept with her or was it one of her

fantasies?—he had shattered his wife's trust. But he was damned if he was going to let her get away.

Kel fully intended to waylay her after the morning's meeting broke up. If Rowena loved their daughter as much as she said she did, she'd better agree to coming back to Regina Downs at least for the length of the school vacation. To hell with her job. What was so fulfilling about being a TV reporter? They were parents with a damaged child. Both of them had to find a way out for their little Tessa before she became enmeshed in her world of silence.

A little after one when the meeting broke for lunch, Kel caught up with Rowena as she walked to an exit. The tailor's dummy, Marshall, was with her, more like glued to her side, but Rowena got the message from his eyes.

"I'll see you later, Josh," she murmured hurriedly, making no attempt to introduce them.

"Are you sure?" Marshall seemed ready to defend the fair lady as he rightly should.

"She's sure," Kel clipped.

"I'll catch you later, then, Ronnie," Marshall said, his eyes wavering away from Kel Warrender's diamond-hard stare. Arrogant devil.

"Quite the white knight, isn't he?" Kel murmured in an amused, irritated voice as Josh Marshall moved off.

"He's tried to be a friend."

"As long as he tries nothing else." Kel took her beneath the elbow and steered her through the crowded foyer, ignoring all the speculative glances that were directed their way.

He was so powerful, so seductive, Ronnie felt all the old desire rise in her blood. This happened every time they met and she had to accept she couldn't control it. Hormones, she explained to herself. Hormones raging through her body. Kel had always affected her that way.

"So, have you time for a bite of lunch?" he asked when they were out on the sunlit pavement. He looked so handsome, so vital, so perfect, she relived her loss all over again.

"Kel, haven't you grasped I don't want to be with you?" she said, trying to hold in her emotions.

"We have things to discuss, Rowena." He took her arm urgently. "I'm appalled by your coldness."

Wasn't she herself? "That's unfair," she protested. "It was you after all...."

His eyes sparked. "I wonder if we could get off the subject of my miserable infidelity and talk about our daughter. I desperately want to see her. Before I go back, if possible.''

"Of course you can see her." Ronnie shook her head in dismay. "Have I ever denied you that?"

"You denied me your body often enough." His own bitterness overflowed.

Ronnie looked away. "Maybe my battered pride had something to do with it."

"I guess so," he said wearily. "We can't stand here slugging it out. For what reason I'll never know, people seem to be very curious about us."

"Being in the public eye makes one very vulnerable, Kel. You can't move freely. Neither can I.''

"So let's get away." He put up his hand, signalling a passing taxi that immediately pulled into the kerb. Kel had always had that knack. "You can spare an hour. I'm staying at the Sheraton. Their restaurant is pretty good."

Despite her concern, Ronnie found herself in the back seat of the cab as it covered the distance from the Convention Centre to the hotel. Being with Kel was like having a dagger to the throat, she thought theatrically. On no account could you defy him. That's what came of being reared as an Outback prince.

In the hotel restaurant, she looked around, spotted a couple of faces she knew socially, husband and wife, gave them a little wave, which they returned before diplomatically going back to the study of their menu.

"What are you going to have?" Kel asked, taking another glance at her lovely, closed face.

She gave a brittle little laugh. "I don't want much."

"Seafood. Could you manage that?"

"You decide, Kel." She was trying to sound cool, but the slight vibrato in her voice was giving her away.

A young waitress approached and gave Kel an adoring smile. "Nice to see you again, Mr Warrender. Would you and the lady care for a drink?"

"Nothing for me, thank you." Ronnie shook her head. Here was someone at least who didn't watch Channel 8.

Kel sank back into his chair, smiled idly at the girl and ordered a beer. "We'll have the menus, too."

"Certainly, Mr Warrender." She hurried away to oblige, returning within seconds, smiling all the while into Kel's eyes.

A man as sexy and dynamic as Kel Warrender should be registered as a danger to women, Ronnie thought wryly. She, too, sat back trying to conceal all the hurt that was in her. How *should* a wife feel knowing the man she adored was having an affair with another woman?

Never look to Sasha Garland to take a high moral stand. Sasha was the victim of sexual obsession. She'd been Kel's girl since forever. Her father, George Garland, was a prominent pastoralist, a millionaire and a lifelong friend of the late Sir Clive Warrender. Sasha had always been a favourite in the Warrender household and both families apparently had cherished hopes one day Sasha and Kel would marry.

Ronnie had blazed onto the scene, shattering everyone's hopes. Small wonder Sasha had been devastated, but in the end she'd had her vengeance.

Now Kel spread his elegant, long-fingered hands. "And how is my little princess? No worse, I hope."

Ronnie adjusted a piece of silverware, her expression deeply concerned. "I had a meeting with her teacher and the school psychologist this morning. That's why I was late getting to the Convention Centre."

"And?" As usual, he leapt to the point.

"Nothing has changed, Kel. I wish I could tell you differently. Tessa maintains her silence with everyone but me. But astonishingly she's keeping up with her work. She's in the top three in the class and she's doing exceptionally well with her drawing.''

"Why wouldn't she be smart?" Kel grated to cover his own pain. "God knows you're bright enough and I managed to pull off a degree or two." In fact, he had an honours degree in commerce and law. "This psychologist can't be any good."

"She's not the only one Tessa sees," Ronnie protested. "I take her to a top professional, Kel."

"Maybe she's trying to teach me a lesson I'll never forget," he said painfully.

"She adores you, Kel. You know that," Ronnie assured him, never mastering her feeling to give him some peace.

"But she won't speak to me. She holds me responsible for our break-up. But I won't accept that entirely." He raised his raven head. "You played your part."

Ronnie let out an anguished sigh. "I had to leave you, Kel. It can't be otherwise."

"The truth is you don't want to front up to your marriage vows," he retorted.

"What if I'd been unfaithful, Kel?"

He looked at her, eyes as dazzling as the sun on ice. "I don't think I'll answer that question. But I can tell you this. I'd make short work of the guy involved, but you'd never get away. I loved you passionately. I married you, and I'm going to stick with my vow. Till death us do part.''

Baffled, she stared at him. "You don't expect much, do you? I'm twenty-nine. I could have a long life ahead of me. I could fall in love again, marry, have more children. I want them. But first I would need a divorce."

"Over what?" he challenged.

She exhaled deeply. "Over Sasha Garland, Kel. Did you ever get around to breaking the tie?"

He sank back wearily in the chair. "That would be damned near impossible. I've known Sasha all my life. Her dad is my godfather, my own father's best friend. Our mothers were always close. Sasha has been very kind to Hilary. She's shown her a lot of understanding. Lord only knows how Hilary finished up so unattractive."

It *was* a mystery. The parent Kel and Hilary had in common, Sir Clive, had been an outstandingly handsome man. Both Kel and Hilary looked a lot like him, but whereas Kel had turned out stunning, Hilary, six feet tall and well built with features too strong for a woman and a gruff, abrasive manner, seemed terribly disadvantaged. Ronnie had always looked on Kel's stepsister with a good deal of sympathy and tried her best to be friendly, but it had taken a while before Hilary had let her in.

"Don't shift the subject to Hilary," Ronnie warned. "And don't think she's entirely loyal."

His tone showed intense irritation. "What the hell do you mean?"

"Insight, Kel. Insight hard won. Hilary has problems. Most you know about. Some you don't. I know she worships the ground you walk on. But you're bigger, stronger, brighter, than she could ever be. And you're a *man*. You're all-powerful. You were your father's heir. Yet Hilary was his firstborn."

"Hell, Ronnie," he exclaimed, in his anguish using his nickname for her. "Hilary could never run Regina Downs, let alone a cattle empire. Worse, the men don't like her. They show her deference and respect, but that's only because they know they have to."

"Hilary knows how to dish out the arrogance," Ronnie said, witness to it countless times. Hilary trying to match up to her stepbrother. Exert his authority. "She's a woman who desperately needs attention."

"All right, I agree with that, but she's very fond of you."

"Is she?" Ronnie asked quietly, feeling Hilary

had somehow betrayed her. "It was Hilary who advised me to leave you after all."

He was visibly shocked. "I don't understand you."

"Then just let it drop."

"How can I?" He set his jaw. "I want to talk."

"That would be fine, only it's all too late."

He stared at her as though trying to see into her soul. "I never heard Hilary say a word against you."

"Are you sure?" Ronnie's eyes flashed bright.

"We agreed you certainly know how to hurt." Faint colour moved under his dark copper skin. "Anyway, Hilary was trying to comfort me. She's devoted to Tessa."

Ronnie nodded. "I know. We're going round in circles. This is solving nothing."

"Then why bring it up?" he challenged her. "I can't believe this! *Hilary* told you to leave me?"

"I'm not lying, Kel." Ronnie lowered her gold head. "I'm sure she didn't mean for long, but she thought you needed teaching a lesson."

"For God's sake!" He shook his head in amazement. "Hilary has gone out of her way to be understanding."

"Maybe she wants to have things the way they were," Ronnie told him bleakly. "You and Sasha, the family choice. As you're Tessa's father and a very influential man with friends in high places, you could get custody of our child. In other words, the whole lot.''

His strongly marked brows drew together. ''I've never heard anything so stupid in my life.''

''Maybe jealousy softens up the brain.'' She gave a brittle laugh. ''I've been reading up a good deal of psychology lately. When I started to put things together, it occurred to me Hilary had some kind of love-hate going where you're concerned. You were the apple of your father's eye. His wonderful son. Your mother idolised you. Sir Clive was always kind to Hilary, but you could see he was trying hard. She has no charm, and you and he had charm galore. Her own mother died when she was a child, which must have been a terrible blow and Hilary and your mother have never really got on, much as Madelaine tries. Such wildly different types. I think, though Hilary appeared to accept me, underneath she may have resented me.''

Kel considered a moment, then came to his stepsister's defence. ''You want to forget the times she went out of her way to help you? To show you the ropes? What you're saying is absurd.''

''I didn't mean to make you angry.'' She looked away across the beautifully appointed room.

He shook his head. "I *am* angry, Rowena. Believe it. I had a meaningless one-night fling with Sasha I don't much remember. No excuse, but I was very drunk with a demon in me. I shamed myself and I hurt you. I've begged for your forgiveness and I'm not a begging man. But you're going to hang me as though I committed a terrible crime."

"Infidelity is a sin," she pointed out quietly, thinking of its terrible effect on her.

"And I've got my punishment," he said. "I accept that, but I can't have our little daughter punished because of what happened between us."

Wasn't that the truth. "What is it you want me to do, Kel?" she asked in a kind of despair.

"Don't hold me to an impossible standard," he flared. "I've missed you more than I can possibly say. I miss my little girl. I want us to be together forever. Not for it to be like this. Haven't you got any love left for me?"

Above all, she had to keep her head. "Kel, I've grown very self-protective," she tried to explain.

"I can see that." The indomitable Kel Warrender sounded drained. "Is there any chance you can come with Tessa for the Christmas vacation? You must know she needs you there. We have to solve this problem of our daughter together."

"I'm scared to come back, Kel." She felt she could crumble with pain.

"Scared? Not you." His vibrant voice softened.

"I don't want to be seduced all over again."

Hostility bristled. "I thought you treasured our sex life."

"That's right. I treasured it." She tried but didn't quite succeed in holding back a glistening tear. "But I can't take it when you lie to me."

"Lie to you? Hell, woman—" he leaned closer "—didn't I confess right up?"

"You did that *one* time." She shook her head.

"There were *no* other times, Ronnie," he gritted. "I promise you."

Not entirely true. She recalled one occasion when she had caught him withdrawing from Sasha's passionate embrace. She remembered vividly her shock, her sick sensations, the way she had to support herself by clutching a chair. She thought of the number of times Hilary had hushed things up for them but later admitted to the couple's meetings under Ronnie's questioning.

The waitress approached again, glancing from one to the other. "Would you be ready to order now, Mr Warrender?"

Kel nodded absently, staring down at the menu for a moment before ordering the catch of the day, red emperor with French fries and a side salad for two. Neither of them was hungry as it happened. Too many disturbing things on their minds.

They fell silent for a few moments while they waited, then Kel began to ask about her job, listening attentively to the things she told him. He always had been a good listener.

"Is that what you think you really want?" he asked eventually.

"I have to live, Kel. It's all I know," she said defensively.

"When you can have all the money you need." He let out a sardonic laugh.

"Except I don't want to take it from you."

"You're my wife," he reminded her, his expression wrenched.

"I'm also my own woman. And a very successful one."

"I don't mean to diminish your ambition, Rowena. You're very compelling on television. But you're not so very successful at covering up your heartache. It's all there in your beautiful dark eyes."

"None of us can evade pain," she replied.

"But we can *confront* it. I want you back, Ronnie. I'll die before I ever let you down again.

And there's more. I want more children. I want them from *you*. I want a son."

Ronnie smiled a little bitterly. "Of course, a man must have a son."

"*I* must have a son, sons, who can take up their heritage," he corrected her. "I adore my daughter, but I would never expect a woman to work a quarter as hard as I do. It's a very physical world, you know that. A dangerous world, too. I love my little Tessa with all my heart. I want the very best for her. That can only happen when her mother and father are together."

It was fruitless trying to defend herself against his powerful charm. "I don't know, Kel. I couldn't bear to go through any more terrible times."

His smile burned. "I'll make it work, Ronnie, I promise."

"Let me think about it," she evaded, shaking her head. "Like you, I'm desperately worried about Tessa, but I have commitments. A contract to honour." In fact her contract was due for renewal with a promised big salary hike.

"You have just over two months left to run." He felt like letting out a great shout of gratitude and triumph. "Surely you can work something out? We'll pay them out if we have to."

What a wonderful thing it was to have lots of

money. "It's a pretty big thing to ask, Kel," she said. "I'm promising absolutely nothing beyond accompanying Tessa. She would want me to, much as she loves coming to you."

He groaned, pain in the sound. "And this is the little girl who used to love all my bedtime stories."

"They were so good they used to send her off to sleep." Despite herself she smiled, showing the single dimple in her cheek.

"That's because she was so little. I'm a great storyteller."

"God help you, yes."

"Ronnie, let up," he rasped. "You've already had me on the rack, but enough's enough. My heart, my head and my bed are empty without you."

He was a true magician. She was weakening. "It seems so long...."

"The worst fourteen months of my life. I've been counting." His response was soft and tender.

Unsettled, she asked, "Is Madelaine at the homestead?"

"Not at the moment." His glance was slightly mocking. "My mother comes and goes, but she'll be back as soon as she finds out you and Tessa are coming home."

"Let's take one thing at a time, Kel." She

feared her own desire. "Don't get any ideas I'm going to move back into our bedroom, either."

One black eyebrow shot up. "You surprise me, Ronnie. When did I ever force you?"

"A couple of times," she lied. Both of them had been playing games.

He shrugged. "I give you my word." He let his eyes move so slowly over her, Ronnie's pulse began to race. It had been an eternity since he'd made love to her. An eternity. Now just his looking at her was like a free fall in space. She was giddy with sensation but afraid of crashing to earth.

"Should I respect it?" She fixed him with large, liquid eyes.

He leaned forward to grasp her hands. "I can't think of anyone you should trust more."

CHAPTER TWO

By THE time they parted company, a kind of fragile peace had been established. Ronnie had to meet up with a staff photographer, while Kel had to return to the Convention Centre.

"What time should I turn up to see my daughter?" His silver-grey eyes ate up her lovely face. There was no life without her. None.

"I'm working until around six-thirty," she responded. "Tessa will be staying with Mamma. Why don't you come there?"

Thinking back, he gave a sardonic laugh. "So Bella can tell me yet again what a fool I've been."

"Most likely," she said wryly. "At the same time, you've got a big place in my mother's heart. She lives for the day we're…" She broke off and turned her head so he wouldn't see the expression in her eyes. "Stay for dinner if you like. Tessa will love it."

"What time does she go to bed?"

"That's not a criticism, is it, Kel?"

"It's a simple question." He smiled down at her, that twist-your-heart-in-your-breast smile.

"Generally around half past seven," she answered. "She can stay up a little later. I'm not sending her to school tomorrow. She has an appointment with Dr O'Neill midmorning."

"That's the child psychologist?" There was pain in his eyes.

"Yes," she replied, quietly confronting her own part in their separation.

"Why don't I take her?" he suggested. "Didn't you tell me he wanted to see me anyway?"

"He knows you're an important man and you're only in the city from time to time, Kel."

"So I'll take her tomorrow," he urged. "I can find the time."

"I'll see." She wasn't about to relent. "Anyway, I'd better be getting back."

"Let me find you a cab." Casually he turned, picked one approaching and hailed it. "Until tonight, then, Rowena."

"Fine." She tried to speak lightly despite holding back so much feeling.

And then he kissed her. Caught her chin, turned up her face and lowered his mouth over hers. Her mind's eye glittered with stars. And her emotions heated with helpless fury. Wasn't this the man who had abused her trust? Would she never be free of her own violent longing? It was so humiliating.

As he released her, Ronnie, conscious of the swirling lunchtime crowd and the fact her face was very well known, smiled up at him with mock sweetness. "Don't *ever* do that again," she gritted from between clenched teeth.

"You taste delicious, Ronnie. You always did."

The cab swept next to the kerb. Kel opened the rear door and waited while Rowena climbed in. Finally he saluted, ever so gallant, ever so chivalrous, a small taunting smile etched on his beautiful, seductive mouth.

Kel Warrender, her husband. Ronnie didn't wave. Didn't look around.

The cab had barely gone a block, moving slowly through the traffic, before it missed the green light. Ronnie stared out the window, her mind in a kind of trance as if a spell had been laid on it. But the spell was well and truly broken as she found herself staring directly at a woman framed in the doorway of an exclusive boutique. It wasn't simply the fact that the woman was eye-catching, this woman's features were etched on Ronnie's memory forever. Early thirties, tall, poised, model thin, very fashionably dressed, designer sunglasses hiding those cat's eyes, her short, stylish bob a lot darker than when Ronnie had last seen it.

Sasha Garland.

Sasha Garland in town. It was all very predictable. Ronnie swallowed hard on the knot in her throat. What a rotten start to the afternoon. Get a grip on yourself, girl, she urged. It could be merely a coincidence. Then just as swiftly, be your age. Sasha's turning up in town at the same time as the convention was exactly the sort of thing she'd do. Kel hadn't said a word about it. Why would he? Ronnie knew for a fact the Garlands were out of the country. No, Sasha was on the loose. Maybe she was even staying in Kel's hotel suite.

Ronnie mulled that over and felt ill. The calming effect of lunchtime harmony was ruined. This was the woman who had destroyed her marriage. The woman who had never forgiven Ronnie for the terrible injury she had done her. Stolen her man. Only Ronnie had never known a thing about Sasha Garland until weeks after Kel had asked her to marry him. Everyone had kept silent. Including Kel.

Her stomach churning, Ronnie leaned forward and asked the taxidriver to let her out. Perhaps if she spoke to Sasha? Like right now. She and Kel were still married. Sasha must listen. Anger and resolution radiated from heart to brain. Thrusting a five-dollar note at the driver, Ronnie stepped out onto the pavement.

"Keep the change," she called, falsely jaunty.

"Thanks, luv." Women! the cabbie thought wryly. Forever changing their minds.

Several feet from Sasha, Ronnie called her name. She was apprehensive now that Sasha would tell her things she didn't want to know, but she was determined on and in need of some sort of confrontation.

Sasha whirled, laughing though Ronnie had no idea why. "If it isn't the glamorous Rowena Warrender in the flesh," she breathed, her voice full of sarcasm. "What is this—an ambush?"

Ronnie didn't hesitate. She went right up to her. "Surely you're not worried? I saw you. I thought I'd say hello."

"How about the truth?" Sasha challenged.

"What are you doing in town?" Ronnie used her professional on-the-spot voice.

"Loitering with intent." Sasha gave a crooked smile.

"Tell me about it," Ronnie urged. "Tell me about the times you've followed my husband all around the country."

"What if I have, Ronnie?" Sasha said genially. "The thing you can't seem to get is that Kel was mine long before he was yours. Men are to blame for everything. Say, why don't we have a cup of coffee, girls together. Everyone staring at us is hurting my eyes. Tell me, are they staring at you or is it me?''

"I don't know and I don't care," Ronnie said briskly. "I've just had lunch with Kel, but I could manage another coffee." A gallon if she could pin this woman down.

"You're angry, Ronnie." Sasha's smile showed pity. "I can see it in your eyes. What about Nicco's?''

"That'll be fine.''

Nicco's at lunchtime was packed with familiar faces, heads swivelling in Ronnie's direction, waves all round. Her good-looking face spelling irritation, Sasha forged ahead, then threw herself into a banquette like an athlete crossing the finish line. A big fish in most ponds, she wasn't used to any other woman catching her waves. As always, it had to be Rowena Warrender.

"So you were telling me you had lunch with Kel?" Sasha lost no time in picking up the conversation, lifting an imperious hand to order espressos for both of them. "Never could kick the habit," she murmured.

Ronnie looked down at her pink polished nails. She wasn't wearing her exquisite diamond engagement ring nor her wedding band, and her hands felt extraordinarily bare. "We may be separated, Sasha, but there are lots of things for us to discuss.

"About Tessa?" Sasha nodded in understanding. "I've been feeling bad about Tessa." She spoke the simple truth.

"I should think you would," Ronnie shot back so sternly Sasha flushed.

"I don't like the idea of hurting her," Sasha said defensively. "She's Kel's daughter after all. But you screwed up your own life, Ronnie," she accused, dark brows puckering.

"How's that?" Ronnie's answer was tight. "We were blissfully happy until you chose to take your vengeance."

"Take my vengeance? God, that sounds melodramatic," Sasha snorted. "It takes two to tango, sweetie. You might have thought you were *it*, but Kel needs a helluva lot of woman to satisfy him."

"You mean someone bigger than both of us," Ronnie retorted sarcastically. "You weren't enough for him, either. He married *me*."

"He was dazzled by you for a while," Sasha said more quietly. "I have to hand it to you, Ronnie. You keep yourself looking great. You're smart, stylish—heck, you're even warm and friendly. I can't help liking you myself, even though what you did to me was horrible. Kel was *my* man. See how you like it now. The thing is, Ronnie, there's no way I'm going to let go. Put it down to my obsessive nature. I grew up believing I was going to marry him. Mumma persevered with it even when you and Kel were standing at the altar. I know it's not a good thing to break up marriages, but I've convinced myself it would never work out. You're an outsider, Ronnie. Hilary and I knew that from day one. It's taken time and I've sent quite a few eligible guys on their way, but they all seem so colourless beside Kel.''

"And Kel's so colourful he's dangerous," Ronnie finished wryly. "Listen, I get the picture, Sasha. I even feel sorry for you. But if my husband cares as much about you as you seem to think, why has he never asked me for a divorce?"

Sasha lowered her glossy dark head, then said in a well-thought-out way, "I know his biggest concern is Tessa. He'll do nothing more to upset her at this time. But he's bonded to me."

"You don't feel it's because you're forever hanging around?" Ronnie suggested.

"Maybe." Sasha looked momentarily upset. "But I'll continue to do so, Ronnie, until Kel shuts the door in my face."

Under her professional composure, Ronnie's

heart sank. "So tell me, where are you staying while you're in town?"

"The Sheraton, where Kel's staying. What do you think?" Sasha drew back while the waiter set down the two rich dark-roast espressos.

"In a way, you've pilloried the man you confess to love," Ronnie offered in retaliation.

"You expect me to give him up?" For a moment, Sasha's golden-green eyes were quite wild.

Ronnie exhaled sharply. "It's a reasonable appeal from a *wife*. That's if you ever had him in the first place, which I'm beginning to doubt."

Petulance came into Sasha's voice. "You don't believe the rumours? Maybe you'd prefer times and places? Hilary could fill you in."

"That's another thing that's bugging me." Ronnie looked Sasha right in the eye. "Doesn't it disturb you, knowing you're twisting Hilary's mind? You pretend to be her *friend*!"

"Oh, to hell with that!" Sasha tossed off irritably, cheeks reddening. "I get my bad moments like everyone else. Hilary can be incredibly wearing even for me. How can she possibly land a man, which is what she desperately wants and what she tries so desperately to hide, with her dreadful gear and sergeant-major abrupt manner? I've been trying for years to jolly her into changing her image."

There was a grain of truth in it. "Hilary needs someone to love. Someone to love her," Ronnie said, always with a sympathetic slant to her mind.

"You're saying there's someone out there?" Sasha jeered, herself so unhappy with the way things had turned out that sarcasm seemed to spring from her as if from a fountain.

"The thing is I trusted Hilary once." Ronnie stared reflectively across the room. "Now it's dawned on me you were using her to undermine me."

"Got it in one!" Sasha mocked. "But I wasn't lying, Ronnie. No matter whether he married you or not, Kel and I were building a life before you were ever dreamed of. These days, the bond is as strong as ever."

"And it does help if you keep following him around," Ronnie emphasised the point gently. "Hilary, of course, with her confused loyalties, keeps spilling the beans. But get ready for a big surprise. I'll be back on Regina for Tessa's school vacation. Kel has begged me to stay."

It was the last news Sasha wanted to hear; in fact, it upset her deeply, but she made a valiant attempt to rally. "Hey, you are Tessa's mother," she pointed out.

"Indeed I am." Ronnie stood up, her expression

one of near serenity. "And you just might remember, I'm still Kel Warrender's wife."

Ronnie arrived at her mother's house some forty minutes before Kel was due. The front door was open and she bent to pat Coco, her mother's King Charles spaniel, who greeted her ecstatically, snagging her right stocking in the process. Tessa followed, smiling at her mother in her heartbreaking fashion, running for the evening ritual of a big hug and kiss.

"Hello, darling, have you been a good girl for Nonna?" Ronnie asked, melting under a torrent of maternal love and protectiveness.

Bella, wearing an apron, appeared in the hallway, a lovely warm smile on her face. "If you can call feeding Coco nearly a packet of Smacko's being good. I'm expecting a grand attack of indigestion later on."

Tessa's lips barely moved. "But don't you think he looks happy, Mummy?" she looked up to whisper, deep in her self-imposed near silence.

Ronnie rested a hand on her little daughter's shining head. "He does indeed, darling." Coco was sitting in front of them, head cocked, tail thumping, the very picture of a contented dog. "But we must look after him and that means sticking to his special diet. Too many treats might make him sick, just as I don't allow you to eat too many sweets. Anyway, good news. Has Nonna told you Daddy is coming for tea tonight?''

Daddy!

Tessa's heart swelled at that infinitely dear name even though Daddy went away and she never saw him again for a long time. Wonderful, wonderful Daddy. Her beautiful, big soulful eyes, so like her father's in shape and colour, conveyed a yes. She would be very, very good so Mummy and Daddy wouldn't fight anymore and the terrible spell on her voice would be broken. She and Mummy would go back to the place she loved more than any other place on earth.

Regina, where the sky was always a vivid, cloudless blue and the endless plains were an extraordinary bright red. And the homestead! The marvellous homestead, so big she couldn't even count the rooms. And the rocking chair Daddy brought down from the attic and put in her bedroom so he could tell her bedtime stories while they rocked back and forth. Regina, the place she called home. The place where she really belonged, the way all the glittering stars belonged in the sky.

''I know you won't feel like going to bed when I tell you...'' Mummy was saying sweetly. She never shouted or got cross. "…but you can't stay up too late, sweetheart. Daddy will tuck you in and tell you one of his Dreamtime stories."

Tiny blue pulses beat in Tessa's vulnerable temples. She clasped her hands, drowning in a mixture of excitement and agony. Every morning she woke, it was to a sense of terrible loss. Once, there had been three of them—a family. She remembered climbing over Daddy in the mornings so she could lie between him and Mummy in the big bed, snuggling up. She missed the strong, handsome father she adored, the way he made everyone else look little. Even Mummy felt sad and alone. She just knew it. Though she smiled every night on the television, Tessa knew her mother was missing Daddy terribly. Tessa was sure an evil magician was at work. Just like in her storybooks.

Acutely aware of her small daughter's train of thought, Ronnie stood for a helpless moment staring down at her. Bella had changed the little girl into a very pretty pink dress for the occasion, and dressed her long hair with a cascade of ribbons falling from the crown. Tessa's whole expression was so sweet and poignant Ronnie felt it like a blow. Their marriage break-up had been very hard on everyone. But it had been disastrous for Tessa.

She and Kel would have to deal with it as a matter of urgency.

Afterwards, with Tessa sitting expectantly by the window awaiting the arrival of her father, Ronnie grabbed a few moments alone with her mother. Bella was in the kitchen, a professional workplace for the dedicated cook, making final arrangements for dinner. Tonight it would start with the exquisite eggplant ravioli Kel always enjoyed. What made Bella's pasta so special was the fact she kneaded it by hand using the very freshest eggs.

Roast leg of lamb with rosemary and garlic sizzled in the oven, while chunks of vegetables roasted together in a baking dish. Bella usually added a drizzle of balsamic vinegar for the last fifteen minutes of roasting the vegetables, lending them a wonderful caramelised flavour.

When Ronnie's father had been alive—an engineer, he had been killed in a tragic on-site accident a scant year before Tessa's birth—there had been much entertaining at their house. Her mother had the marvellous Italian knack of putting wonderful food together, then setting an exceptional table. Ronnie looked at her now with great love and admiration. Her mother had been so brave. Ronnie went to her mother, put her arm around her trim waist and hugged her.

"How was Tessa, really?" she asked. "Apart from the incident with Coco."

"I only turned my back for two minutes," Bella said, laughing. "She's okay. She solved the new jigsaw puzzle I bought her in what I thought was record time. It said on the box seven to eight years and she's only five."

"She hasn't spoken a word?" Ronnie raised her eyes to her mother's profile, thinking as always how beautiful she was, how timeless. Isabella was in her mid-fifties now, hair as dark and abundant as ever, olive skin unlined, the fine dark eyes Ronnie had inherited full of warmth and wisdom, her figure full but perfectly proportioned.

"I'm sorry, my darling," Bella said, herself a mass of emotion. "It breaks my heart as much as it does yours. She had a long, whispered conversation with her little friend."

"Nicholas?"

"I'm not sure if Nicholas isn't her guardian angel," Bella suggested. "Have you ever asked her?"

Ronnie sat down in a chair at the long table. "I've asked her lots of times, but she withdraws on the subject of Nicholas. He's always there for her. She doesn't know why."

"And Dr O'Neill tomorrow?" Bella checked on the roast.

"Kel wants to take her this time."

"Why don't you let him?" Bella thought it was a particularly good idea. "The doctor's told you he wants to see Tessa's father."

"Tessa's adored father." For a moment, Ronnie's large dark eyes filled with tears almost as though she didn't know what was happening to her.

Bella watched her with deep sympathy. "Kel is one of those men it's very easy to have great affection for."

"Even when he betrayed me, Mamma?"

"Come, come, my darling," Bella went to her daughter and laid a hand on her shoulder. "It seems to me on reflection that perhaps the punishment didn't fit the crime."

"Now, Mamma, you played a part in it," Ronnie protested. "You agreed with me when I left."

Bella's expression grew sad and pensive. "I didn't know it was going to go on this long. I didn't know the effect on my little Tessa. It happened, *cara*. I don't even think Kel knows why. It was one of those accidental things."

"It was planned," Ronnie said, and her voice

had a ring to it. "It was planned all along. When I left Kel after lunch, I ran into—"

"Don't tell me. Sasha Garland?" Bella looked agitated.

"She said she's staying at the Sheraton where Kel is this week."

"She would volunteer that information," Bella said with fine scorn.

Ronnie nodded. "She is. I checked."

"How I despise her," Bella groaned. "This is wicked. Did you have it out with her?"

"I managed a few words. She claims Kel is still involved with her. She'll never let go."

Ronnie could see the anger rise through her mother's body. "She's a fool, then. I'll stake my life on it. Kel loves you. It's about time that woman fixated on somebody else. You can't tell me Kel is begging you to come back to him and continuing an affair. I won't have it."

"What am I to do, Mamma?" Ronnie asked in some bewilderment. "He broke my heart."

Bella shook her head, her hair arranged in a classic knot. "You have no life without him, my darling. I know you too well. Tessa is suffering badly. Her world that was so full of sunshine has become dark and menacing. She desperately needs her mother and father to be together."

"So I forgive him now. Is that it?" Ronnie asked in a kind of despair. Pride versus longing.

"What else can you do?" Bella said. "He's human, flesh and blood. He's had his punishment. This Sasha, painful as it is for her to accept, must mean nothing to him. He had plenty of time to marry her and he didn't. He's made no move towards getting a divorce. On the contrary, he has told you many times over he wants a reconciliation."

"So this can happen to me again?" Irritably Ronnie brushed the trace of tears away. "If not with Sasha, someone just like her. Let's face it, Kel is a very sexy man. A rich sex life is very important to him."

"I think, actually, it is to you too. I don't relish saying this, my darling, but you told me yourself you had shut the bedroom door on him."

Ronnie felt chilled by her memories. "That was only after Hilary told me what was going on behind my back."

"Ah, Hilary." Bella gave a deep, ironic laugh. "Sasha and Hilary have been friends for a long, long time. That's just the way it is. These landed people always stick together. Nevertheless, I think now Hilary must have been swallowing Sasha's lies."

Ronnie shrugged darkly. "Except I did see something to confirm it. Something that disturbed me terribly."

"When was this?" Bella stared down at her in consternation.

"It was after a weekend party, a couple of years ago. Kel's team had won the polo cup. I went in search of him, full of pride and love, only to find him in Sasha's arms. It looked like they'd been kissing passionately."

"It was a trick of course!" Bella huffed. "Did you have it out with them? Did you confront them?" she asked sharply, her eyes very dark.

"I'm not a confrontational person, Mamma. You know that," Ronnie sighed. "Coming on that after all Hilary's hints, I was afraid of my own thoughts. What was I supposed to do? Break up my marriage? Turn the other cheek? I found myself slinking away."

"I don't understand why you didn't tell me." Bella was trying to get it all sorted out.

"You've shed enough tears, Mamma. I'm not a child. I had to work it out for myself."

"So meanwhile, all the tension built up. You became more and more insecure until you finally packed up."

"That's about it." Ronnie shrugged. "I refused

Kel my bed as a last resort. Something he bitterly resented. Nothing seemed to add up. Did he really need *two* women? A wife and a mistress?''

''It was Sasha who worked at being the mistress,'' Bella observed shrewdly. ''She's immensely cunning. She may well have seen you coming that night and thrown her arms around Kel. She could easily have made it appear they were kissing. To an insecure young wife, such a thing would be very incriminating. I only know when you first brought Kel to meet your dear father and me, we thought the two of you were made for each other. Both Hilary and Sasha each in their own way have tried very hard to spoil things for you. I don't think you should let them get away with it.''

The sound of Tessa's footsteps as she pattered through the parqueted hallway alerted them to Kel's arrival. Even then, the little girl didn't call out, which all three adults desperately hoped for, but her face was wreathed in smiles as Ronnie let Kel through the front door. He was dressed with casual elegance in a double-breasted jacket worn over a soft blue shirt and dress jeans. He was carrying wine, roses, chocolates and a brightly wrapped and beribboned present that was obviously for Tessa. His wonderful vitality flowed from him to his womenfolk.

He picked Tessa up and kissed her until she giggled helplessly with excitement, funny little gasps coming up from her throat as if she was exploding with joy, but no longed-for words. Finally Kel let his eyes rest on his wife, courting her all over again, before Bella came from the kitchen to greet him, her apron removed, arms outstretched.

"Kel, how lovely to see you." It was a gesture of reconciliation and affection.

This resulted in more kisses all round. "Bella, you get more beautiful with every passing day," Kel said so sincerely it filled Bella with pleasure.

"I try to make a life for myself," she said.

"And nothing would delight me more than for you to come to us at Christmas." Kel turned to smile into Tessa's small face, drawing her head onto his shoulder. "Wouldn't you love Nonna to come and stay with us on Regina?"

Hardly daring to breathe, Tessa touched his chest, greatly comforted by the strong thud of his heart.

"Wonderful. Then it's all fixed." Kel spoke warmly, confidently, though he yearned for conversation with his little girl. "Now what about us opening your present, princess?"

"Of course." Ronnie smiled. When he was being good, Kel was utterly irresistible.

Dinner was like the old days, great culinary enjoyment, laughter and good conversation. Later, Kel and Ronnie took Tessa up to bed. It had been decided Ronnie and Tessa would stay with Bella for the night. Kel tucked his daughter in, then sat by her bed telling her one of his store of Aboriginal legends while she drifted off to sleep. He didn't look ruthless, a man without a husbandly conscience; he looked like a deeply devoted father, lingering lovingly at the bedside of his sleeping child.

"I can't believe she's persisting with this silence," he said to Ronnie when they were out in the hallway. "Obviously it's all my fault. One mindless act and I put my whole family at risk. I hate myself, Ronnie." His eyes were as deep as the ocean as he looked at her. She had changed her suit for a short georgette dress in deep blue, a shade he loved on her. Her long blonde hair was tucked behind her ears to show off her lovely diamond-and-pearl earrings. He had given them to her along with a matching necklace when Tessa was born. A beautiful woman who was forcing him to live in celibacy.

"I tried hating you, too. An impossible thing to do."

"So neither of us has escaped our bonds?" He

looked into her vulnerable eyes, seeing the aching desire.

"How could we? We have our child." She had a terrible urge to lean forward and rest her head against his chest.

"And we have one another," he exhorted her. "Our marriage is the most important step I've taken in my life. It wasn't just some escapade I engaged in. I married you determined our marriage would last forever. You cut me off, Rowena, long before Sasha flew a thousand miles to turn up at my hotel."

The knowledge made her flare into sudden anger. "I know all about your desires, Kel."

His sparkling eyes roamed every feature of her face. "Yes, I remember. But my desire was all for *you*."

"Yet Sasha is still in your life." She knew she sounded like a tape that wouldn't stop, but she couldn't help it.

He speared long fingers into his raven hair. "I think we'll have to call it arrested development with Sasha," he said, his patience running out. "Mothers don't realise what they do talking marriage from the cradle. At this stage, I couldn't get rid of Sasha with a fire hose."

"Apparently not," Ronnie returned acidly. "She's staying at the Sheraton."

"What the hell! What are you saying?"

"I ran into her a few minutes after I left you. Didn't she tell you?" Ronnie's eyes widened.

"Don't be so stupid, okay?" His voice turned hard. "Sasha's free to stay anywhere she likes. I'll speak to her if I have to, but I'll never fall into her trap again."

Her trap. The words had a terrible ring.

"You're free to divorce me, Kel, any time you like," Ronnie said bleakly.

"For God's sake, haven't you been listening?" He seized her powerfully and drew her towards him. "What is it with you? Some deep-seated insecurity? When are you going to learn I want you. No one else. God knows why when you're treating me so badly."

"Don't do this, Kel," she protested, trying in vain to break free.

"Why not? You're my wife."

Blazing with anger and a desire that fairly crackled, he lowered his head, pressing her against his body so she felt his arousal, kissing her until she was drained of all resistance.

"Let me love you," he muttered. "Let me start all over again." His hand, which trapped her breast and caressed it through the filmy material, became more insistent as the nipple peaked beneath his grazing thumb. "Ronnie, God!" He shaped her arched back, kissing her searchingly, playing her like a violin. "Love, my lover, I want to be deep inside of you," he groaned.

Her resistance, after all, was as fragile as glass. Only the fact they were in her mother's house gave her a vestige of control.

"Kel, you've got to stop," she implored, so full of emotion her voice broke.

"How do I do that?" His deep laugh was edgy.

"Mamma might come." Now he pinned her lower body against his, and for a moment she felt herself in flames, utterly naked.

"Bella never barges in," he told her. "She's too sensitive, too experienced to do such a thing. We can't go on like this, Rowena. We want each other. We always did. Nothing else matters." He began kissing her throat with close urgency. "That's a great dress, but I want it off you. I've never stopped thinking of your beautiful body and how if feels under my hands."

It was as it had always been. He was sweeping her away. "You're dangerous to love, Kel. I've found that to my cost."

"*Forgive me*. That's all I ask. I promise if you

come back to me, I'll take great care of you and our child. I'll never allow anyone to come between us again. Promise, Ronnie."

She broke away, gasping. "Kel, stop pressuring me. Moving me about like a pawn. You've always been good at it. I've been through an agonising process of trying to get my life together."

"It's no life for Tessa without her father around," he countered just as urgently.

"Do you think I don't know that?" She looked up at the tall, powerful strength of him. "You're asking me to put my career on hold."

"I'm asking you to abandon it all together," he said flatly.

"When I'm not even at the height of my powers?" she asked with bitter humour. "Not even in my prime?"

"Is that how you see it?" he asked, eyes flashing in the bronze sheen of his face. "Is this your *dream*, Ronnie? To be a passing star on television news?"

Put like that, it didn't sound like much. "I'm good at what I do, Kel," she answered quietly.

He made a little sound of apology. "I know you are, but it's a job another clever, good-looking woman could handle. And there are plenty coming up. Your *unique* job, a job no one else on this earth can do is being Tessa's mother. We hear all the time how children are so resilient. How they can bounce back from anything. I don't feel happy with that. Plenty don't. Most children can't handle the sad breakdown of a family.'' He stared at her with his silver eyes, his charisma so lavish she felt like buckling at the knees.

"Kel, I know all this,'' she said numbly. "I know it only too well. But life with you will never be quiet. It's like battling a big surf. The thrill, the excitement, the wonderful exhilaration, then the inevitable crash.''

Perversely she never mentioned the countless times he had been so exquisitely gentle and comforting. Kel, the big, powerful cattle baron cosseting her as if she was someone ineffably precious. Kel kissing her face, her throat, every inch of her body. The ecstasy!

"Let's try a period of reconciliation first,'' she suggested, afraid she would never withstand him once back on Regina.

"I'll try anything you like.'' He was enormously moved, pulling her to him with quiet, controlled strength. "But don't shut me out, Ronnie. I can't take it again. I bitterly regret my mistake. It was shameful and crazy. I don't have much memory of it.'' He sighed ruefully as if even he couldn't take it in. "It does me no good to bring this up, but I was really messed up and pretty damned drunk."

"Nice try, Kel, but it won't work." Ronnie shook her blonde head.

"So there's no use my insisting?"

"No." She had heard it all before. His denials. Hilary's admissions. What she had seen with her own eyes.

"Are you going to allow me to take Tessa to the psychologist tomorrow?" he asked in a different, more clipped tone.

"Mamma thinks it's a very good idea."

"Thank God Bella is on my side," he said wryly. "She doesn't want this separation to go on."

"Mamma doesn't believe in divorce."

"Neither do I," he said forcefully. "And neither do *you*, Ronnie, when all's said and done. The only thing I'm asking is for you to give me another chance."

She bit her lip. "I've been very badly hurt by all this, Kel. I'll probably lose my job if I ask for a lot of time off. My contract is up for renewal. Most likely they won't take up the option."

"At this point, Ronnie, our daughter is more important than your contract," he said, his hands closing on her shoulders.

Ronnie nodded but didn't speak for a moment. His hands were warm and hard on her skin and she felt desire cut through her like a knife. She was young. He had taught her everything there was to know about passion. Now this. This barren wilderness.

"I'll come with you tomorrow," she said finally. "Both of us should be there. I never dreamed what happened to us would have such terrible repercussions. Dr O'Neill is treating Tessa's case very seriously."

"I'm sure he is." Kel squared his wide shoulders. "I've checked his credentials. They're beyond reproach, but I feel our being reunited as a family would be far more therapeutic than all the counselling."

He took her hand and began walking with her down the corridor to the central staircase. "So what time?"

"Would it be a problem to pick us up here at ten?" she asked.

"No problem at all." He turned at the top of the stairs then took her slender body all the way into his arms. His blood surged with sensuality. *Bellissima*," he said softly. "You are so lovely. Hair glittering all shades of gold. Eyes like dark velvet. Skin like flowers. Your beautiful breasts just out of sight. I hurt a lot, Rowena. There's the demands of my body but also here inside my head.''

He was speaking from the heart, but Ronnie warned softly, ''Don't think I'm going to fall straight into your bed.'' Pathetic, when her whole body was shaking.

''God forbid I should make you.'' He was aware of the pulse that beat so frantically in the small hollow of her neck.

''I mean it, Kel. You must respect my wishes.''

''I always did. Trust me, darling,'' he urged. ''If you don't, it will kill me.'' He lowered his head, kissing her very gently at first, then not gently at all, moving his hands hungrily up and down her lower back as her clothes moved and her short skirt rode high.

Finally he put her away from him not a little disoriented, seeing her eyes tightly closed, her mouth trembling, her breath ragged. Their desire still had the same rushing momentum.

''Lord,'' he breathed onto the top of her head. ''It's the same story every time I touch you. I'd better go.'' His hand grasped the polished newel on the banister. ''We've got to be together, Rowena. I give you my solemn promise I won't touch you until you ask me.'' There was genuine commitment as well as a little smile in his voice.

And I probably will, Ronnie thought. Not ask. *Beg.* The day wouldn't dawn when she would be free of her husband's spell.

CHAPTER THREE

HE ARRIVED back at the hotel, passing but not seeing Sasha tucked into a deep armchair, nursing another nightcap to get up her courage. God knows the multicultural river city of Brisbane was alive with attractive men, Sasha thought, many bearing the dark, striking good looks of their Mediterranean heritage, but as soon as she saw Kel Warrender striding purposefully through the lobby, Sasha felt the same old shock of need through her body. No one could eclipse him. No one. That was her tragedy.

A young woman near her whispered to her friend, "Isn't he a dream?"

"Heck, he's famous." The other woman nudged her companion's arm playfully. "Kel Warrender. You *know*. The cattle baron. Don't you remember he married Rowena Warrender? But the marriage broke up."

"How terrible," the first young woman said, sounding shocked. "I expect another woman got in the way. Who wouldn't try with a guy like that?"

Exactly, Sasha thought grimly. I'm one tough, persistent woman and this is my last-ditch stand. She waited exactly seven minutes, then stood up a little unsteadily and smoothed her short black crepe evening dress with the shoestring satin straps. Kel had always admired her legs. He favoured black, too. It suited her sophisticated looks and the cut was anything but austere. Any article about her in the glossy magazines always mentioned she was one sharp dresser.

Bolstered by the admiring glances that came her way, Sasha made for the lifts aware of the trembling that shook her body. It seemed to her she had always been engaged in some elaborate scheme to get Kel to commit to her. It really was a chronic condition. But for a while there, she'd had him until golden-haired Ronnie had stolen him away. At that time, she and her mother had been counting their chickens before they were hatched. They'd been sure they could pull off an engagement. Women did it all the time. Even married to his precious Ronnie, Kel hadn't actually renounced her.

Kel came to the door of his suite at the second knock. He stared down at her—magnetic, exciting, smouldering blackly.

"Sasha," he said, shaking his head, "keep this up and you can consider yourself a call girl."

"Naughty, darling," she said, wincing. "I live the way I want, Kel. I like to make things happen."

"Tell me about it." He stared past her down the corridor. "Have you brought a photographer with you?"

"Don't be like that," she cajoled, pretty sure he would ease up. "I'd never hurt you or your precious reputation."

He shrugged, bleakly amused. "You exaggerate, of course. One of the things I've learned about you, Sasha, is you don't give a damn who gets hurt."

Her eyes flickered as she felt his mood. "For pity's sake, Kel, after all these years, are you trying to tell me I'm nothing? You allowed me to love you. We were lovers. Now you're telling me I'm no good. Why are you guys so insensitive to a woman's pain? Hell, I love you so much I'd let you carve me up. What happened at the Sandpiper Inn wasn't entirely my fault."

"Especially your fault," he corrected. "You schemed, plotted, planned it."

Her chin shot up. "I had to do it, Kel. I don't care if you are married. Marriage isn't what it used to be."

Kel pitched his voice almost kindly. "Sasha,

you must accept this once and for all. I love Rowena. Got it? I love our child. I have not given up on my marriage. I never wanted to hurt you or puncture your pride. I didn't deceive you. You got no talk of marriage out of me no matter how hard you and your mother tried to rope me in. I'm very fond of you. Why wouldn't I be? We grew up together. We share the same roots. But for God's sake, get on with your life and let me get on with mine."

Sasha looked like she had received a body blow. "What a miserable ingrate you are. You can't dismiss me like that. I gave you the best years of my life. Let me in."

Kel's silver eyes turned to slate. "The answer is a great big no. I'm in enough trouble already."

"Scared of doe-eyed Ronnie?" she mocked, slipping her arms playfully around his waist.

"Don't play the fool, Sasha." He drew away. "I'm angry."

Abruptly her confident facade crumpled. "I'm not happy, either. I just want to apologise. Sort this thing out. Life's too short to turn your back on your friends. Please, Kel..." Neatly she bobbed under his arm and entered the suite. "Say, this is great!" she said, looking around.

"Sasha!" he nearly yelled at her, then thought

better of it. There was no telling what Sasha would do with a few drinks in her. "I've never ill-treated a woman in my life, but I'm about to throw you out."

"No." She fixed her eyes on him, then threw herself into an armchair, bunking in. "Hang on a sec, Kel. I'm not out to seduce you."

"Really?" His eyebrow shot up. "I thought that was the whole idea."

"Up to now, Kel, you've been my whole existence," Sasha said quietly.

"Then I'm sorry." He couldn't keep the pitying note out of his voice. "But you've been spoiled rotten, Sasha. It's not a case of your never knowing when to give up. You *have* to have what you want. It doesn't matter whose happiness is at stake. I know you're genuinely fond of Tessa, but look what's happened to her since Ronnie and I separated. Doesn't Tessa matter?"

"Of course she matters." Sasha sounded sorely wronged. "I know it's horrendous, but it's not my fault alone. You were with me at the Sandpiper Inn."

"Ah, the Sandpiper Inn," Kel responded flatly. "All I recall is waking up and finding you in my bed. You told me we had one helluva night, but I don't remember a damn thing. All I remember is leaving while you were having a conversation with one of my colleagues.''

"Bob Wilding." She nodded. ''We were drinking partners.''

"I remember telling you to get out of my bed. I also distinctly remember your odd answer. 'I'm on my way.' Is it possible you got into my room via the veranda?'' He stared at her so accusingly Sasha began to fidget, then as he came closer, his handsome face positively threatening, she began to radiate guilt.

"Ah, well, you were bound to find out sooner or later,'' she admitted, suddenly collapsing into confession, her normally strong, clear voice wavering like a child's.

"So I didn't betray Ronnie after all.'' In the middle of his shock and anger, Kel felt elation.

"Keep your dreams, sweetheart," she said bitterly. ''You didn't. You were out of it.''

"My God!'' He turned way from the sight of her. ''The damage that's been done. For what? I don't love you, Sasha. I love Rowena. And both of us have been worried sick about Tessa.''

"But, my dear,'' Sasha gritted, ''I thought you could love me with Ronnie out of the way. I pictured it so often I convinced myself it was true.'' She rose groggily, her eyes huge in her pale face.

"I'd better go. I need a drink to ease the pain." She began to walk slowly across the room, starting back a little as the phone shrilled close beside her.

"Don't touch it," Kel warned, alerted by something in her expression. There was a distinct possibility it could be Ronnie with a change of plan. "Sasha..."

Without hesitation, her contrary nature at work, Sasha snatched up the phone and spoke seductively into it, eyeing Kel all the while. "Kel Warrender's suite, Sasha speaking," she added unforgivably.

"Bitch!" Kel breathed, visualising Ronnie's stricken, shocked face at the other end.

"Well, what do you know, no answer!" Sasha crowed, though her pinched expression gave the jauntiness of her tone the lie. Finally, finally, she realised no ploy on earth would ever work. She couldn't make Kel love to order. The bravest thing she could do was take herself off to the other side of the moon.

Kel wanted to believe very much it wasn't Ronnie who had rung, but he knew in his bones his hunch was correct. When he arrived at Bella's, she met him at the door, taking him conspiratorially by the elbow and drawing him into the living room.

"Gosh, I can do without all this, Kel," she said

in her rich, beguiling voice. "Rowena isn't here. You'll have to take Tessa by yourself."

"That's no problem, Bella." He turned to stare down at her. "Where in hell *is* Ronnie?"

Bella returned his challenging look fairly and squarely. "Her boss at the station has sent her on a job. He left a message last night. He wants nobody else but Ronnie. She's so good at her job."

"So that's why she rang me at the hotel," he groaned.

Bella swung on him, dark eyes flashing, memories of her daughter's heartache flooding her mind. "Do you think it wise to let that woman into your room, Kel? That brazen Sasha. The woman needs a shrink. She's a terrible troublemaker."

He did his best to keep cool. "Tell me something I don't know. I wasn't entertaining her, Bella. She turned up on my doorstep, ducked under my arm and took up a defensive position in an armchair."

"You didn't throw her out?" Bella asked with blazing eyes. "You so big and strong?"

"I could have," he agreed, "but to tell the truth, I was a bit concerned about bloodcurdling shrieks. Some women are shocking when things don't work out for them."

Bella savoured that for a moment, then asked more mildly, "You're asking me to believe this?"

"I'm not asking. I'm *expecting* you to believe it—and a lot more," Kel answered bluntly. "Sasha's turning up last night might have caused more problems, but it freed me from a lot of heartache. She finally admitted nothing happened that night at the Sandpiper Inn. Absolutely nothing. She suckered me in, damn her. So much suffering, but in the end it was no more than Sasha trying to play Delilah."

"She's prepared to tell Ronnie?" Bella asked hopefully. She had met Sasha Garland enough times to know how far she would go to get what she wanted.

"She doesn't feel *that* bad about it, Bella." His tone was ironic.

"So it's your word against hers?"

"It is, and Ronnie's gone off like a firecracker, right?"

"She was breathing flames," Bella said in confirmation, "and feeling tremendously upset. Can you blame her when that Sasha is taking control of the situation?"

"Why didn't Ronnie speak?" he countered.

"You damned well know why. She's haunted by that woman."

"Not anymore," Kel said grimly. "Ronnie's going to have to trust me."

When Kel and Tessa arrived at Dr O'Neill's, it was to find Rowena unexpectedly waiting for them.

"I thought you had an assignment," Kel said, ignoring her closed expression.

"It'll keep," she answered briefly without looking at him. She bent to kiss Tessa on her small perfect nose. "How are you, darling?"

In answer, Tessa sighed deeply. She had picked up instantly on the vibrations that pulsed between her parents. Little as she was, she could sense what went on behind her mother's soft, tender eyes. She knew exactly how her mother felt and how much she loved Daddy. But she wouldn't let him know about it. The saddest part was that Tessa *knew* Daddy was wonderful. It distressed her terribly that they lived apart, which was one of the reasons why the evil magician had taken her voice. Tessa couldn't remember when it happened. Or even how. She just seemed to stop talking. She knew she would make Mummy cry if she told her all about it. When she saw Daddy, it was like a tight string was wrapped around her tonsils. The magician had done that. She loathed him. Lots of times she felt like talking to Nonna, but the words wouldn't come. Nonna would only tell Mummy.

Mummy and Nonna talked every single minute they spent together. They were the greatest *friends*. Finally Nicholas came to help her. Nicholas, her guiding spirit. Nicholas helped her push away the panic when her voice wouldn't work. It was *so* peculiar.

A few minutes later, Dr O'Neill came to the door smiling, shaking hands with her tall, wonderful daddy before asking her to join him for a little talk. Dr O'Neill was so nice, with sparkly blue eyes and lovely white hair even when he wasn't old. Mummy said he had a great sense of humour. Talk! Wasn't that funny when she was caught in the spell? But the magician couldn't stop her from drawing things for her nice doctor.

While their small daughter with her intense thoughts disappeared into Dr O'Neill's office, Kel took a seat beside his wife on the comfortable leather couch. A collection of beautiful prints all touching on childhood scenes hung on the walls.

"Would you care for coffee?" Judy Richmond, the sweet-faced, rather old-fashioned receptionist, asked, always managing to realise when parents needed a few moments alone together.

"That'd be wonderful." Kel slipped easily into a charming smile.

"I'll be a few minutes," she returned. "You needn't worry about the phone ringing. I'll take it on the extension."

"That was nice of her," Kel murmured after the receptionist had moved into an adjoining room.

"She's a very nice woman," Ronnie confided coolly. "She needs to be since Dr O'Neill works with children."

"What's wrong, Ronnie?" he broached her attitude swiftly. "There's frost coming off you."

She gave a low, brittle laugh. "I'll never warm to *you* again," she said with exquisite contempt.

He nodded, careful to see things from her point of view. "If you give me a moment, I could explain about Sasha last night."

"I doubt if you could explain it even if we had all the time in the world, Kel. What I find difficult to understand is why you *want* to explain."

"It's impossible here," he said, listening to sounds of cups clinking in the next room.

"I'm glad you realise that," Ronnie responded, feeling her own energy absorbed by his.

His rush of anger was quickly followed by a far deeper tide of hurt. "I intend to tell you before I go back,'' Kel announced, glancing at her set profile.

"Which is when?"

"The conference finishes tomorrow. I flew in in the Beech Baron. I'm due out midafternoon."

"At least the conference has been a success," Ronnie said tonelessly, staring at her ringless hands. "Regina has defied the gloom."

"Not just Regina," he corrected her. "Market prices are at a twelve-month high. We've had the best season in years and the lower dollar gives us a big advantage. We all need something positive after the tough years, or have you forgotten?"

"Cattle are only part of your big portfolio of interests, Kel," she pointed out.

"Maybe." He shrugged. "We've had to diversify, but the cattle business is our life. That's what I am before anything else, Ronnie, a cattleman like my father and my grandfather and his father before him. You assured me it was the life *you* wanted."

"Ah, but I didn't believe then that our marriage could fail." Unable to resist, she gazed briefly into his silvery eyes, seeing them darken.

"It will only fail if you let it, Ronnie."

"Oh, that's good coming from you," she murmured, and closed her eyes.

"Let's sort it out outside," he suggested, badly

wanting to pull her into his arms. "What we're both here for is our child. Her welfare comes before our needs. Agreed?"

"Of course I agree." It was the sad truth she had faced. "Whatever happens to us and our relationship appears to be over, our parenthood is not."

His tone was low but his attitude was clear. "*I* don't accept that our relationship is over, Ronnie. You're as much in need of comfort and security as Tessa. I want us to sit down afterwards and discuss this."

She clasped her hands together on her lap. "I have to go back to work, Kel. You appear to want me to accept Sasha Garland as part of your life. I'll never do that."

His striking face tautened by several degrees. "The truth is that Sasha is out of my life."

"Extraordinary way she has of showing it," she snapped back.

"Rowena," he said in an intense undertone, "I've been branded something I'm not. I never did believe it. But I've been made to suffer. That's all over. I want my daughter. The impact of our separation has been disastrous for her. I know you recognise that. I want you back. Make no mistake about that. And take a few minutes to consider the enormous stresses of divorce litigation. You won't take my child from me. I don't intend to be a part-time father. You'd better grasp that.''

''So I'm to tolerate your infidelities or battle you for custody?''

Her hands were shaking and he reached for them, holding them firmly. ''Don't push me too far, Ronnie, and don't dump infidelities on me. That's just a beat-up. What about that tailor's dummy, Josh Marshall? Isn't he mooning after you?''

''Don't be ridiculous.'' She pulled her hands away when she craved his touch.

''Hell, Ronnie, I saw the way he was looking at you.''

''You don't like the notion of another man look-ing at me?'' Her chin came up.

''They could just get themselves strung up,'' he drawled, glancing at her with mocking eyes. ''I happen to know you've been faithful to me, Ronnie.''

Colour stained her lovely skin. ''Ah, yes! I bet you even paid someone to keep an eye on me!''

''What do you think,'' he scoffed, ''when you've been talking divorce? Like I said, Ronnie, I'm not cut out to be a part-time father. If you're not going to show me any trust, I'll have to get at you through emotional blackmail. In a few minutes, I expect Dr O'Neill is going to tell us the answer to our daughter's problem lies squarely with us.''

The following morning propelled by their talk with Dr O'Neill, Ronnie decided to take action, requesting a meeting with Channel 8's management. No matter her blossoming career, her daughter's welfare meant far, far more to her. In a quiet tone, she told those sitting around the boardroom table that she would not be renewing her contract at this time, a bombshell that made backs stiffen with shock and dismay. The ''personal reasons'' she cited didn't appear to cut much ice. People in television tended to be very self-centred, she remembered. Within a highly competitive industry, the number-one priority was ratings.

''That's a pretty heavy thing to spring on us, Ronnie,'' her immediate boss censured her. ''You've got a great future. If it's money...?''

Ronnie shook her head. ''I've thought this over very carefully, Joe. Obviously I don't want to let the station down, but my daughter has developed a few problems that must be straightened out.''

''Surely we can discuss this,'' he persisted,

mouth drawn down. "There must be other options available."

Basically he was insensitive to her personal problems, she realised. "I'm sorry, Joe," she apologised. "I can give you four full weeks so you can get someone else to replace me. Then it's the Christmas vacation. Tessa and I will be returning to my husband's property in the Channel Country."

"You mean you've patched things up?" one of the station's top executives questioned, causing Ronnie a momentary flash of resentment.

"To be honest, there's no talk of permanent reconciliation," she answered. "The thing is, both of us are deeply concerned about our daughter."

"Of course, Ronnie," Joe Gannon broke in abruptly. "We understand, but I wish this weren't happening. After all, we've done so much for you."

"And I'm very grateful." Ronnie looked sincerely at each man in turn. "I do mean that. You've been wonderful in promoting me, but I'm a mother before I'm anything else."

She wasn't surprised when she answered the telephone some hours later to be told by Joe they wouldn't need her to stay on until December.

Miranda Frost would take over until they found a new "face".

That sounds about right, Ronnie thought wryly. No one is indispensable. She cleared out her desk by midafternoon, smiling a little tightly to herself.

"They'll never take you on again, Rowena," a female colleague who had been passed over for Ronnie told her with some satisfaction. "You did a pretty good job, I have to grant you, but they'll find someone better. They always do. Our five minutes of fame is so fleeting."

She found her mother in the garden planting dozens and dozens of white impatiens along a shady border.

"My darling girl!" Bella looked up in surprise. "I was just thinking about going for Tessa."

"That's okay. I'll go for her, Mamma," Ronnie said, sinking onto the curved white stone bench. "Bit of news. I'm not working for Channel 8 anymore."

Bella's rich, low voice rose to dramatic soprano. "Wh-what!" She shook her dark head, bemused.

"I can't say I'm surprised," Ronnie said philosophically. "They did it to Grant Symons, don't you remember?"

"It's a ruthless business, this television news."

Bella straightened up, pulling off her gardening gloves. "What brought it on?" she said sounding outraged.

"I started the ball rolling, Mamma," Ronnie explained. "I told them I wouldn't be renewing my contract. Dr O'Neill didn't mince words yesterday. Tessa's problems reflect the fact we're a dysfunctional family."

Bella looked down at her hands, examining them for wear and tear. "I guess not that many children take refuge in becoming mute," she agreed quietly, sitting down beside her daughter.

Ronnie's velvet eyes stung with tears she wouldn't allow to flow. "Dr O'Neill said such alienation from her family, her peers, teachers and the like must be viewed very seriously."

"As though we don't!" Bella was filled with an overwhelming sense of frustration. A devoted grandmother who had been faced with many problems in life and she couldn't liberate her own little granddaughter.

A strong breeze blew across the garden and Ronnie held her long hair with one hand. "It's reached the stage where I think Tessa is powerless to free herself from this self-imposed sanctuary of silence," she said. "She told me only the other day she 'froze like an ice block' when someone wanted her to talk. It made my heart break. I can't go on like this, Mamma. I'm flooded by anxiety all the time. Tessa is so small and helpless. She adores her father, yet such a confusion of emotions surround her she appears to dread to speak.''

Bella drew her daughter to her, pressing her head onto her shoulder. "She'll talk again, *cara mia*, when she feels safe. I know this. I am praying for it. I think maybe we won't let her watch too much television for a while. She's such an imaginative child I'm coming to believe she feels like some little storybook character with a spell on her. One day, she was sitting on the swing with her back to me and murmuring to her invisible friend. She was in tears when she was telling Nicholas about it.''

"I'm sure Nicholas isn't hurting her. He's helping her,'' Ronnie said with certainty. "Invisible friends are important in this world.'' Like fairies. Or angels.

"She wants her father,'' Bella said. "She wants her parents together the way it used to be. She demands continuous daily contact with both of you. Another thing she's badly missing is Regina. That's *her* beloved environment. She draws so many pictures of it all the time. The land, the sand hills, the animals, the birds, the wildflowers.''

"I know," Ronnie sighed deeply while her mother patted her arm. "It expresses her longing to be back there. She does lots of drawings of the stars and those humanlike spirits Kel tells her all about. She loves the Aboriginal legends. She grew up on them." As Ronnie spoke, so many wonderful memories filtered back to her.

"Both of you are very intelligent, deeply caring people." Bella kissed her daughter's cheek. "I know you can work through to a solution. As for Sasha Garland, she's to be pitied. She's one of those women who can't accept when a love affair is over. But don't let her destroy your marriage, Rowena, I beg of you. Don't cut your husband off from your trust. Allow him to speak to you."

Ronnie gave another deep sigh. "Mamma, Kel can charm the birds from the trees. He could convince you white was black. Whatever happens, both of us have to put aside our conflicts for Tessa's sake. You're coming for Christmas, aren't you?"

"Try to stop me." Bella's beautiful dark eyes flashed and she thumped her breast. "More than that, *cara*, I want Tessa to greet me with a big shout of joy. I believe this will happen as surely as I believe God is in His Heaven."

So the husband who had driven her away now lured Ronnie back to his own private kingdom.

CHAPTER FOUR

I'M HOME, Tessa thought, wanting to shout and shout with joy and excitement, but the evil magician somehow managed to stop her. Instead, she pointed downwards with her hand, down to her proper home, the place where she was born. The enchanted landscape shimmered in the quicksilver heat of mirage. Mirage was a wonderful illusory thing that created phantom billabongs and lakes right in the heart of the desert. Many an explorer had perished following these beautiful but treacherous apparitions, but nothing would happen to her.

Tessa knew and loved her homeland with a passion. Forever, forever the land would be with her. One day she would paint this place, so magical, so old—ancient, Daddy called it. This Timeless Land steeped in Aboriginal legend. She would become very famous for it. People would say, ''Ah, yes, Tessa Warrender. She's a member of one of Australia's great pioneering families.''

Driven by their vision, her ancestors had taken up this vast, isolated holding in the far south-west of colonial Queensland. In the middle of the great wilderness they had built a splendid house like the home they had left on the other side of the world. They called it Regina after the first English bride. Just eighteen years old but brave enough to confront an overpowering wild landscape, Regina Warrender had aristocratic blood in her veins and eyes like mine, Tessa thought. Eyes like Daddy's. Shining, lake-coloured eyes that had come down through the generations. Regina Warrender was an unforgettable woman. No evil magician could have driven the voice out of her.

It's important I find my voice, Tessa thought, her heart fluttering around in her chest like a wild little budgerigar. Regina was the place it would be found. She was sure of it. But it was too soon for the curse to be lifted. Why else didn't she cry out?

For one heart-stopping moment as they soared over the steep pink-and-orange walls of Jinka Bluff and commenced their descent onto the station's all-weather runway, Ronnie really thought Tessa was about to speak. She could feel the waves of excitement that emanated from her child.

Lord, hear my plea. Let Tessa speak, Ronnie prayed, her eyes glued to her daughter's profile. She crushed her long fingernails into the palms of her hands as Tessa's rosebud mouth opened as if to shout aloud. Her expression was so joyous it was beatific. This was Tessa's physical and spiritual home. This splendid, untamed *infinity*. Baked red-ochre plains that ran on forever, lightly clothed with golden grasses, spinifex, mulga and mallee under the canopy of a blazing cobalt-blue sky. Painted on the roof of the huge hangar was the station's logo—a magnificent breeding bull, head lowered, tail swishing, beneath the boomerang-shaped caption, Regina Downs.

Tessa's huge silver eyes were stars in her delicate face. She reached for Ronnie's hand, squeezing it. Loving touches were an important part of their communication, as well as lots of hand holding, but for all Tessa's obvious rapture she never uttered a word or breathed a single cry.

Be patient, Ronnie thought. Let this wonderful place heal her. Below them, a long, snaking trail of cattle was being guided to water by stockmen on horseback; clouds of red dust rose from the trampled earth and turned into willy-willies that spiralled like a top over the endless sea of sand.

"Get ready for the big welcome, princess," Kel called to his little daughter, so precious to his heart. "You're *home*!" The fierce joy of his tone gave powerful emphasis to the word. *Home*. But he, too, was aware that Tessa, for all his willing her, hadn't broken her silence. Consternation and frustration were momentarily etched into his strong, handsome features. Surely home was the best treatment in the world. Tessa had a powerful connection to the land. As he did. The land would do its own counselling. Its power was great.

Ronnie, like her daughter was aware of a building excitement deep in her body. It had always been so. This utter fascination with a man and the wild grandeur of his desert home…Kel Warrender and Regina. You couldn't separate one from the other. Fifth generation of a colonial dynasty dedicated to the land. The Warrenders' English ancestors had had this same commitment over many centuries. It was in the blood.

Ronnie knew only too well the extended Warrender family hadn't been overly pleased when Kel had chosen a city girl to be his bride, but Ronnie hadn't just fallen head over heels in love with Kel Warrender. She had fallen completely under the spell of his desert kingdom.

Regina was Channel Country. The home of the cattle kings. A powerful place full of history and legend. This was the best cattle land on the continent, 350,000 square kilometres of Queensland's far south-west, so called because of the great network of braided channels that when fed by monsoonal rains of the tropical north turned the vast area into one magnificent, lush feeding lot.

It was an awesome place, Ronnie thought, this riverine desert, not only for its sheer size and time-less landscape, the terrifying spectacles of drought and flood, but also for its tremendous mystique. This was the most ancient geology on earth, little changed in thousands of years, with little or no intrusion by man. Just to walk over it was to feel it profoundly with all the senses. Then the most sublime factor of all—the coming of the wildflow-ers. It was a time she and Tessa adored, the beauty and vastness of the floral displays unparalleled on earth. Was it any wonder Tessa felt starved for the sight of her desert home? The city was alien, friendless to her. This was Tessa's world.

On the ground they were greeted by lines of stockmen standing to attention like soldiers on pa-rade. The teacher at the station school, Annie Connelly, without peer at her job, was there with her young charges, children of the station staff, who when they were old enough would be sent off to boarding schools. Ronnie caught sight of Tom and Desley Gibbs. Tom, retired from his job of head stockman after a bad fall, now filled the role of major-domo with his wife, Desley, the long-time station housekeeper. Beside Desley were three of the Aboriginal house girls smiling merrily behind their thin, elegant hands. And last but far from least...Hilary. Hilary with her strong personality but no ''give'' in her nature. She was dressed as ever in unisex gear. In fact, with her commanding height, her Akubra pulled right down over her dark, short-cropped hair, she could at a distance have been mistaken for a lean young man.

Tessa made no move to run to her aunt, even as a child recognising the eccentricity in her, holding tightly to her mother's hand. But her face was turned like a sunflower's to the station line-up.

I must say hello to them, Tessa thought, with her free hand making rapid little finger signals to them, greetings, like deaf children used to communicate. Of course, the station people recognised her signals immediately, every last one of them. She knew they would, thrilling as they began to respond. Lovely! Some with one hand, others with two, the Aboriginal girls with their marvellous natural talent as dancers and mimers making of their little movements something hauntingly beautiful like a ballet.

She and Mummy loved this impromptu response, but Aunt Hilary strode towards them, the expression on her stern face making her look like she was about to call them all to order like a schoolteacher.

"Rowena, Tessa, welcome home," she said, putting out her hand. She shook Ronnie's resoundingly, then took Tessa's hand in her own. "Well now, you haven't grown much, have you?" she said with a gruffness that still held affection. "I was thinking I might get a great big hello."

The evil magician seized Tessa's throat. "I'm sure she'll speak when she's ready, Hilary," Ronnie said, responding to her little daughter's desperate touch, her tone calm and friendly.

Hilary shrugged. "I guess so." She turned her head, her strongly defined features softening unbelievably as Kel, who had been organising the luggage, moved towards them. "Hi, Bro! What sort of a trip was it?" she asked.

"Smooth. We all love flying." Kel stretched out a hand and gently tweaked his daughter's long blonde ponytail. "That was a great way to say hello, flower face. You must be able to feel how happy everyone is to have you home. You and Mummy." His gaze caressed Ronnie, her lovely face and her slender body. "Life is going to be more fun, tons more exciting. I promise. Now it's December we're going to get out the Christmas tree and decorate it right up to the ceiling. Would you like that?''

Tessa gave him a great big smile and grasped his hand.

So it was as a family they went forward to greet everyone in turn. Ronnie was reduced to tears by her welcome, touched by the tide of liking and warmth that flowed towards her. It was genuine goodwill and a uniform protectiveness towards Tessa, who smiled very sweetly while tough, weather-beaten stockmen grinned at her encouragingly from ear to ear. Finally Tessa went to stand among the children, who stared at her with a kind of worship. She let Desley exclaim over her, then returned her hug before spontaneously beginning to play a hand-tapping game with the Aboriginal girls, who were always perfectly attuned to her.

It will come, Ronnie thought. It's *got* to come.

"I love them all," Tessa confided to her mother as they drove to the homestead, her small, upturned face so bubbling with joy that Ronnie planted a big kiss on her cheek.

"Speak up, Tessa. Let's all hear," Hilary brusquely urged from the front seat of the Jeep.

"She's okay, Hilary," Kel intervened tersely. "Just leave her alone."

"I'm only trying to help her. I want to do things

for her.'' Hilary frowned. "Get her back to reality. We can't go around cosseting her.''

"Just let her relax, Hilary.'' There was a decided edge of irritation in Kel's voice. "This is Tessa's first day home. The most wonderful Christmas present a father can have.''

In the back seat, Tessa, who had lost a little of her exuberance at the sound of her aunt's tone, brightened up again. Her father was *overjoyed* at her return. Christmas was such a lovely time. She had dreamed of this, her mother and father living happily together again. She and Nicholas had prayed together. She glanced off to her left to see if he was still there.

He was. The whole universe was his home.

Ronnie lifted her rapt face to Regina homestead as though it were her first experience. Nothing had changed. It looked as marvellous as ever. A huge house, a proud house by anyone's standards, built substantially of brick rendered and painted white with wings added over the years so it sprawled over a considerable area.

The frontage comprising the original homestead and the major extensions to either side was broken by a series of beautiful bays, the whole structure completely surrounded by deeply shaded verandas. These verandas in turn were decorated by elegant wrought-iron lace, pillars, balustrades, brackets, fretwork, all opening to the verandas by way of French doors with shutters painted midnight-blue.

A creek ran at the homestead's feet, meandering through ten acres of home gardens kept lush and green by the use of bore water. The gardens had been planned in the 1860s by the legendary Regina. It was she who had determined it would bloom and survive in what was then and remained today a great desert wilderness. Masses and masses of scarlet bougainvillea flamed in the sunlight and a flowering jasmine that had been used as ground cover rose above the piers that lifted the single-storey building off the ground and decked the veranda balustrades in great waves of bridal white.

"Beautiful, isn't it?" Ronnie laughed. "Absolutely beautiful. So substantial it could stand for eternity."

Beautiful as you are, her husband thought, his eyes on her in the rear-vision mirror. She wore white linen slacks, a sleeveless linen shirt and a stylish studded belt around her narrow waist. Her long hair, pulled back and tied at the nape with a scarf, gleamed pure gold in a shaft of sunlight. She looked a delicate creature, even fragile. He would have to treat her with kid gloves.

"I'll show them through to their rooms, shall

I?'' Hilary asked, taking control the moment they were inside the front door.

"No need," her stepbrother answered. "You can see that lunch is ready on time, if you wouldn't mind."

"I've put Tessa across from her mother," Hilary informed him in clipped tones, beginning to move off.

Kel put the luggage down and shot a rapier look at her. "Tessa can sleep wherever she wants."

And what about me? Ronnie thought. Hilary had taken a long time to get used to another woman being mistress of the house. Now it was uncertain how Hilary felt about her being back in the picture. Certainly Hilary was acting as though she and Tessa were guests.

"Don't let her upset you," Kel said quietly, watching Ronnie's expression, the way her long lashes fluttered down onto her cheeks. "She means well. It's just——"

"She's never really wanted me here, Kel," Ronnie answered with simple truth. "Hilary badly needs to be mistress of her own home."

"God help the lucky fellow," Kel murmured in a voice that cracked with laughter. "Where did Tessa scoot off to?"

"She's just saying hello to the house again." Ronnie smiled.

"What about you? How do you feel?" His silver eyes moved intently over her face.

"Hyped up," she said honestly, full of hidden hungers and shadows. "When is Madelaine coming?"

He smiled at her, aware she was marshalling all her defences. "She promised faithfully she'd be here by next week. I told her Bella would be with us for Christmas. In fact, I think we might be crowded out with family. Mabs was delighted. She and Bella always did get on well."

He was right. Despite the great differences in their lifestyles, both women were at ease with one another. Both had suffered the sad fate of losing their husbands in agonising accidents. Sir Clive had died in a light-plane crash when the pilot, who was ferrying him around his various properties, ploughed into an escarpment during a fierce electrical storm. That had been several years ago, devastating the family. Sir Clive had been such a big, strong, dynamic man that everyone had come to believe he would last forever. Sir Clive's outright approval had been very important to Ronnie. The fact that he had seen her as the right sort of wife for his son had mellowed the entire family.

"Come into the drawing room." Kel reached for her hand. "The house has missed you. I was thinking maybe it could do with a little refurbishment before Christmas."

"Hasn't Hilary arranged that?" she asked quickly, not wanting to cross that strong-willed, abrasive woman. "I don't want to put her out."

"What are we talking about here?" Kel glanced down at her, surprised. "You're my *wife*, Rowena. It's not a position you can put aside. Besides, you have exquisite taste. Decorating isn't Hilary's scene," he added dryly.

"So what do you have in mind?" Though it bothered her greatly, Ronnie didn't pull away. She felt the same old desire rushing to the surface of her skin like the bubbles in champagne. Still, she kept her poise, speaking in an almost professional voice. "It looks very grand as it is. One doesn't interfere with a beautiful historic home too much. Perhaps a few gentle changes. Actually I always did want to get rid of the wallpaper." She smiled wryly. "It's very beautiful in itself, but it's not the best backdrop for the paintings. They're important paintings. The eye shouldn't be distracted by the wallpaper design."

"I agree," Kel said.

It was her turn to be surprised. "But you *never* wanted the wallpaper removed."

"That was then," he said mildly, lifting her hand, looking down at their linked fingers. As usual, his body was responding to her. "Suddenly I can see what you saw all the time. One gets very used to one's home. You looked at it with fresh eyes."

"So I'm to be given free rein?" Pleasure and excitement beat in her blood. She turned her head, her gaze ranging over the long, spacious room with the series of French doors giving on to the veranda. As always, the large, ornately framed portrait of Regina Warrender that hung above the white marble fireplace caught her eye. It was a glorious portrait, the subject's skin so glowing Ronnie felt it would be warm to the touch.

Regina was dressed in a magnificent low-cut, ruby-red ball gown, diamonds and rubies at her throat and ears. She looked what she was—a woman of breeding. She had left her ancestral home in Lincolnshire, England, to marry her adventure-loving second cousin, who had the outrageous idea he could build his own empire in colonial Australia. As a result, the Warrender family with freehold stations in every mainland State controlled an area as large as the country from whence they had come. The portrait of Regina commissioned by her adoring husband had been painted on a trip "home" when she was in her late thirties and at the height of her beauty. Less than six years later, leaving a husband and six children—four sons and two daughters—she had been laid to rest in the family cemetery some half a mile from the main compound, her death the result of being bitten by a taipan, one of the deadliest snakes in the world. These days, with antivenenes and the Royal Flying Doctor service, she might have survived. Then, such a bite meant certain death.

"How beautiful she was," Ronnie said quietly, staring up at the portrait. "How beautiful and how strong. A gentlewoman despite all she had to endure in a harsh new world. Childbirth in such isolation, deprivation, little female company of her own standing, her husband gone over long periods of time. Drought, flood, fire, illness. The mind boggles at what she had to cope with."

"She had a dream," Kel reminded her. "God knows the English are an indomitable lot. We know from her diaries she shared everything with her husband."

"'One reason why we get on so wonderfully well,'" Ronnie quoted from the diaries. "They were true partners in everything. Remember what she wrote when they wanted to acquire Parinka Run? 'Harry and I talked about it right through the night.'"

Kel gave her a long, speculative look. "I've a feeling they did that in bed."

"Probably. He was a very sexy man." Even saying it, her body began a slow burn.

"Speaking of beds," Kel said blandly, "perhaps we should consider moving back together?"

She closed her eyes and took a deep breath. "Shut up, Kel."

"We could, of course, establish a strict territorial line. Perhaps not quite down the middle. I'm a lot bigger than you."

"*No!*" She wasn't about to be taunted.

"Okay, so what is Tessa going to think?" he asked in a too gentle voice.

Ronnie shook her head. "I don't...I can't..." She felt the tension flowing out of her. When she was in his arms, he was her world.

"Of course, it will be just a front," Kel continued. "There's always the day bed. It's plenty big enough to accommodate little ole you."

"Don't joke," she warned.

"Don't you want to do everything you can to help Tessa?" he asked, genuinely believing the huge demand on his self-control was worth it.

"You know I do." Ronnie's dark eyes skimmed away from him. "But I don't want you jumping me in the dark."

He kept hold of her by one wrist. "You don't, eh? We used to do it all the time."

And I haven't forgotten, she thought. The turbulent clamouring of the senses, the ecstatic release. I'll never lose the memory of you, my lover.

He lifted her fingers to his mouth and kissed them. "Ronnie, I swear to you I will respect your wishes. I know what you've been through." The scent of her light perfume, her own skin, was wrapping itself around him like tendrils. Desire put a sheen on the fine, hard planes and angles of his face.

"You can't," she murmured, mind and heart at war. "Men and women see things differently. I've learned a very painful lesson. I never want to repeat it."

"You choose to continue to believe the worst of me, don't you?" he challenged, responding to her melancholy.

"God, Kel, I loved you so much!" You were all my hopes and dreams.

"You *still* love me." Aroused by her soft cry, he found himself grasping her slender arms and drawing her tight against his hungry body. "Lord, I can feel it."

For a moment, she put up a frenzied little struggle, trying to hold back the gathering momentum, but sensation built and broke over her like a giant wave. "I absolutely hate this," she gritted. Perversity was an extension of passion.

"Shut up." His voice was tight. Once they had been such glorious lovers. That couldn't possibly be lost, he thought. He lowered his head, malelike demanding her submission, his blood running redhot. Anything was permissable between them. She had been away too long.

Kel wondered how he could contain himself not to catch her up. Carry her through to their beautiful bedroom overlooking the creek, make love so frenetically she would have to plead with him to take her to a place where there was only liberation from all conflict and a rapturous pleasure.

"Ronnie." Space and time receded. He poured every atom of a dynamic persona into the powerful sweetness of his kiss. He wanted to be so gentle with her. He had talked to himself so often about this very thing. Everything depended on it. Yet he needed her so badly just having her near him brought his control to the brink.

Ronnie, too, found herself near sobbing even

when she was starved for the magic. Pride. Sometimes she had it. Sometimes she didn't. The trouble was, she loved him with a passion that blinded her.

"I'm sorry, I'm sorry," he crooned over her in contrition, feeling her heart fluttering under his hand like a trapped butterfly. "I want you so badly. You know I can't resist you."

The very air had turned electric. Ronnie felt her body rising to his in waves. His arms wrapped around her as though he would never let her get away. She wondered what would happen, but just then, light skipping footsteps sounded on the parquet of the hallway. The next moment, Tessa rushed into the drawing room, fresh from her exploration. When she saw her parents together, her mother locked in her father's strong arms, Tessa's mouth curved up in a big smile.

They'd been kissing—she knew it! Pure exaltation made her apple-blossom cheeks glow. It had to be all those prayers she and Nicholas were saying. She made a funny little noise in a throat that felt as smooth as honey. Not quite a word but a sound that had her parents smiling. She ran to them and grasped them around the knees, her small face uplifted, her long hair out of its ponytail like a golden flame. As a baby, they called it a group cuddle. She tried desperately to get the familiar request out, wondering if her father heard her. They were a family of three. Her father had to come back to them. Being apart had badly frightened her.

Looking down into his daughter's exquisite little face, Kel felt his heart melt. "My little love." He reached for her and swung her up into his arms. Tessa let her head fall forwards onto his broad shoulders, then snuggled in. It made her so happy to be back on Regina. So happy to see her mother's dark eyes glowing like pansies, safe within her father's arms.

The moment of togetherness warmed Tessa like the glorious Outback sun. It filled her with the brilliant radiance of its light. This was going to be the best Christmas ever. Mummy and Daddy loved each other. They loved her. Like Nicholas promised, she would soon win her voice back from the cruel magician so it would reach everyone's ears.

Lunch, set up in the breakfast room with its extensive views of the creek and the coolibah trees lining its banks, was surprisingly pleasant. Hilary, after an initial brusqueness, settled down to a more relaxed manner for which Ronnie was very grateful. Afterwards, while Tessa helped Desley, the housekeeper, clear away, Kel took Ronnie by the arm and guided her out the front door. "Look, I'd love to stay but there are a thousand and one things I have to attend to," he apologised, setting his pearl-grey Akubra at a rakish angle.

Ronnie nodded in agreement. "I understand perfectly, Kel." She knew as well as anyone the size of his job.

"About the bedrooms…" He smiled a little, his face handsome, debonair, mocking. "We're agreed on solidarity, right? We're Tessa's parents. That means as far as she's concerned, we sleep in the same bed. We always did."

"Are you considering tying me up?" she asked sarcastically even as her body pulsed. Her husband, her lover, her torment.

"Are we talking wrists to the bedposts?" he quipped, letting his sparkling eyes slide over her.

"No, we're not!"

"Really?" He raised his dark eyebrows. "Wouldn't you like me to tickle you all over with a feather? Make you laugh and cry and tremble and moan?"

He had done that before today, she thought, excitement skittling down her spine. "There's a simple answer," she managed coolly. "No." Then as an afterthought, "You devil!"

One arm snaked out around her narrow waist,

pulling her into him. "You used to love me for it."

"Tell me about it." She was helpless against him. Him and his magnetism.

"Move into our bedroom, Ronnie," he urged. "The fact you're going to sleep on the couch can be *our* secret."

God, didn't she want it? Right or wrong, she was the victim of emotional and sexual deprivation. Slowly, aware of how she was giving in to him at every turn, Ronnie began to shake her head. It was then that he kissed her, stealing her will and her breath. He had such hunger, such energy, such passion—the powerful charisma she had fallen in love with. She was probably mad, but she knew Tessa would draw great comfort from seeing her parents together in their old bedroom. Consequently, when Tom came in with the rest of the luggage, she had him put what was hers in the main suite. The rest belonging to Tessa was left in the very pretty bedroom sometimes used as a guestroom almost directly opposite.

It was when she was settling Tessa, who had succumbed to the effects of their journey, for a nap when Hilary reappeared, standing in surprise at the doorway.

"What, no nursery?" she asked. The nursery was where Tessa had always slept.

Ronnie turned her head to smile. "Not anymore. Tessa has always loved this room."

"Well, it *is* pretty," Hilary agreed. "A bit too feminine for my taste. I expect it's the mural."

Eyes heavy, already half-asleep, Tessa nodded her head. Behind the beautifully carved bed that stood on a raised platform were two huge murals of Regina at the time of the wildflowers. They had been painted by a well-known Australian artist who'd often enjoyed hospitality on the station. Fantastic paintings, a touch surreal, they depicted the red plains thickly patterned in the white and gold glory of the everlasting daisies, the pink parakeelya, the scarlet desert peas, the blue gillyflowers, the native hibiscus and many more. It was a wonderful world of colour with the peacock-blue sky adorned with flights of outback birds—the brilliant parrots, the rose-pink galahs, the orange-and-crimson chats and, the phenomenon of the Outback, the flashing green fire of the budgerigar.

"Worth a fortune, those murals," Hilary observed, watching Ronnie walk so gracefully towards her. Ballet lessons, Ronnie always said. Now Hilary wished she had taken a few. She stood back, allowing her sister-in-law the lead, disguising her surprise when Ronnie walked into the main suite and immediately began to tackle the task of unpacking her luggage.

"It's wonderful to be back," Ronnie said diplomatically, watching Hilary subside into an armchair. "Thank you so much, Hilary, for all you've done. The flowers in all the rooms are lovely." She inclined her head towards a huge bowl of pink and cream roses on the circular library table.

"Desley handled all that," Hilary admitted wryly. "She's good at that sort of thing. I'm for the outdoors as you know."

"A splendid horsewoman," Ronnie said sincerely. Hilary had won countless trophies in her youth and up until a few years ago. Dressage, cross-country events, endurance races—you name it. In the right setting, Hilary shone.

"Which reminds me, Tessa must get back to her lessons." Hilary frowned. "Kel bought her the most beautiful pony. Did he tell you?"

"Not as yet." Ronnie felt disappointed and it showed.

"Hell, trust me to spoil the surprise," Hilary groaned. "And it was to be a big surprise."

"I won't let on." Relaxing, Ronnie smiled. "It's easy for these things to slip out." She removed several linen shirts from the case, then walked into the dressing-room for hangers.

"You're always so damned nice," Hilary said, remembering many other times. "I don't deserve it. Look, Ronnie—" she leaned forward "—can we lay things on the table? This is Christmas. A time of peace and goodwill."

"Suits me." Ronnie wondered what was coming.

"You're home for good, I take it?" Hilary asked, preparing to launch into her story.

"Well, we're trying to settle things, Hilary," Ronnie said. "Give it our best shot for Tessa's sake."

Hilary sighed deeply. "I was lied to, Ronnie," she said. "I was lied to and used. I should have acted as a conciliator. Instead, I fell for every last one of Sasha's phoney stories."

Ronnie turned around fully to stare at her. "Hilary, you persuaded me to *leave*, remember? Are you telling me now you lied?"

Hilary put her face down into her hands. Another woman would have cried. "I didn't *lie*, Ronnie. I'm never that bad. I truly believed what Sasha told me. Sasha was my friend. One of us. Lord, Ronnie, if you hadn't come along, Sasha would've been *family*. She and Kel were lovers at one time.

I thought he'd gone back to her. She persuaded me of that. But I've since realised Sasha is an accomplished liar. She thought it *funny*, mind you, to use me. You have to remember when Kel went away on his trip, so did Sasha. I've since confirmed she only caught up with him that one time at the Sandpiper, wasn't it? To my endless remorse, I always let her know his exact whereabouts."

Ronnie felt ill. For more than a year... "This is hurting terribly, Hilary," she said. "Kel and I have lost precious time in our lives. Far more serious, look at what's happened to Tessa."

Hilary jumped up in angry despair. "I know, and I want to apologise most abjectly. But I had to tell you *my* side of the story, Ronnie. I was a fool. I was duped. You're everything I'm not, Ronnie. I've always liked you. I couldn't help it, but I was frightfully jealous of you. No man has ever looked at me as Kel looks at you. No man ever will."

Ronnie looked at her with haunted eyes. "You won't *let* anyone reach you, Hilary. I understand how it's been for you. You hide a vulnerable heart behind a brusque manner. If you'd only take a little advice, you could turn yourself into a striking-looking woman overnight. Everything you need is there, but you want a recognised style. I could help you. Mamma could help you.''

"Bella?'' Hilary's smile was hopeless. "She has offered in the past. I could *never* look like Bella. She's a very beautiful woman.''

"I think so.'' Ronnie sank onto the bed, greatly upset but beyond anger. "You want to get out from under, Hilary. Take complete charge of your own life. You're blessed with looks, splendid health and a lot of money. Why don't you make it work for you?''

"I'm too scared.'' Hilary finally faced her fear.

"Never! A woman who can do what you can do?''

Hilary shrugged her physical skills off. "I don't have any charm like Kel. He's got it all.''

"What you have to do, Hilary, is become more approachable,'' Ronnie suggested. "Relax and let people in.''

Hilary resumed her chair. "Sasha used to laugh about me behind my back. To my face, for that matter, but I pretended not to see it.''

"Maybe I should've pointed that out,'' Ronnie said wryly. "Have you discussed this with Kel? How Sasha lied to you?''

"Now you're talking really scared.'' Hilary slumped in her seat, dismay in her eyes. "I adore my brother. He fills the greatest place in my heart, but when he gets going he's as formidable as Dad. He would hate me for wrecking his life.''

"There's a chance he might tear a few strips off you," Ronnie had to admit. "But I think it's something you must do, Hilary. For all our sakes."

Hilary met Ronnie's eyes. "I'm *so* sorry." No tears, but her mouth trembled.

"I believe you, Hilary," said Ronnie of the soft heart, "and I accept your apology. It's Christmas, and forgiveness is the order of the day. I'm just wondering, though, how you found out about it."

Hilary gave a strained smile. "Sasha actually had the hide to fly in while Kel was away. She suggested she and Kel had picked up where they'd left off in Brisbane. I knew then for a fact she was lying. I was bitterly upset and angry. Kel never really loved Sasha. I see that now. She was simply *there*. Both families were promoting a match. We had it out, I can tell you. She failed every test. As did I. Every test of loyalty and integrity."

"I didn't behave all that sensibly, either," Ronnie said. "You sowed the seeds of doubt, I guess, but if I'd used half my brain—"

"Don't lose Kel," Hilary said.

CHAPTER FIVE

THEY had the most wonderful time decorating the tree that evening. It rose in splendour to the beautiful plastered ceiling of the hall, the ceiling's scrollwork delicately picked out in muted tones of gold, ivory and blue. Tom Gibbs had brought the artificial tree in from the storeroom and assembled its many green branches while Tessa enjoyed her afternoon nap. But it was left to the family to decorate the tree.

There were glittering baubles, bells and ornaments galore, all packed away in boxes from year to year. Metres and metres of silver and gold, emerald and ruby roping were unwound to twine around the pendulous branches of the lofty pyramid as the enchanting sound of classic Christmas carols of the world resonated through the rooms. Even Hilary got into the spirit of it, handing sparkling ornaments to Tessa as she ran to and fro.

Finally it was time for Kel to place the Christmas angel at the top of the tree, and Tessa's huge silvery eyes, so poignant in repose, filled with joy. She subsided to the floor beside her mother, the ankle-length skirt of her pretty cotton voile dress pooling around her.

"That's Nicholas on top." Tessa leaned in to her mother confidentially. "Not really Nicholas, of course. Nicholas is too big. Big as Daddy."

This was news. "Nicholas is big?" Given up to surprise, Ronnie stared into her daughter's eyes. "But I thought Nicholas was the same size as you. Smaller even. Elf-sized."

"No, no, Mummy." Tessa shook her head. "He's tall and so *wonderful*! He's not like us. He's more a shape. Like a shape inside a light bulb. Only his wings are very clear. They have feathers like the swans, but they're all tipped with gold. And they're *big*! They go up past his shoulders and almost down to the ground."

A child's fantasy, of course. "Such a vivid imagination, my darling." Ronnie hugged her daughter to her. "How marvellous it is to see with the eyes of a child."

"But he's right there beside you, Mummy." Tessa looked matter-of-factly to Ronnie's left.

"*Is* he?" For a few seconds, Ronnie actually felt her mind reel. It was even the least bit scary.

"Don't worry, Mummy," Tessa said, a gentle, reassuring hand on her mother's shoulder. "Everything will be all right."

"How's it look, girls?" Kel called, breaking up the rapt moment and capturing their attention.

Tessa was so excessively happy that Ronnie really thought her daughter might call out an answer, but though she sprang to her feet and clapped her hands in delight, she stopped short of putting her feelings into words.

"Well, that's it. I'm off to bed," Hilary announced, smothering a yawn. "Got to be up at dawn. Where is it tomorrow, Kel?"

By this time, Kel had descended the ladder and snapped it back together. "The Twenty Mile. You don't *have* to come if you don't want to. You might prefer to stay at home. We'll have lots of people flying in from now on. Most folk like to deliver their Christmas greetings in person."

"Don't I know. But I like to be outdoors. Ronnie's here to take care of everything." Hilary rose to her feet, then bestowed on them all a surprisingly warm smile. "We'll have to have a billabong barby soon, Tessa," she suggested. "Remember how great they were?"

Remembering, Tessa started forwards and gave her aunt a big hug, causing Hilary to experience a tremendous rush of affection not unmixed with her many regrets.

"Come on, sweetheart." Kel spoke to Tessa

gently, grateful things were going so well. "Time for you to hit the sack. We have wonderful things planned for tomorrow."

Tessa went willingly, holding tightly to her parents' hands. Here on Regina she was no longer uncertain and afraid. God really did love her. He would set her free.

Ronnie spent a long time in the bath, luxuriating in the scented bubbles even when her mind kept turning over all the events that had almost brought her marriage to the brink. The web of lies and deceit, the different relationships that had caused it, her own inexperience in handling the situation. She should have marched up to Kel and Sasha that night she'd found them withdrawing from an embrace—or *thought* she had. Her mother had probably been right. Sasha had engineered the whole thing. She should have demanded facts not fantasies. She should have confided in her husband when it all began to happen instead of simply accepting the situation.

She had never spoken to Kel about it. She had cloistered her intense fears about the stability of her marriage, feeding her natural jealousy and feelings of betrayal, denying him her body even as she burned with her own fierce desire.

She had known all about Sir Clive's affairs. The

terrible mistake she had made was her readiness to condemn Kel simply because he was his father's son. Now remembering, she realised Kel, for all his strong passions, was a far more caring and deeply committed man. A rock to lean on. Pity Hilary when she had to tell him her part in the whole sorry business! But from the misery and remorse locked up in Hilary, she would have to speak out if she wanted to stay fairly sane.

It might help, Ronnie thought, if she asked her mother to bring several outfits with her for Hilary. Bella would love that. She had often spoken sympathetically about Hilary's failure to exploit her potential. Style and design were born in Bella.

Kel had been so sensitive tonight. So sensitive and tender. A magician with Tessa. Why Tessa wouldn't speak to her father when she adored him was the greatest mystery. Maybe Tessa's fears and anxieties had almost literally choked her. And that talk about Nicholas! Tessa had undoubtedly got it all from Ronnie's own beautifully illustrated book on angels through the ages. Tessa had artistic talent. Tessa had great imagination. The two had come together. Even the shape inside the light bulb. That would be the halo of light artists usually employed in their paintings of angels. The radiance. If it wasn't so wonderful, it would be bizarre.

When she finally emerged from the bathroom, her matching peach satin robe over her satin-and-lace nightgown, she could see Kel's tall, lean frame silhouetted against the silvery moonlight that slanted across the veranda.

Despite the fact her bare feet made little sound on the carpet, he turned his head and called to her. "Come on out. It's the most beautiful night. The Southern Cross is right over the house."

How many times had they stood on the same veranda, Kel with his arms wrapped around her, watching the night sky? The stars were breathtakingly beautiful over the desert. They crammed the sky, glittering like great handfuls of diamonds thrown down on black velvet.

"You smell delicious," he said when she came to stand near his shoulder, for a moment closing his eyes in bliss.

"Gardenia."

"And you. I've always loved the woman scent of you." Try to keep it light, he thought desperately as desire knifed into him. The breeze made a little rush for them, whipping Ronnie's blonde hair back over her shoulders. The moonlight pearled her beautiful skin.

"Tessa had a wonderful time tonight," she said

with evident gratitude. "Her eyes shone. You're marvellous with her, Kel. You always were."

"So when is she going to speak to me?" he asked resignedly.

"I know she will," Ronnie promised. "She's super sensitive. We have to give her more time. Regina will do its healing."

The certainty of her tone moved him profoundly. "You sound as if you really believe that."

"I do." She stared up at the purple sky, the glorious embroidery of stars. "Regina and her friend Nicholas."

"Ah, Nicholas." He laughed indulgently. "She's always had a wonderful imagination." He was filled with the urge to draw his wife into his arms and take what was his.

"She sees him as an angel," Ronnie was saying as though it was a mystery.

"Then I'm glad of it." He made himself turn towards the bedroom. "The angels are here to help us. You must be tired, Ronnie. It's been a long day."

"I am a bit," she told him while her whole body vibrated for his touch. "Tessa should sleep well. She goes right through the night."

He allowed himself to lightly brush her with his

lips. "You're trembling. Please don't. I promised you I'd make no demands on you."

So why don't you? she wanted to cry out in perversity, lacking the right words. "So it's the day bed?" she asked.

"Darling, it *has* to be," he said wryly. "I'm not made of steel. Come into bed with me and I'll totally lose it. You know where my heart lies."

She watched him for a moment, looking so at a loss he thought he would never overcome the doubt in her.

"This is damned ridiculous," he burst out, the bronze skin of his splendid torso gleaming in the light. Once, *she* had worn the top of his pyjamas. "You sleep in the bed. I was only having you on. I have a sleeping-bag tucked away in the dressing-room. I've slept on hard ground countless times."

She put out a hand to stop him. "No, Kel. I'll curl up here. I'm so tired I'll go straight to sleep. You need your rest. You're up at dawn."

Just so he wouldn't argue the point, she lay down on the comfortable day bed and pulled the light rug over her.

"Aren't you going to take off your robe?" he asked her.

"Of course." She threw the rug off and stood up again, letting the luscious garment slip down her arms. She stood there, slim and lovely in her shimmering nightdress, so lovely he drew in a single ragged breath, his face taut.

"Welcome home, girl. Here, give me that." He all but snatched the robe from her and settled it over a chair. "Good night, Ronnie," he added. "Sleep well." While I take another cold shower, he thought, his frustration boundless.

Ronnie burrowed her head into the pillow, making herself small. What sort of fool was she to shut out love?

She woke up with a wail not unlike Tessa's when she'd had a bad dream.

"Ronnie, sweetheart, what's the matter?" Kel was on his feet immediately, fully alert, guarding the sleeping princess. His wife. He snapped on a lamp, then went down on his haunches and stared at her. "Darling, you're crying." Tears tracked down her cheeks. She appeared to be foundering in grief. "Ronnie!"

On a great wave of love, he hauled her into his arms, feeling her fragility. He carried her to the bed and settled her head against the pillows before sitting down on the side of the bed and taking her hands. "Can't you tell me?"

In the glow from the lamp, her velvety dark eyes

were huge, long lashes stuck together in spikes. She looked almost as young as Tessa. Defenceless, vulnerable. He lifted her hands to his mouth and kissed every finger. "Don't you give me a hard time," he groaned.

"I love you, Kel," she said, his very touch making her tremulous. "Yet I've treated you so badly. I should have had more wisdom, more experience. I should have challenged Sasha's claims of an illicit affair. I should have talked the whole thing over with you. Instead, I bottled up all my fears. I was sick at heart I might lose you."

Emotion caught at his throat-a deep understanding of what she had been through. "My darling, that's never going to happen," he answered with compelling fervour. "Don't be so hard on yourself. I made plenty of mistakes. The thing was, we were trying to settle into our marriage after a whirlwind engagement. What should have been so simple— the growth of trust and confidence in one another—was being eroded by deliberate deception."

"I realise that now," Ronnie sighed. "Sasha sabotaged me at every turn. I made it easy for her by letting her play on my insecurities. She fooled Hilary, too. I know Hilary is sorry for that."

His laugh was a little rough. "And so she should be."

"Then I thought I saw you and Sasha together," she finally confessed, her voice low and somewhat hesitant. "Or rather I saw the two of you withdrawing from what I interpreted as a passionate embrace."

His quick, indrawn breath moved her hair. "When was this?" He made no attempt to hide the dismay that overwhelmed him.

She looked into his eyes, finding them very direct and crystal clear. "I'm going back a few years," she explained. "It was when the Monaro Cup finals were held on Regina. We had a gala weekend, remember?"

"Of course I remember." His black brows knotted. "And you caught me kissing Sasha?" he asked in simple disbelief. It had never happened.

"She was in your arms," Ronnie whispered, leaning forward so her upper body fused with his.

"Sweetheart!" Kel's arms closed strongly around her. "I beg you to believe there was no affair going on behind your back. Goodness, woman, did I ever conceal my love and longing from you? You were and remain the only woman in my life. You're everything I want. As for Sasha, I can't honestly recall anything much about her that weekend. She does as she damned well pleases. Some people are like that. All I can recall is having a wonderful time with you, watching the way you enchanted all my friends. Sasha is one reckless character. Married or not, she'd think nothing of trying to coax a kiss out of a man. That's the way she is. But as far as I'm concerned, you could never have seen me kissing her. It simply didn't happen. What's far more likely is you saw me attempting to maybe cool her ardour. In other words, holding her off.

"You should have kept on coming, Ronnie, instead of steering away. You should have yelled 'Hands off, Sasha. That man is my husband.'" A gentle smile curled up his mouth.

"I suppose." She smiled ruefully at his tone. "But think for a moment, Kel. They were early days in our marriage. I was trying to establish myself as your wife. I know no one expected you to marry a city girl. Sasha tried to undermine our marriage almost as soon as it began. She manipulated Hilary into helping her."

"I know." For a moment, his striking face looked grim. "She did a lot of unforgivable things, Ronnie. It comes under the heading of obsession. But I'm sure we won't be bothered by Sasha any more. She's done her sorry dash and she knows it. When she tricked her way into my hotel room in Brisbane, she finally confessed she'd been lying about what allegedly happened at the Sandpiper. I've been waiting for the right moment to tell you. To put all your doubts to rest.

"Sasha got into my room then via the veranda that runs around the top suites. In her own words, I was out of it and she took advantage of the situation. Her claim I made love to her wasn't true. It was a cheap, dangerous, ugly lie. I think in her heart of hearts she's ashamed."

Ronnie closed her eyes, feeling the healing power of his love and loyalty. "I can't bring myself to forgive her."

"Not when it caused so much pain," he agreed. "Not when our separation damaged our child. Anyway…" With one smooth, purposeful movement, he was in bed beside her, drawing her trembling body powerfully into his arms. "…we're not going to waste another word on Sasha. She has nothing to do with our life. I want to talk about us."

"Oh, yes!" She turned her face into his bare chest, feeling the delicious tickle of the hair that matted it on her soft cheeks. "We've lost so much time," she groaned, hugging his lean, strong body that had given her so much ecstasy.

"Darling, there's still so much time for us," he reassured her. "Lots of love. Lots of living. I want you, Ronnie, more than I can ever tell you. No one and nothing is ever going to part us again." He lifted her hand and pressed his lips to her palm. "We're together. Alone together. And I'm half mad for you."

"Shall we test that?" she urged huskily.

"My God, yes!" His hands moved to shape her breasts, luxuriating in their sweet, tender weight before locking her closer, half-covering her arching, yearning body with his own. "My wife! My darling heart!" A powerful force was gathering in him, the glorious intensity of the dominant male. "I'm going to love you...love you...!" His blood was glowing, fired by the fuel of his boundless desire.

We can make a baby, Ronnie thought, winding her slender arms around his neck like the tendrils of a vine. The time is just right. She was dazzled by how beautiful the idea seemed. Truly inspired. A son to make their family complete.

She opened her mouth, her heart, her warm woman's body, feeling it pinned by her husband's dynamic strength. The flood of moonlight in the room was like heaven—unutterably beautiful. A miracle. This was truly a miracle.

One of many.

EPILOGUE

THE weeks before Christmas rushed through Ronnie's fingers like the sands of the desert. Family arrived. Madelaine first, laden with presents that she and Tessa set under the tree. Then Bella with her complement of things and a new surprise wardrobe for Hilary that would set her back a few thousand dollars, followed by aunts, uncles, cousins. The huge old homestead embraced them all. People from all over the Outback flew in and out, an annual migration every Christmas to deliver personal greetings.

Desley and her staff were kept busy providing morning and afternoon tea. Magnificent rich Christmas cakes were cut. Toasts drunk. Goodwill and good humour flowed. It was a hectic but a happy time even though the great blessing they all prayed for had been denied them.

Though every last member of the family kissed Tessa and folded her in their arms, she never spoke to them. A tragedy, they thought, the only hope lying in her communications with her mother. Everyone had worried dreadfully that Kel's marriage might be over. Rowena, after all, had walked out, but that little episode was very obviously over. They appeared to be more in love than ever. A few within the circle knew of Sasha's treachery, but they weren't talking. The great thing was that this marriage endured.

Ronnie decided to make Christmas Eve very special. She poured over recipes with Desley, both deciding on a buffet to be served in the long, screened rear terrace overlooking the turquoise swimming pool. The pool was being given lots of use in the Christmas heat. Tessa was allowed to stay up until nine-thirty, but she was made aware she had to be well and truly in bed before Santa Claus made his rounds.

She had been very excited all day, spurred on by the presence of three of her cousins, all a little younger but bundles of joyful energy. The children were to be given adorable, handcrafted teddy bears all dressed up in Christmas finery—white ''fur''-trimmed crimson velvet coats and matching bonnets. The wonderful presents would come later on Christmas morning. Tessa went to bed that afternoon for a nap with a singing heart, tears of joy and thankfulness in her eyes. Her imprisoned voice was about to escape.

Ronnie took great care dressing that evening.

She wanted to look a dream for her husband. Her final choices narrowed down to two dresses for evening. Pink sequined stretch tulle over an under slip, the other rose-red silk georgette, hand beaded and sequined around the low oval neck and around the sleeveless armholes, the exquisite fabric decorated with sparkling beaded and sequined open scrollwork.

It was Christmas so the red won out. She would wear the South Sea drop pearl earrings Kel had given her, leave her hair out but brushed back over her shoulders. Like Tessa, she was so excited her stomach felt full of shooting stars. It was an extraordinary feeling. One she remembered experiencing before.

Kel came back to their bedroom just as she was putting on her earrings. They had all decided to dress for the party, so he wore a sand-coloured summer suit with a fine quality open-necked blue dress shirt. He looked so vivid, so vital, so handsome and elegant she felt like falling against him in rapture. They were deliriously happy. It was like being transported. They made love all the time, in their bed, twice in the deep green seclusion of Pink Lady Lagoon. They might have been newly married, aching for each other, insatiable.

"Now that's what I call a dress," he said, whistling under his breath. "You look ravishing, Mrs. Warrender."

"All for you." Ronnie twirled.

"I'll remember long after my hair turns white." He went over to her and stood so close their bodies were brushing.

Ronnie put up her hand and touched his mouth very gently with her fingers while he blew softly against them. A tender gesture but incredibly erotic.

"I want you again," he murmured, his tone so loverlike it lit her eyes. They had made love very early that morning when the dove-grey sky was streaked with pink and lemon.

"And you can have me," she replied quietly but emotionally. "Any day. Any time."

"I think I might hold you to that." His hands came up to lightly caress her beautiful breasts. They seemed a little fuller, the nipples swelling like tiny raspberries against his palms. "Ronnie, my love, I love you so much."

She sighed, closing her eyes with rapture. "Do you have any idea what happens when you touch me?"

"I'm good at this sort of thing." He studied her with intense feeling.

"Oh, you *are*!" With a considerable effort, she

opened her eyes. Her stomach jabbed her again with those funny shooting stars.

"All right." He was acutely aware of her, the extraordinary sheen on her, the emotional depth of her black-lashed eyes.

"I'm fine." She gave a little bubbling laugh. "Maybe running a bit on full throttle. It's been a very exciting time."

"None better," he agreed fervently, dropping a quick kiss on her brow. "But for now we'd better go join the family. The celebrations are already under way."

It was a wonderful time for all, adults and children. Everyone had their photographs taken in their Christmas finery in front of the tree; the Christmas carols were replaced with other tunes so those who wanted to could dance. Kel with his power and grace was a marvellous partner. He was a born dancer as Ronnie had often told him, but he shrugged that off as a joke. It was at one point when he spun her towards the shadowy end of the terrace that she felt her breath almost leave her, so dizzy only for Kel's support, she would have fallen to her knees. In fact, he had to catch her as she slumped into a faint.

Shocked and dismayed, Kel swept her up into his arms almost unnoticed, then carried her into the library and laid her down on the leather couch. He sank onto his knees, gently slapping her wrists. "Ronnie, Ronnie…" He had seen these faints before and his heart gave a great bound. "Darling, speak to me."

In the next moment, Ronnie rallied, opening her eyes on her husband's face. She had never seen him so pale. "Heavens, did I faint?"

"You sure did. Frightened the hell out of me."

"I'm so sorry."

Tessa raced into the room, anxiety imprinted on every delicate feature of her face and in every line of her small body. What was the matter with Mummy? She had nearly fallen over. Surely all the enchantment she had seen around them wasn't over?

Her father directed a swift look at her. "Stay with Mummy for a moment, sweetheart. She's all right, but I'll get Sam to take a look at her." Sam, Tessa knew, was Daddy's cousin, a doctor.

While her father hurried out of the room, Tessa went to her mother and stared at her with anguished eyes. "Are you sick, Mummy?" Her heart pounded in her chest. "Are they going to take you away?"

This brought Ronnie, who had been lying quietly exploring all the sensations in her body, to her senses. She pulled her little daughter into her arms and kissed her cheek repeatedly. "My precious girl, don't be silly. Mummy's fine." To her astonishment, she found herself adding, "I always faint when I'm pregnant. I did it with you."

Had she really said that? For all her daydreaming, was it true? In an instant, Ronnie accepted its certainty from a great joyous power.

"What?" Looking ecstatic, Tessa laid her hand on her mother's shoulder. "What did you say, Mummy?"

"I'm pregnant, my darling," Ronnie smiled tremulously. "Are you happy?"

Am I happy? Tessa thought. I'm delirious with joy. She kissed her mother's cheek resoundingly, then raced purposefully for the door, her feet sprouting wings, her small body full of vigour.

"Daddy, Daddy," she shouted so loudly it galvanised the small group who were hurrying along the corridor—her father, her two grandmothers and Dr Sam. "Mummy's pregnant!" she announced on a tidal wave of happiness. Her grey eyes sparkled like stars; a lovely big smile curved her mouth. "Did you hear me?" she cried with the same wonderfully animated pitch, launching herself headlong into her father's waiting arms. "Mummy's going to have a baby. A little brother for me. It's wonderful! Nonna, Mabs?'' She looked to her grandmothers for confirmation. ''I'm going to name him Nicholas. For Christmas.''

Kel bowed his head with profound gratitude, kissing his daughter's blonde head. ''So you shall, princess,'' he promised, his vibrant voice thick with emotion. ''So you shall.''

On the terrace, someone changed the dance tunes back to Christmas carols. Immediately, familiar, heartwarming strains soared through the house, touching them all with magic.

''Joy to the World.''

Sarah's First Christmas
Rebecca Winters

Dear Reader,

A few years ago I was downtown doing some last-minute Christmas shopping. It was freezing out and had started snowing. I was rushing to my car, parked in an area behind a large office building, when I heard some children crying their hearts out. I looked around and saw a little boy and girl wandering around the cars without coats, crying for their grandma. Apparently a male relative had left them locked in the car for hours and had never come back, but they managed to get out.

Well, I bustled them inside the back entrance of a nearby furniture store to get them warm while I called the police. All the employees took pity on the children and fed them doughnuts and drinks. But the whole time, the children would not be comforted and kept crying for their grandma. The police found and jailed the relative responsible, and they also found the grandma. A little while later this grandma, frantic to find them, came running into the store. When those dear little children saw her, they fairly flew into her arms and I have to tell you—the joy on their faces made that particular Christmas absolute magic for me. From that moment on, my mind was busy composing *Sarah's First Christmas*.

I hope all of you readers have a magical Christmas this year. God bless you.

Rebecca Winters

CHAPTER ONE

"GOOD night, Brooke. Thanks again for the bonus. It was very generous. I appreciate it more than you know. Merry Christmas!"

"You're welcome, Dave. Merry Christmas to you and your family, too. See you on Monday."

A gust of snow swept through the store before Brooke Longley's favorite employee could close the door of Longley's Western Outfitters. Over the past week the tiny community of West Yellowstone, Montana, had already been pummeled by two blizzards. Now it seemed a third one was building.

Though the grandfather clock showed only a few minutes after seven, it felt like midnight. Brooke normally kept the store open until ten, but not on Christmas Eve.

Tonight the Garnetts were hosting their annual holiday party for the locals at the Cowhide Bar and Grill just a couple of blocks down the main street from the store. Brooke had no particular desire to go. But her good friend, Julia Morton, who lived with her husband, Kyle, at the other end of town, had made her promise to meet them there.

"Just because you've sworn off men for good, Brooke, it doesn't mean you want people thinking you've become antisocial since your broken engagement."

When Julia put it like that, Brooke could see her point. Therefore she decided she would attend the party for an hour, then head on home in her father's reliable four-wheel-drive Blazer.

After turning off the lights and locking up, she started to trudge through the blinding snow in her sealskin boots. Despite the constant shoveling by her neighbors who worked in the other shops, snow had drifted across the walkways impeding her progress.

The thermometer under the eaves of the local drugstore registered two below zero. No doubt the temperature would fall to at least ten below before morning. Last year at this time, the weather conditions had been similar.

Thank heavens it wasn't last year.

Thank heavens you're not waiting for Mark to arrive from California.

She and her fiancé had planned to be married at the little Church of the Pines in West Yellowstone between Christmas and New Year's. Then came the nightmarish phone call. Her fiancé wasn't coming for the holidays after all. He'd met someone else and hoped she would understand. It was better to end their engagement now rather than face a divorce later on down the road.

A month later, her father died after a sudden fatal heart attack, leaving her totally alone to grieve. At the lowest point in her life, she couldn't imagine living long enough to see another year come and go.

But life had played a trick on her. To her surprise, twelve months of hard work running the family business had passed. In that amount of time, the company had prospered and she'd turned twenty-four. Not only was she still alive to see another Christmas through, Julia and Kyle, who'd moved down from Great Falls during the summer, had become her best friends. Since the girls she'd been closest to through junior high and high school had ended up moving to a big city or out of the state altogether, it would be nice to spend part of Christmas Eve with the Mortons.

She picked up her pace but the blizzard seemed to be gaining in intensity. With whiteout conditions like this, no one was driving anywhere. Everything had come to a standstill. A world of unrelenting white. Quite beautiful if you knew you could reach shelter.

As she was crossing the first street, which resembled a cow path, she thought she could hear a child crying. But the wind often mimicked human sounds so she dismissed the notion and kept moving, anxious to get out of the ferocious elements.

By the time she'd reached the other side of the street, the crying sounded again, only much louder. Brooke stopped to listen. There could be no mistake. The sounds were definitely mortal. A terrified child was out in this storm.

But *whose* child? *Where*?

Sensing the sound was coming from a side street, Brooke wheeled around and started in that direction. She hadn't gone a dozen feet when she spied a small figure beating on the glass of Clark's Indian jewelry storefront window. The place was dark. No doubt Harmon Clark had closed up early and either gone home to his ranch or already headed for the Garnetts' party. The little girl couldn't be more than five years old. In between sobs she kept crying out a name, but Brooke couldn't understand her. The poor child was dressed in flimsy tennis shoes, no socks, a wisp of a dress and a paper-thin windbreaker that provided no insulation against the blinding snow. Another few minutes and she would freeze to death.

Without hesitation, Brooke knelt beside her and put a protective arm around her slender shoulders. "My name's Brooke. I want to help you. Who are you looking for, darling?"

The little girl kept slapping at the window with her bare hands. It sounded like she was saying something about Charlie.

"Sweetheart...nobody is inside. If you'll come with me, I'll help you find Charlie. Okay?"

"Nooooo! Not Charlie! D-don't let him t-take me!"

Brooke wasn't immune to the fear in the child's desperate plea. Without wasting another second, she picked her up and started running through the snow toward the family store. Inside it would be warm. There was a telephone.

Several times she almost fell in her race for shelter. The rigid body she held in her arms shivered without cessation. "It's going to be all right," she murmured over and over again in her attempt to reassure the comfortless child.

A dozen scenarios of what might have happened to bring this innocent, defenseless little person to this point passed through Brooke's mind, none of them good. She'd never thought of herself as a violent human being, but whoever this Charlie was, the urge to kill him had grown into a driving need.

"Here we are, safe and sound."

She pulled out her keys and unlocked the door. Blessed warmth enveloped them as she kicked it shut with the back of her boot, then flicked on the lights and hurried through the interior to the kitchen in the rear of the store.

An air duct from the furnace came up through the floor. Brooke placed a chair next to the vent and lowered the little girl. When she was seated, Brooke rushed into the other room to pull a thermal blanket from the shelf.

By the time she returned to the kitchen, the hysterical crying had turned into a spate of whimpers. The little girl's teeth were chattering. Brooke got on her knees and pulled off the worn, frozen tennis shoes. After relieving the child of her windbreaker, she wrapped the blanket around her and began to rub her icy feet, applying gentle pressure.

"What's your name, darling?" The snow hadn't yet melted off her straggly, dark brown hair.

"S-Sarah."

"Sarah what?"

She rubbed her eyes with the back of her hand. "I don't know."

Horrified by the revelation, Brooke wanted to go

after the man responsible and strangle him with her bare hands. But her first priority was to give this child the care she needed.

"I'm going to make you some nice warm cocoa. Would you like that?"

Between the sobs, Brooke couldn't tell if the girl had answered her or not. It didn't matter. She jumped up, mixed a packet of instant cocoa with water, then heated the contents in the microwave.

When it was ready, she put the cup to the girl's lips and told her to drink. To her relief, Sarah held the mug by herself and drank every drop. She wasn't just thirsty; she was starving!

"I bet that tasted good."

She nodded.

"Where's your mommy?"

"C-Charlie says I don't have a m-mommy."

"Who's Charlie?"

"H-he was mad b-because the car s-stopped." As Sarah spoke, Brooke detected a soft Southern drawl. The girl was a long way from home. "When he got out, I climbed out the other door and r-ran away." Her lower lip trembled. "It was c-cold in the s-snow. I—I c-couldn't see." She started crying again. Huge tears fell from dark blue eyes.

Sickness welled in Brooke's throat. Her heart went out to this precious little soul. She put her arms around her and rocked her back and forth. "I'm going to take care of you. Everything's going to be all right."

"Do you think C-Charlie's looking f-for me?"

"I don't know."

"He'll get mad and h-hit me when he finds me. Don't let me him f-find me," she begged.

Brooke knew instantly that this was no game of make-believe or a child's exaggeration—the little girl was telling the truth. She had to bite her tongue before she said, "He's never going to get near you again. Do you believe me?"

She hugged Brooke in response.

"It feels good in here, doesn't it?" she asked, trying desperately to change the subject.

"Yes."

"Would you like some crackers?"

"Yes."

Reaching for a box left over from lunch, she placed it in the girl's lap. "Eat as many as you want while I go into the other room and make a phone call."

"Don't leave me!" she cried out in panic.

Too late, Brooke realized her mistake. She scooped up the little girl, crackers and all, and carried her into the front of the store. After setting her on the counter, she picked up the receiver and pushed the buttons for the police.

"Julia?" she cried out when she heard her friend's voice. "How come you're on duty tonight? I thought you were going to meet me at the Garnetts' party."

"I am, but Ruth asked if I would fill in for her until nine. I was just going to call you and tell you to meet Kyle and me there later."

"I'm afraid I won't be going. An emergency has cropped up."

"Tell me what's wrong." Suddenly her friend was all business. As soon as she heard Brooke's story, Julia told her to take the little girl home with her and they'd send an officer out to the house later tomorrow or the next day to begin an investigation.

Apparently there'd been a number of car accidents on the highway and now the roads were closed in every direction. All available patrolmen were busy. What she would do right now was relay the information to the state police.

Julia was paid to think fast and come up with the right decision. Being that it was Christmas Eve, Brooke could only praise her friend's wisdom. Since there was no hospital in West Yellowstone and the roads were closed, home was the next best place to see to Sarah's needs. In a remote area like this, especially in winter, practicality was every bit as important as the letter of the law.

"Whoever this Charlie is—" Brooke's voice shook "—he has traumatized this child and should be made to pay for what he's done."

"I agree," Julia muttered with equal venom. "That poor little thing. She was lucky you came along when you did. If anyone can make a little child feel better, it's you. I'll stay in close touch with you. When I get off work, Kyle and I will drive over to your house and see if there's anything we can do to help."

"That would be wonderful." Brooke thanked her friend, then hung up the phone and gathered Sarah in her arms once more. "How would you like to come to my house tonight? It's not very far from here. We'll have a nice dinner. Does that sound good?"

Sarah nodded.

"Before we go, we need to get you some clothes. You can pick out whatever you'd like."

Obviously the little girl had never been given a choice of things to wear before. At first, she didn't seem to understand, but after some prodding on Brooke's part, Sarah picked out a red plaid shirt, jeans, stockings, cowboy boots, a Western-cut parka with a hood and ski gloves. While she was putting on her new clothes, Brooke stashed some other items in a sack to be wrapped later.

Once Sarah was dressed, Brooke said, "My truck is right outside. It's going to be cold before I can get it warmed up, so I think we'll take the blanket. Are you ready?"

She hadn't needed to asked the question. Her little shadow followed her out of the store, clinging to her hand for dear life.

CHAPTER TWO

THE small but cozy Longley house surrounded by jack pines sat on the outskirts of West Yellowstone away from the street. Besides central heating, it had a stone fireplace, which if necessary, could keep the whole interior warm in winter.

Despite the blizzard, which might last several more hours, Brooke found her way home in the Blazer without difficulty. There was something rather comforting about knowing she wouldn't be alone this Christmas Eve. The stranded child seated next to her needed Brooke if she were going to survive. It felt good to be needed on this night of all nights. And her friends would be over later.

"Sarah? Did you know tonight was Christmas Eve?"

"What's that?" the little girl asked as their feet sank in the snow leading up to the front porch.

Another pain seared Brooke's heart. "Just a minute and I'll show you." She helped the little girl up the stairs, then found her key and let them inside. The second the door was shut she flicked the wall switch that automatically turned on the Christmas-tree lights.

"*Ooh*," Sarah cried softly, her eyes shiny bright as she beheld the twinkly colored lights and balls dotting the freshly cut blue spruce.

"Come look at this ornament, Sarah."

The little girl approached with an air of reverence. "There's a *baby* inside!"

"That's right. It's the little Lord Jesus. Tomorrow is His birthday. We call it Christmas. The day Christ was born. We give each other presents and it's a very special day. Later on tonight after I've got you tucked in bed all comfy, I'll tell you about Him. How He lived and died, and how He loves everyone on the earth and blesses us when we're in trouble."

Sarah cocked her head. "What's *bless*?"

"He makes us happy when no one else can."

While Sarah contemplated what Brooke considered a less-than-adequate explanation, Brooke turned on her battery-operated tape player and put in a medley of Christmas carols. Soon the house was filled with music. She was rewarded by Sarah's sweet smile. "Can we sleep by the baby Jesus *all night*?"

Brooke swallowed hard. "If you want to. I'll get a fire lit, then we'll go into the kitchen and fix dinner. I hope you like scalloped potatoes. I made a lot of food last night. The only thing we have to do is warm it up and we can eat.''

The girl did a little skip at Brooke's side, like a child who was happy. The movement tugged at Brooke's heart.

''What's *skolupped*?''

''It's creamed potatoes, one of my favorite foods, but it's kind of hard to explain. You just have to eat some and you'll see how good they are. I think you'll like them a lot.''

While Sarah set the table following Brooke's instructions, Brooke warmed their food and heated some apple juice with cinnamon sticks and cloves. In no time, they were able to tuck in.

Sarah had started on her second helping of potatoes when Brooke heard a knock on the front door. The fear in Sarah's eyes grew tangible. ''M-maybe that's Charlie!'' she cried out before dropping her fork. The next thing Brooke knew, Sarah had left her chair to run around and cling to her. ''Don't let him take me.''

Brooke gave her a squeeze to mask her own fear. ''It's probably my friend Julia and her husband. They said they would come by tonight.''

Julia had made it clear that the police wouldn't be able to drive out to the house before morning at least. Though Brooke knew her friends were going to drop in, it seemed too soon for Julia to be here. *Unless* she'd gotten off work earlier than planned. Brooke supposed it could be a neighbor, though she thought it unlikely when everyone was either at home or at the Garnetts' by now.

Then again, *that monster might have followed Sarah here.*

"Charlie won't get the chance to hurt you," she vowed in a fierce whisper. "But just to be safe, you stay in here while I find out who it is."

For once, the little girl didn't try to follow her.

With pounding heart, Brooke entered the living room. Out of a sense of self-preservation, she made a detour to the fireplace for her father's loaded hunting rifle. No stranger to a gun, she'd gone target shooting with her father ever since she was a little girl. He'd always complimented her on her wicked accuracy. Though she didn't hunt, she was thankful he had taught her how to shoot in case of an emergency.

The rap on the front door sounded again. If it had been one of the neighbors or Julia, they would have called out and made a lot of noise by now.

Brooke advanced to the window to find out who was there, but the snow was still coming down hard, making it impossible to see anything beyond the glass. The words, "Silent night, holy night, All is calm, all is bright," permeated the living room's interior. The irony of the situation staggered Brooke. "Who's there?" she called out.

"Deputy Marshal McClain."

McClain. McClain...

That was the name of Julia's cousin who was a federal marshal. What would *he* be doing in West Yellowstone on Christmas Eve? Maybe she hadn't heard the man correctly.

According to Julia, the marshals had different business than the police or the state troopers. More and more she began to think Charlie could be standing on the other side of the door attempting to impersonate a marshal.

"I was told you found an abandoned child in town. I'd like to talk to both of you." His deep, vibrant voice had a silky quality, arousing her suspicions even more.

I just bet you would.

Cocking the rifle, she turned on the porch light and slowly opened the door. She had to look up a long way to see a pair of flame-blue eyes beneath the rim of a federal marshal's hat staring down at her with an intensity that took her breath away. So did the rest of his rugged features and magnificent male physique dressed in full winter uniform. His badge glinted in the glow from the Christmas lights.

He flashed her his picture ID. "Merry Christmas to you, too, Brooke Longley." His hard, masculine mouth twitched provocatively.

"You *are* Julia's cousin! When you called out your name, I thought I must have been mistaken because she told me you don't work around here."

"Normally that's true."

As she continued to stare at him, she remembered several conversations with Julia, who was forever trying to get her to start dating again.

"Honestly, Brooke. With that blond hair and those green eyes, you're a real knockout. It makes no sense that you refuse to give the guys around here a chance. I think you're as determined to remain single as my cousin.

"He's not only Montana's most gorgeous bachelor, he's also the most elusive male on the planet. The two of you make a real pair, you know that? If you both weren't so damned stubborn, you'd probably find out you were perfect for each other."

"I—I'm sorry," she whispered when it dawned on her she was still pointing the rifle at his face. Feeling rather foolish, she rested it over her left shoulder. "Please, come in."

"Thank you."

It had been a long time since she'd been this aware of a man. He had to be in his mid-thirties. In retrospect, Mark had been a boy by comparison.

At a precarious moment like this, she was shocked that she would be entertaining any thoughts at all about Julia's cousin, who for reasons of his own had no desire to get involved with a woman. She could understand that. After Mark's rejection, she never wanted to feel that vulnerable again, either.

While she put the rifle back over the fireplace, he stepped inside and shut the door. As he took in the sight of the Christmas tree, she noticed his eyes light up exactly like Sarah's. His broad chest rose and fell as he breathed in the warmth and spicy smells coming from the kitchen. Something told her he'd been out in the storm a long time and was enjoying the respite from the harsh elements.

"Please make yourself comfortable, Deputy." She turned on a lamp to give them more light.

"I wish you hadn't done that," he murmured as he shrugged out of his parka with consummate male grace. "I feel like I've just walked inside a Christmas card. You know the kind. There's this tiny house all snug in the woods. Through the frosted windows, it looks warm and inviting, like fairyland."

That's exactly how I feel about my home. Inexplicable chills chased across her skin. Her breath caught again as he removed his hat to reveal a healthy head of hair that gleamed like dark, shiny chestnuts in the firelight. He was even more attractive than she'd realized. Julia hadn't exaggerated her cousin's masculine charms. In fact—

"Where's the little girl?"

"She's hiding in the kitchen. How is it you're in West Yellowstone? If I remember correctly, Julia said her extended family lived in Great Falls, as well."

He sat down on one of the overstuffed chairs. "That's true. But I belong to the Special Operations Group within the federal marshal's office. The nature of my work takes me all over the country. I'm rarely home."

Because you don't want to be? Though it was none of Brooke's business, she couldn't help but be intrigued by a man who was so inaccessible.

"I've been following up a new lead on a two-year-old case. It brought me into town tonight. When I found the car in question abandoned in the middle of the street, I phoned the local police and discovered Julia was working dispatch.

"As soon as she told me about the little girl you found, everything fitted into place, particularly when I asked for details and heard that the child was about five years old and spoke with a Southern drawl.

''After hearing that news, I had an APB put out on the man who'd been driving the abandoned car, then I told Julia I would drive over here to talk to the little girl. Her testimony could give us much needed information.''

Brooke pressed her palms together. ''Right now, Sarah is so terrified I don't know how much help she could be. Can you tell me something about this case before I ask her to come in the living room?''

He eyed her pensively before nodding. ''It could be a long shot, but I have a gut feeling this might be the little girl who was stolen a couple of years ago by two convicted killers from Mississippi.''

Brooke's gasp reverberated throughout the living room.

''They escaped while federal marshals were transporting them across state lines.''

At the thought of Sarah being at the mercy of lunatics like that, Brooke couldn't remain seated.

''The two men took off and since then have eluded the law time and again. They were last spotted in Utah, where I was put on the case. I picked up their trail out of Santaquin. The child could be the daughter of one of the prisoner's victims shot in Mississippi.''

"You mean the mother is dead?'' Brooke cried out quietly.

"That's right. She wasn't married, so we have no idea who the birth father is. Somewhere in Utah the murderers split up, or else one of them killed the other. So far, no body has been found. One of the convicts has been posing as the girl's father for cover.''

Shuddering in horror, Brooke rubbed the side of her hips in a nervous gesture. The deputy's gaze appeared to take in the motion with male appreciation though he wasn't obvious about it.

"Sarah calls him Charlie, but she's never referred to him as her father. She said he told her she didn't have a mother. When I asked her, she didn't seem to know her last name.''

His jaw hardened. "It fits, but over the past two years a lot of promising tips have turned into false leads. Still, if he's one of the prisoners we're looking for, and he has the right survival equipment, what better place to hide out for the winter than Yellowstone Park where it would be difficult to track him.''

She felt light-headed and sank onto a matching chair. "Sarah said the car stopped. When he got out to see what was wrong, she ran away as fast as she could.''

"She must have been terrified of him to risk facing a blizzard of this magnitude." He rubbed his lower lip with the back of his thumb. "No matter who this man is, we can thank Providence she had the intelligence to run before it was too late. Tell me how you came to find her."

In a few minutes, Brooke had given him every bit of information she could think of.

"I'd like to talk to her, but I don't want to frighten her. Obviously she trusts you. What do you think would be the best way to handle it?"

The fact that the deputy cared enough about Sarah's fears to want Brooke's input first said a great deal about his sensitivity and kindness. It seemed to be a trait that ran in Julia's family.

Except for his male appeal, which was too potent to ignore, there was nothing wrong with him. In their arrogance, some law-enforcement types might have given her a hard time for answering the door with a loaded rifle staring them in the face, particularly because she was a woman.

This man took the incident in stride, displaying a calm temperament combined with a sense of humor she found rare in most people, male or female.

"It's too bad you have to be on duty. I think

everything would go better if she thought you were simply a friend from town who'd dropped over to enjoy Christmas Eve with me. It might make her less suspicious if she believed we'd known each other before tonight. But since that isn't the—''

"It is now," he broke in on her before pulling out a cellular phone. "Besides, Julia has raved so much about this fantastic friend she's made in West Yellowstone, I feel like I already know you."

"That's nice to hear. About the raved part," she added before she realized she'd probably made another blunder. A blush stole over her face. "I mean—''

"Don't try to fix it." His mouth twitched before he started to chuckle.

Brooke didn't think there was a sight more attractive to a woman than to watch an attractive man smile with his eyes as well as his lips. "I feel like I know you, too. Or at least I know about you. In Julia's eyes, you're a living legend."

"Is that right?" His grin indicated he didn't take himself or his cousin's compliment seriously.

"I know she worries about you," Brooke added on a more sober note. "According to your cousin, you perform some of the most dangerous work in the world. I believe it. Tonight is Christmas Eve. While other men are safe at home putting up the

Christmas tree, your presence here because of those two murderers is a case in point. As far as Sarah and I are concerned, your cousin is right. You *are* a hero."

There was an enigmatic expression in his eyes before he said, "Tell me that after I've caught those felons, then I'll be happy to bask in your praise, Ms. Longley. Speaking of which, you deserve all the credit for discovering Sarah when you did, and coming to her rescue."

"Anyone would have done what I did!"

He shook his head. "I wish I could say that were true, but unfortunately, it isn't, and I speak from experience. Julia told me you didn't make a sound of protest when she asked if you would keep the little girl with you until tomorrow or the next day. Most people would find that request a great inconvenience at any time, but particularly on Christmas Eve."

It was her turn to dismiss his praise. "Don't make me out to be some kind of a saint. The truth is, I'm glad I'm the one who found her. I happen to believe Christmas is for children. Without her, I would be alone tonight, and it just wouldn't be the same." She could hear the wobble in her voice. *Damn.*

"My cousin said this would be your first Christmas without your father. She knew it would be a difficult time for you.''

"She's right.''

"Julia also said you suffered a broken engagement at this time last year.''

Julia! Brooke averted her eyes.

CHAPTER THREE

"I'M SORRY if I've made you uncomfortable. I simply wanted you to know that I've been through my own hell over a situation involving a woman I had considered marrying. Believe me, I understand how bleak the prospect of the holidays sounds with no one to share in such a special time."

His admission was a revelation. She didn't think Julia knew he'd ever been close to being engaged, let alone married. Obviously his pain had been too great to discuss, even with his cousin.

"If you and I want Sarah to believe we're good friends, I think it's important we understand where the other person is coming from. It will make for a more harmonious relationship all the way around."

"I agree," she said quietly.

While Brooke digested the wisdom of his frank remarks, he talked into the phone and left word that he was taking the rest of the night off and would contact them in the morning. In case of an emergency, they could always call him.

He put the phone back in his parka pocket, then

sat forward, his eyes narrowing as his gaze traveled over her upturned features. "Thanks to my cousin, you and I know some of the essentials about each other's life. For Sarah's sake, maybe now would be a good time to fill in the rest of the information we ought to know about one another. In case Julia never mentioned it, my name is Vance."

"Yes, I know. And you're thirty-six."

They smiled in mutual amusement.

"That's right. In case Sarah asks, I was born and raised on the Circle Q Ranch a few miles south of Great Falls, Montana. I have three brothers, all of whom are married with children and help Dad run the place. Since Julia has done a lot of talking, I have to assume you've learned I'm the loose cannon of the family."

"On the contrary, she's in awe of you. According to her, out of all the children, you're the brilliant one. She told me you're the reason she's working in law enforcement. Didn't you know that?"

"That's hard to believe, but I have to admit I'm flattered. The fact is, it took me a long time to find myself. I received my degree in mining engineering from the University of Utah, but once I was out of college, I decided I didn't want engineering because it didn't provide the adventure I was craving.''

''That happens to a lot of people, Vance. I'm sure they don't consider themselves a loose cannon because of it.''

''You haven't heard the rest,'' he muttered in self-abnegation. ''Then a good friend suggested I try law enforcement. After a time, I found I didn't like normal police work in a city, either. I decided I needed challenging work, but something that would keep me out-of-doors.''

She smiled. ''You sound exactly like my dad. He grew up in New York and became a Wall Street broker. After a time, he felt stifled by the stress of business but couldn't see his way out.

''When he happened to come to Yellowstone on a vacation, he said he knew he'd found paradise. So he moved out here and invested all the money he could scrape up to buy into Ted Wilson's store.

''By the time I was born, Ted retired. Dad bought out his half and changed the name to Longley's. He never regretted the move. According to him, it made a new man out of him.

''It was here he met my mother and married her. People who knew him in New York, and then came here for visits, couldn't believe the change in him. He was finally content.''

Vance nodded. "I know the feeling. I would've liked to meet your father. It sounds like we had a lot in common. When an official from the district federal marshal's office in Great Falls suggested a deputy marshal's job might be just the thing for a renegade like me, I looked into it and found out he was right. I've been with the marshal's office ever since."

"As long as you're happy, nothing else really matters."

"Amen to that. So, is Brooke Longley happy running her father's store?"

When he flashed her that devastating smile, Brooke's heart turned over. *No. This couldn't be happening. It just couldn't be. Not when she'd promised herself never again!*

"Yes and no. I was an only child born late in my parents' marriage and I've lived most of my life in West Yellowstone. I received my degree to teach English from the University of Wyoming.

"When an opportunity came along to teach English in Japan for a year, I took it. But upon my return, I discovered my mother was ill with pneumonia. Under the circumstances, I put off finding a permanent teaching job here in Montana so I could care for her."

Tears threatened. She had to clear her throat. *Damn* again.

"After my mom died, I helped Dad at the store. He never stopped grieving over the loss of my mother. Late last winter he suffered a fatal heart attack. I've been running the business ever since. That's about it."

The compassion in his eyes caused her to look away.

"You've had to deal with a lot of grief. I'm sorry."

"It's all right." She tossed back her head. "The worst is behind me. When I think of Sarah's situation, I could never complain about anything."

"I was thinking the same thing. Therefore, now that we're good friends—" he winked "—I have to tell you I'm famished. How about inviting me to your Christmas feast?"

She blinked. "What feast?"

"The one I could smell the moment you opened the door. I've been salivating ever since."

Brooke's pulse raced. "I'm afraid it's just meat loaf."

"Did Julia tell you that was my favorite meal?"

She couldn't be certain if he were teasing or not. But a dedicated bachelor never stopped being suspicious of a feminine trap.

"I'm afraid our conversations never got quite that detailed. What she did tell me over and over again is that you are as against marriage as I am against ever getting involved with a man again."

His mouth quirked in genuine amusement. "That's good. It means she's decided to give up playing Cupid at least."

Brooke nodded. "She's tried that unsuccessfully with me several times in the past, too. I finally had to put my foot down. You don't think she purposely sent you over here tonight hoping something might happen between us, do you?" For no good reason, Brooke derived the greatest enjoyment out of goading him.

There was an unreadable expression in his eyes. "I'm afraid the idea to come over here was all mine, but no doubt she's already planned our wedding by now."

Brooke nodded. "If I know Julia, she's probably estimated how many children we're going to have and where we're going to live." With false sweetness, she added, "You'll have to forgive your cousin. She and Kyle are still newlyweds, totally blind to the pitfalls of romance."

"You're right about that," he muttered with such deep conviction, Brooke knew his disillusionment was every bit as severe as her own. Knowing he'd been burned by a love affair that didn't work out touched a sensitive chord inside her. Now that her compassion had been aroused, she had no desire to bait him.

"I think I've left Sarah alone long enough. Maybe if you were to remove your badge and weapon, she won't notice you're in uniform. You can put everything, including your hat and parka, in the front hall closet."

Once again his shuttered eyes gave her a thorough appraisal. "Good idea, Ms. Longley. If I need to protect you, I can always reach for the rifle."

His comment had a sobering effect on Brooke. "Do you think that murderer is out there looking for Sarah?"

The mirth left his eyes. "Probably not. He's a desperate fugitive. Since she got away from him, he's more likely to keep on running. I have a gut feeling he's headed for the Park. We'll catch him."

The conviction in his deep voice sent a shiver of a different kind through her body. She could well understand someone's fear if they found themselves on the wrong side of the law where he was concerned. He exuded unquestioned confidence and authority not possessed by many men.

Needing to do something with her hands, she reached for the tape player and turned the cassette to the other side. "I'll just tell Sarah you're staying for dinner. You're welcome to freshen up in the guest bathroom. It's the first door on the right as you go down the hall."

Without waiting for a response, she hurried into the kitchen. "Sarah?" she called out. "You don't have to be afraid. That was one of my good friends who's come..." She stopped talking when she realized there was no sign of her little guest.

Maybe she was hiding under the table. But when Brooke lifted the hem of the red tablecloth to look, she found nothing. *Please don't tell me you were so terrified you ran out the back door into the blizzard.*

Panic-stricken, Brooke wheeled around, then almost fainted in relief when she discovered the door was still locked. "*Sarah*? Where are you, darling?"

"In h-here," a fear-filled voice sounded from the area of the utility closet near the back entrance.

Slowly Brooke opened the door. Sarah was well hidden behind the vacuum, but part of one red cowboy boot was showing. Another pain passed through Brooke's body when she reflected on the abuse this adorable child had been forced to suffer. "It's all right, sweetheart. Charlie has gone far away. You can come out now. My friend, Vance, dropped over to spend Christmas Eve with us. He's really nice.''

"I tell stories, too," came a low, masculine voice from behind Brooke's shoulder. She could feel the warmth from his hard male body all the way to her insides. "In fact, I have a special Christmas story I always tell my nephews and nieces."

The tenderness in his tone caught at Brooke's emotions. Obviously it struck a responsive chord in Sarah, as well. Pretty soon two little red boots could be seen as she crawled out backward from behind the vacuum and stood up.

"What's the story about?"

"A lonely tree growing up in the forest."

Sarah took a trusting step toward them. "How come it was lonely?"

"A big snowstorm like the one tonight blew all the other trees over and left it standing by itself on the mountain."

"What did it do?"

Brooke fought tears and couldn't wait to hear the answer herself. By now, Sarah had reached the threshold of the closet. Vance's compelling voice and story had caused her to forget her fear.

"Why don't we sit down at the table? Then I'll tell you the rest of it. The problem is, I could smell

Brooke's meat loaf all the way outside and I'm hungry. It's my favorite food."

Sarah's mouth curved upward. "It's my favorite, too."

"Did you save me some?"

"Did we?" Sarah asked Brooke in an anxious voice, grasping her hand.

The child's dearness warmed Brooke's heart. "I think there's enough. If not, we'll load him up with biscuits."

"They're good. 'Specially with hukla...'" She stopped, then looked up at Brooke. "What kind of jam?"

"Huckleberry."

"Huckleberry jam. Brooke made it all by herself!" Sarah informed their guest proudly.

Vance's eyes gleamed as they lighted on Brooke. "Is that a fact? Well now, huckleberries just happen to be my favorite fruit in the whole wide world."

"They are?" Sarah's eyes had rounded.

"That's right. They only grow in certain places during part of the summer here in Montana. You're lucky if you can find them. When I was your age, my brothers and I used to go out in the woods hunting for them. We would eat as many as we could, then we'd take the rest home in sacks and smother our pancakes with them."

"What's pancakes?"

"Well, if you don't know, I bet we can talk Brooke into making them for our breakfast in the morning."

Sarah clapped her hands. With shining eyes, she asked, "Can Vance stay all night with us?" While Brooke stood there in shock, Sarah turned to Vance. "We're going to sleep by the Christmas tree. Brooke said so."

"I haven't done that since I was a boy." Near Brooke's ear he murmured, "I know I told you that I believe Charlie is long gone, but I can't be a hundred percent certain of it. Therefore, to make sure everyone's safe, I'm going to stay overnight to protect you."

CHAPTER FOUR

THOUGH Vance McClain's intentions were prompted by his sense of duty, Brooke's face went hot. "All right," she answered in a shaky voice. "Sarah? Why don't you set a place at the table for Vance so I can serve him dinner?"

Sarah nodded and darted to the drawer for the silverware, her anxiety forgotten for the moment. Vance had a way with children every father ought to patent, she mused in awe.

While Brooke worked at the stove, she could feel his intense gaze. But she refused to meet it or answer his question, which hovered in the air as she prepared a plate of food still hot from the oven. A minute later, they were seated at the table, but this time it was Vance instead of Sarah who devoured his food as if he hadn't had a real meal in ages.

Brooke watched him through veiled eyes while she sipped some more hot cider. Sarah found him an unending source of fascination, as well. Why not? He was easily the most attractive man in the state of Montana, maybe the whole country.

Brooke ought to know. Thousands of good-looking American and foreign men had passed through Longley's over the years. Mark, a graduate student at UCLA, had been a case in point, with his California surfer's tan, his blond hair bleached even whiter by the sun. Like fool's gold, he was all flash, and Brooke had been taken in.

The dark-haired Adonis pointing out Sarah's dimples to her with his index finger needed no artifice to light a fire in Brooke. His hard-muscled six-foot-three physique and vibrant male voice alone made mincemeat of her insides. As her gaze wandered over his intelligent face, she realized that the lines of experience around his mouth, his five o'clock shadow, only made him that much more appealing. There ought to be a law against such a man—

"Did you say something, Brooke?"

Good heavens! Did I? Another wave of heat swept over her. "Sarah and I want to hear the rest of your story, don't we, darling?" she dissembled quickly to cover her embarrassment.

The little girl nodded.

"All right. Where were we?"

"After the storm, the tree was alone on the mountain," Sarah supplied.

She had the steel-trap mind of a precocious

child. *Did Sarah have a father who'd been searching for her? Siblings? Extended family? Had they been waiting frantically these two years for any word of her?* A dozen unanswered questions filled Brooke's mind.

"The tree," he began, "stayed on the mountain for years and years. As it got older, it provided shade for people who needed shelter from the sun, and it gave a home to a family of squirrels and robins. Children could play in it. Some people used its leaves to make medicine for sick people, and villagers took some of its old branches to make a warm fire."

"It was a nice tree, huh, Vance."

"It was the best," he concurred in a thick-toned voice. Brooke could tell little Sarah had gotten under his skin and was tugging away at his emotions as well. "But the tree still didn't feel important. Not until Christmas Eve."

"What happened?" Sarah had been so enthralled by the story, she'd slipped off her chair and had come to stand at Vance's side. He put an arm around her shoulder and lowered his head as if to confide in her. "A new baby boy had just been born. A very special baby. He needed a bed, but his parents didn't have one. So the father came up the mountain and cut down the only tree left to make one for him."

"Did the tree cry?"

"No, honey." He tousled her hair. "The tree had never been so happy in its life."

"How come?"

"Because its wood was used to make the bed for the Baby Jesus."

"I know!" she cried, and jumped up and down excitedly. "Brooke showed me the baby. Come and see it!" She pulled on Vance's arm.

In an unguarded moment, he captured Brooke's gaze. His seemed to say that he, too, recognized Sarah was a very special little girl who desperately needed the love and attention of caring people after what she'd been forced to endure for the past two years. If a look could convey a promise, she sensed that he'd just told her he would do everything in his power to handle this precarious situation with as much finesse as possible. In that moment, Brooke's admiration for him took on new life. Vance McClain was no ordinary man. Her heart knew it. Her soul knew it.

The revelation left her weak as she got up from the table and followed him and Sarah into the living room. Because the little girl absorbed any new information like a sponge, she remembered exactly which ornament depicted the crèche scene and proceeded to point it out to Vance.

"How come Jesus isn't afraid of the dogs?"

Again Brooke's troubled eyes met the unspoken question in Vance's before she knelt next to Sarah. "Those are cows, darling. Jesus was born in a stable where the cows live. They give milk."

"Do they bite?"

"No. They are kind. They love the baby Jesus, too."

Sarah moved closer and put her arm around Brooke's neck. "Do you have a dog?"

"No."

"I don't like dogs."

"Why not?"

"Charlie's friend had a dog that looked like those cows. He said it would bite me if I went out of the house."

Dear God.

Brooke swallowed the sob in her throat.

"What happened to the man and his dog?" Vance asked in a quiet voice.

"I don't know. One day, Charlie and the man got in a big fight. Then Charlie made me get in the car."

"Then you never saw the other man after that?"

"No. But I'm scared they'll come and find me." She burrowed into Brooke's shoulder and clung to her.

"Don't worry, Sarah. They don't know where you are. Besides, I wouldn't allow them to ever come near you again," Vance vowed in the most chilling voice Brooke had ever heard.

Sarah lifted her head from Brooke's shoulder, her eyes soulful as she looked up Vance. "Do you promise?"

By now, he was on his haunches. "I wouldn't lie to you, especially not on Christmas Eve," he whispered solemnly.

"You're not afraid of anything, huh?"

Brooke heard him suck in his breath. "Sure I am."

"*You are*?"

"Yup. For instance, I'm afraid Brooke wants you all to herself and won't let me stay here with you tonight."

Brooke had already said he could sleep over, but in his wisdom, he wanted Sarah's permission.

Her dark head whipped around. With pleading eyes, she cried, "He can stay with us, can't he, Brooke?"

Since he knew how Brooke felt about letting a man into her life, she didn't need to look at Vance to realize he was probably enjoying this chance to take advantage of her hospitality against her will. But in her heart of hearts, she couldn't be angry with him. He had a job to perform where Sarah was concerned.

Winning her trust would supply him with the kind of facts he needed to solve this case. In fact, he'd already gleaned information because Sarah trusted him. Because of that, Brooke knew she had to do everything in her power to help even if it meant letting him spend the night. Even if it meant putting her emotions at risk once more.

But only for tonight, Brooke. Only for this one time. Only for Sarah's sake. "Of course he's welcome. I'll even find him my father's sleeping bag to put by the fire. You and I will take the Hide-A-Bed."

"The Hide-A-*what*?"

"There's a bed inside that couch." Brooke pointed to the couch set against the wall a few feet away.

Sarah stared at it. "I don't see it."

"That's because it's hiding from us," Vance explained with an amused smile. In an economy of movement, he stood up and went over to it. Like magic, he turned it into a bed already made up with sheets and a blanket. Sarah clapped her hands in obvious delight. "Now I can look at the tree all night, huh."

"You can if you don't get too tired," Vance

teased. "But I see a little girl whose eyes are getting sleepy."

"They are?"

A low chuckle escaped his throat. The warm sound found its way beneath Brooke's skin. Everything he said and did was forcing her to think about him too much.

"Come with me, Sarah. We girls have to get ready for bed." The mysterious gleam in his eyes was making her legs wobble.

"While I'm waiting for you, I'll do the dishes."

"That won't be necessary," Brooke said quietly.

"I'm still hungry." He more or less growled, causing Sarah to giggle. "You wouldn't deny me the opportunity to finish off the leftovers, would you?"

The charm of the man took her breath away. As for Sarah, she was totally enamored of him.

"You're welcome to anything I have," she said before she realized how reckless that sounded.

"Is that a fact?" he returned, his drawling voice following her out of the living room.

Embarrassed, she grabbed Sarah with one hand, the sack she'd brought from the store with the other, and headed for the staircase in the front hall. "I was talking about the food," she called over her shoulder during her grand exit. She practically flew up the stairs dragging Sarah with her.

"You disappoint me, Brooke." His voice continued to find her. "Here you got me all excited and then you—"

She slammed her bedroom door to shut out the rest of his words.

"Are you mad?" Sarah stared up at Brooke with anxious eyes.

Brooke could have kicked herself. "No, darling," she rushed to reassure her. "Not at all. Sometimes Vance says things I don't want to hear. That's why I shut the door hard, so he would know how I felt. But I could never be mad at him. In fact, if we could take a peek downstairs, he would probably be laughing."

A new smile appeared. "That's good. I like him."

"So do I."

Sarah followed her into the closet where Brooke changed into a long, plaid flannel nightgown with a ruffled hem. "I wish he was my daddy and you were my mommy."

Oh, Sarah. You poor thing. You're so starved for affection, you would love anyone who's nice to you. "If I had a daughter, I'd want her to be just like you."

"I don't have a mommy. Can I be your little girl?"

Brooke cleared her throat. "I'm not married, Sarah."

"You can marry Vance."

"Vance is a confirmed bachelor."

"What's that mean?"

"It means he doesn't want to be married." The truth of those words didn't improve Brooke's mood. "Now let's get you in the tub and wash your hair."

Distracted by the prospect, Sarah stopped asking questions long enough to follow her into the bathroom. Ten minutes later, she emerged from the water as clean as a whistle with shiny brown hair that Brooke tied back in a ponytail.

After making sure the little girl had brushed her teeth with a spare toothbrush Brooke kept on hand in the cabinet, she reached in the sack for the red-and-white Christmas pajamas and matching slippers she'd pulled from the store shelves. "Let's see if *these* fit."

Soon the child paraded around the room in her new night wear with Rudolph the red-nosed Yellowstone reindeer on the front. A red bulb had been sewn into the fabric of the top, and the slippers, as well.

"Come here a minute, sweetie. There's one more thing I have to do."

Sarah's eyes sparkled with excitement. "What is it?"

"*This*!" Brooke reached out and pressed a tiny switch. Then she did the same thing to the shoes. Now the red nose flicked on and off in three places. "Go look in the mirror on the back of the door."

The second the child did her bidding, she squealed in delight and began jumping up and down. "Can I show Vance?" she cried out breathlessly.

"Of course. Go ahead."

As Sarah shouted his name to the rafters, Brooke grabbed the pillows from the bed, then hurried down the staircase to her parents' bedroom to find the sleeping bag and air mattress for Vance.

By the time she'd brought everything into the living room, he'd found Rudolph the red-nosed reindeer's song on the tape and was teaching Sarah the words to the music. Though he was involved with her, his gaze didn't miss Brooke's entry into the living room. His searching regard made her heart trip over itself. To cover her emotions, she joined in the chorus before filling the mattress with air, using her old bicycle-tire pump. Sarah seemed oblivious to everything and acted so happy, her face resembled a sunbeam. She had pretty features and a feminine demeanor. One day she would grow up to be an attractive woman.

Amid the music and singing, Brooke thought she heard a knock at the front door. Vance and Sarah must have heard it, too. As Sarah froze, he darted Brooke a narrowed glance that said he would handle this.

"Brooke? It's Julia and Kyle!" familiar voices rang out. The knocking grew louder.

By now, Sarah was in Vance's arms.

"It's all right, Sarah," Brooke assured her. "I told you my friends were coming over."

Until she opened the door and saw the look in Julia's eyes as she took in everything and everyone, Brooke had forgotten just how intimate and cozy this domestic scene must appear to her friends. Especially when she'd answered the door in her nightgown.

A suspicious gleam entered Julia's eyes as she and Kyle stepped over the threshold and shut the door. "Merry Christmas to all, especially to *you*, cousin."

CHAPTER FIVE

"MERRY Christmas to you, too, *cousin*," Vance mocked, then nodded at Kyle with a distinct twinkle in his eyes. "Sarah honey, this is my cousin, Julia, and her husband, Kyle. They're close friends of Brooke's who decided to drop over to meet you."

A smile broke out on Sarah's sweet face. "You did?"

"We sure did," Kyle piped up. "In fact, we brought you a present."

Kyle had been holding something behind his back. Now he produced a giant package wrapped in white tissue paper with a red-and-green ribbon. It was as big as Sarah. He stood it in front of her. "Do you want to open it now or tomorrow morning?"

The child looked ecstatic. Her blue eyes stared first at Vance, then Brooke. "What should I do?"

Again Brooke felt her heart melt because Sarah deferred to her almost as if she were her mother. It was a humbling moment in more ways than one, particularly because Sarah had stopped stammering.

"Whatever your little heart desires, darling."

"Then I think I'll open it now."

"I'm glad you said that," Vance reassured her and started helping her undo the ribbons. "I don't think I could have waited until Christmas morning, either." His comment produced an infectious laugh.

As soon as they'd peeled away the tissue, Sarah squealed with delight to discover a huge golden teddy bear wearing a plaid vest and Western hat that had West Yellowstone, Montana, sewn on the brim. It was the kind of bear sold at Taylor's Emporium in town. Julia must have prevailed on the owners to open their store after hours to produce the gift.

"His fingers and toes are all there," Vance said, pretending to give him a quick exam. "He's kind of cute. What are you going to name your very own bear?"

"Jimmy."

"Jimmy." Again Vance sought Brooke's gaze as unspoken questions passed between them. The word had slipped out so easily from her memory it was possible that Jimmy was the name of a family member. "That's a nice name, honey."

Sarah nodded and squeezed her bear the best she could, but her arms could hardly go around him. She burrowed her face against the soft fake fur. "Can Jimmy sleep with me, Brooke?"

"I don't see why not." Brooke wondered how the words managed to slip past the lump in her throat.

"I love him." With sparkling eyes, she stared up at Kyle and Julia. "Thank you for the present."

The little girl's good manners meant someone had taught her well. *Was this the little girl whose mother had been murdered by those escaped convicts?*

"You're very welcome," Julia responded.

"Where's *my* present, Cousin?" Vance's deep voice thrilled Brooke against her will.

Julia grinned at Vance. "My, my. How greedy we've become. It seems to me you have all the presents you could ever want right here. But I think I could manage to give you a cousinly kiss under the mistletoe."

"Me first!" Kyle drew his wife back toward the front door until they were standing under the traditional sprig of green with its white berries. In front of everyone, she gave him a resounding smack.

"Come on, Sarah honey. It's your turn." Vance picked her up in his arms and carried her across the room to the mistletoe. "When we stand underneath this together, you have to give me a kiss."

"Okay." To everyone's amusement, Sarah proceeded to imitate Julie and gave Vance a huge kiss on the jaw.

"It's Brooke's turn!" the little girl cried out when Vance had lowered her to the floor once more.

Heat flowed through Brooke like a river of fire. "I think there's been enough kissing for one night."

"I think you think too much," Vance muttered. Before she knew what was happening, he'd reached her side and pulled her directly under the green sprig.

Brooke had put it up yesterday in memory of her parents who'd always shared a kiss beneath it on Christmas Eve. Little did she dream she'd find herself in the arms of an exciting man like Vance, anticipating his kiss.

"Since you're so shy, I'll do the honors," he whispered before kissing her soundly on the mouth.

It was all meant to entertain Sarah and be taken

in the spirit of fun. But his compelling mouth lingered longer than Brooke had expected. Like a sudden burst of flame, she felt desire ignite her body. The unexpected sensation shocked her so much she clung to him for a brief moment. When she realized what she was doing, sanity returned and she pulled abruptly away from him. Humiliated over her unguarded response, she turned to Julia, red-faced. "Let me take your wraps. I—I've got some nice hot cider and Christmas cookies."

"Sounds good," Kyle murmured.

He started to help his wife off with her coat, but she moved out of reach and said unexpectedly, "No, no. We can't stay. I have a lot to do before morning. We just wanted to stop by and give Sarah her Christmas present. Why don't the three of you plan to come over for dinner tomorrow? We'll be having turkey with all the trimmings. How does twoish sound?"

"Can we, Brooke?" An eager Sarah jumped up and down in anticipation, still holding on to her bear.

This was supposed to be for overnight only. Remember? "I—I think—"

"We'd love to come," Vance announced. "Especially if you're making Aunt Nancy's cranberry ice. She's probably the greatest cook this side of the Continental Divide.''

Sarah craned her neck to look up at him in worship. ''What's cramby ice?''

''It's like ice cream only better.''

''I like ice cream.''

''So do I, honey. So do I.''

Julia's smile of satisfaction was almost embarrassing. ''Then we'll see you tomorrow. Merry Christmas everybody!''

''Merry Christmas!'' Sarah shouted the loudest, her eyes and face glowing with happiness.

Brooke wanted to call her friends back and beg them not to leave yet. But of course she didn't do that. Instead, she shut the door after them and locked it.

For a moment, she could believe that the two people in her living room were her husband and child, that they were a loving family who had just said good-night to dear friends after a Christmas Eve party. The situation felt so normal. *Too* normal when you considered that the three of them had been perfect strangers a few hours earlier. Worried that Vance might be afraid she was getting ideas, especially after the kiss they'd just shared, Brooke whirled around, anxious to disabuse him of any notions on that score.

"Obviously your cousin was delighted to see us under the same roof and didn't want to spoil it by overstaying her welcome."

His lips twitched. "You're right. But she tipped her hand when she invited us for dinner. Still, I don't mind. She cooks like my aunt. Kyle's a lucky man."

"In more ways than one," Brooke agreed, championing her friend.

"*If* you overlook her matchmaking mania," he added in a dry tone of voice.

"What's that 'match' word mean?"

Sarah's question jerked Brooke back to some semblance of reality. "It means she tries to make people be happy the way she is with Kyle."

"You and Vance are happy, huh?"

Red flags scorched Brooke's cheeks once more. "Yes."

"I want to be your little girl and live with you."

That was the second time Sarah had brought up the subject. Now she'd said it in front of Vance. To Brooke's chagrin, she couldn't tell her young houseguest that she already had parents or family somewhere else waiting for her to be returned to them. And judging by the sober expression on

Vance's face, he didn't have a ready comeback, either. The situation couldn't be more precarious.

"Let's not worry about that right now, not on Christmas Eve. I think it's time for bed. Vance? In my parents' room you'll find my dad's clothes in the drawers and closet. You're welcome to put on anything you need."

Since her father's death, she hadn't been able to part with his things. Now she was glad that they were still available.

"Thanks. I'll just take a look."

"When you're ready for bed, pull the blanket and comforter off his bed and bring them in here."

After he nodded, she noticed he made a detour to the hall closet, probably to retrieve his cell phone.

"Come on, young lady. As soon as we're settled under the covers, I'll tell you one of my favorite Christmas stories."

"Can we wait for Vance so he'll be able to hear it, too?"

It could be a long wait if he planned to talk to someone at the federal marshal's office in Great Falls. "I think he's heard this one before. When he comes to bed, maybe he'll tell us a story."

Brooke's explanation seemed to appease Sarah,

who climbed into bed and snuggled under the sheet and blanket. There was barely room for Brooke with the bear between them, but somehow she managed to fit on the very edge of the mattress.

"Are you and Jimmy ready to hear about the Grinch who stole Christmas?"

"What's a Grinch?"

"A creature who wasn't very happy, and he didn't want any of the people in Whoville to be happy, either. So he decided to ruin their Christmas. It all started on Christmas Eve."

"Like tonight, huh?"

"Exactly like tonight. All the parents in Whoville had put their little Whos to bed to dream about Christmas morning and the fun they would have opening the presents Santa Claus had left them."

"Who's Santa Claus?"

After Brooke had explained, Sarah asked, "Will Santa bring me presents tomorrow, too?"

"You'll have to wait and see," Brooke murmured in a gentle tone. Her mind raced to think of things she could wrap for Sarah to be put under the tree before morning.

Thank heavens the people who lived in town had stopped by the house earlier in the week with food and homemade gifts of various kinds. As soon as the little girl fell asleep, Brooke would get busy sorting through the items she could wrap for Sarah.

"But does Santa Claus know *I'm* here?"

At the same time Brooke's lips smiled, her eyes filled with tears. "He knows everything."

"That's good. Now can I hear about the Grinch?"

By the time Brooke came to the part where all the people in the town had joined hands to welcome Christmas morning, Sarah had fallen into a deep sleep. Carefully Brooke moved Jimmy to the floor, then covered Sarah's shoulders with the down comforter before she got out of bed. For the first time in her life, she understood what parents went through to get everything ready for their children before Christmas morning, and accomplish it without making any noise.

Vance entered the living room as she was stealing into the kitchen with some of the presents she'd taken from beneath the tree. In an instant, he figured out what she was doing, and he brought in the rest of the packages without her having to say a word. "What else can I do?"

She lifted her head and met his brilliant blue gaze, which appeared to be appraising her rather thoroughly. It made the breath catch in her throat. "There's a package from the store I left upstairs in my bedroom. If you'd bring that down, I'll get the tape and scissors and we'll see what we can come up with for her."

"You're an amazing woman, Brooke Longley. I'll be right back."

Don't let the compliment turn your head. To-morrow he'll be on about his marshal business and you'll never see him again.

While he was gone, she took the opportunity to make him some coffee before she started unwrapping gifts. To her delight, people had brought over coffee cake, homemade fudge, candy canes and popcorn balls. The grocer, Mr. Wheeler, had given her a box of royal pears.

Vance reappeared with a cowboy hat and a pair of toy silver spurs. En route, he'd also gone into her father's room to produce a long navy stocking. He eyed her steadily. "I figure Christmas isn't Christmas without one. Do you mind?"

Her heart swelled within her. "Of course not. Dad would've been the first to offer it if he were still around. Why don't you start filling it with the fruit and candy while I wrap the store gifts with this leftover Christmas paper?" Out of the corner of her eye, she watched him work and couldn't help admiring his well-honed body, the play of muscles across his shoulders and arms beneath his dark brown uniform. His warm, male scent permeated the small kitchen. A man of his physical size and strength dwarfed the space between them. Being this close to him made her think many forbidden thoughts. She prayed he couldn't read her mind. "There's coffee if you want some."

"I was hoping you would offer. As a matter of fact, I think I'll help myself to some of this coffee cake, as well."

"Louise Pritchard made it. Her husband runs the saddlery shop."

He broke off a piece and put it in his mouth. "Umm. That's tasty." He wandered over to the stove and poured himself a mug of coffee. After strolling back, he said, "That kiss beneath the mistletoe was mighty tasty, too. I think I've got to have another one." Without waiting for her permission, he lowered his head and stole another kiss from her astonished lips.

"You know what?" he said when he lifted his mouth from hers. "Kissing you could be habit-forming. You have a perfect mouth. To tell you the truth, I can't remember the last time I had this much fun on Christmas Eve."

Neither can I, Vance McClain. Only the word "fun" no longer covered what she was feeling. Brooke knew something earthshaking was happening to her.

CHAPTER SIX

"AS SOON as I finish eating, Ms. Longley, I'll help you rewrap the gifts. Sarah will never know what we've been up to."

The evening had been so perfect Brooke didn't want to spoil it, but anxiety got the better of her. "Do you think Sarah's the girl who was stolen by those convicts?"

His dark brows met in a frown. "I don't know yet. She's already given us some good clues, but we won't hear anything definitive until headquarters does the research at their end."

Brooke took a fortifying breath. "She's a highly intelligent girl, but"

"She lacks common knowledge about the most basic things," he finished for her. "Believe me, I've noticed the gaping holes in her education."

"If she's been dragged around by those horrible men all this time—" emotion made it difficult for her to articulate "—then she's lost two vital years of nurturing. Such an experience would explain the gaps."

He nodded his dark head. "Her vulnerability stands out a mile."

"I know." Brooke let out another troubled sigh. "At this point, she's ready to cling to anyone who shows her the smallest kindness."

He flashed her an all-encompassing glance. "She's already crazy about you. That's why it's imperative we unite her with her family as soon as possible. Otherwise she won't want to leave you."

"Or you," she added in a trembling voice. "You heard her. She's already confided that she wishes you and I were her parents."

"Like the child that she is, she wants to deny everything bad and wish for everything good."

Because Vance was a confirmed bachelor, he obviously hadn't liked the sound of Sarah's wish. It shouldn't have hurt Brooke, but somehow it did. Of course, the feelings Brooke was experiencing weren't shared by him! And why should they be? *You're a fool, Brooke Longley!*

"It's possible that Sarah is the kidnapping victim of another situation altogether," he theorized. "She probably has a mother and father who will be out of their minds with joy when they learn that she's being returned to them."

"But what if she's the little girl whose mother was killed? Does Sarah have a father?"

A look she couldn't decipher entered his intelligent eyes.

"According to my sources, the mother was never married and the father ran off a long time ago."

A slight gasp escaped Brooke's throat. "So Sarah's all alone in the world?"

"Not necessarily. She could have extended family. Aunts and uncles. I've already asked headquarters to look into it."

"But what if there isn't anyone to claim her?" she cried softly.

His features hardened. "Let's not jump to conclusions unless we're forced to."

"She'd be placed in foster care until she was adopted, wouldn't she?" Brooke persisted. The idea of Sarah having to live with total strangers haunted her. "Those people couldn't possibly understand the trauma she's been through, Vance." By now, Brooke had become totally emotional. "She's so young and innocent. So sweet. I couldn't bear it if—"

"*Brooke*," he murmured in a husky tone. The next thing she knew she was in his strong arms, her face burrowed against his shoulder, where she broke down completely.

"If you could have heard her crying during the storm, if you could have seen those bare, thin, frozen legs barely holding her up while she pounded on the window of that storefront with her icy cold hands, you—"

"Hush," he admonished gently into her silky blond hair and pulled her closer. "You found her in time. She's safe and warm beneath your roof. Don't borrow trouble. It's Christmas, remember? A time of miracles."

"You're right," she hiccuped. "It was a miracle I even heard her out in that blizzard. If I hadn't—"

"But you did." Now his voice sounded husky.

She clutched at his arms. "Promise me something, Vance."

"What is it?"

"Promise me that if she has no family, you'll use your influence to make certain she goes to the best foster parents there are." In her earnestness, she lifted her head, not realizing until too late how close it brought their faces together. She could feel the warmth of his breath on her cheek. "Promise me the right people will end up taking care of her."

His intense gaze roamed over her upturned features before boring into her translucent green eyes. "I promise."

She felt his avowal permeate her body to its very core. "Thank you," she whispered, trying unsuccessfully to stop the tears.

"You don't need to thank me." He brushed his mouth against hers one more time before letting her go, almost as if he couldn't help himself. She felt strangely bereft without his arms round her. "I want the same thing for Sarah," he added as he started gathering the gifts to take back to the living room.

Brooke believed him. She'd watched and heard the two of them bond, which was a miracle in itself considering Sarah had been at the mercy of such awful men until tonight. After that experience, Brooke would have thought Sarah would be terrified of all men. But Vance had a way...

And not just with children, her heart cried out. The closeness of their bodies had felt too right. Having him sleep under her roof tonight seemed the most natural thing in the world. If she were being totally honest with herself, she never wanted the magic of this Christmas to end.

Last year at this time, she'd wanted to die.

This year...

This year, Vance and Sarah could be the family she'd always dreamed of. It didn't seem possible such a thing could have happened, yet here they all were, the three of them together.

Vance couldn't find out how she felt! She would have to put on the greatest acting performance of her life.

Because everything in her cried out to follow him to the living room and spend the rest of the night talking to him, she realized she must forgo that pleasure.

Determined as she'd never been in her life, she stayed in the kitchen to clean up the mess they'd made. To be on the safe side, she made some dough for the scones she planned to serve in the morning.

After giving Vance a half hour's lead time, she turned out the light and tiptoed into the living room. All was quiet on Sarah's part. By the deep, even sounds of his breathing, Vance had fallen asleep, too.

Brooke resisted the almost overpowering urge to inspect him up close. Forcing herself to turn away from him, she climbed into bed next to Jimmy and Sarah.

Last night at this time, she couldn't have imagined this situation. Tonight, she couldn't imagine it being any other way.

Turning on her stomach, she positioned herself so she could feast on Vance's reclining physique beneath his covers. She had no idea how long she lay there dreaming about him, maybe a half hour. But at some point, she must have fallen asleep.

Toward morning, she became aware of someone calling out. At first, she thought she was dreaming, but finally she realized it was Sarah's voice she could hear. "Don't hit me, Charlie. I'll be good. I'll be good."

Brooke sat straight up in the bed, brushing the hair out of her eyes. Her watch said five-thirty. Apparently Sarah, who had twisted around in her covers, was having a bad dream. Though sound asleep, her arms covered her head as if to avoid a blow.

A few feet away, the glow from the Christmas tree lights revealed Vance's chiseled features and upper body clothed in a white T-shirt. He, too, must have heard Sarah's cries and had come wide awake. Soon he'd turned on one of the lamps to brighten the room.

Their eyes met in horrified understanding before Brooke reached for Sarah and wrapped her in her arms. "It's all right, darling. It was just a dream," she crooned to the little girl. By this time, Vance, who was wearing the bottom half of her dad's blue pajamas, closed the distance between them and sat on Sarah's other side where he put an arm around both of them.

The gesture was meant to comfort the little girl. But it made Brooke acutely aware of his physical nearness. With the slightest provocation, she would curl right up in his arms and stay there.

At first, Sarah seemed disoriented. She stared up at Brooke, then transferred her attention to Vance, who lowered his head and kissed the tip of her nose. This brought a broad smile to her face, snapping her out of her trancelike state.

"Merry Christmas, Sarah. It looks like Santa Claus came last night."

She regarded him in complete wonder. "Did he bring *me* presents?"

"Take a look under the tree."

In an instant, Sarah scrambled out of his arms, leaped off the bed and rushed over to examine all the packages, squealing in delight over each one.

"I see something else for you hanging on the fireplace," Brooke interjected.

As Sarah ran to the hearth to investigate, Vance caught Brooke's gaze. She saw many things in his eyes, among them a look of indescribable tenderness. During that private moment of silence, she felt she'd glimpsed the essence of the man who probably didn't show this vulnerable side very often. It was a revelation.

"It's a stocking! Can I pull it down?" Sarah was fairly jumping with excitement.

Vance chuckled before he turned his attention to the little girl. "Of course. Santa Claus left it full of good things to eat, especially for you."

Watching Sarah was like rediscovering the joy of Christmas with all its attendant excitement. Brooke didn't need to look at Vance to know he was experiencing the same feeling.

The little girl plopped down on the floor with her treasure. Like any eager child, she tipped the stocking upside down and shook it until everything dropped out on the carpet.

"What do you bet she goes for the candy cane first?" Vance whispered near Brooke's ear, sending delicious chills through her sensitized body.

No sooner had Vance made his conjecture than Sarah reached for the cane and started to lick it. "Umm," they heard her remark as she started to unwrap a piece of fudge.

"That fudge came from Grunby's," Brooke confided in a quiet voice. "It's so famous they can't keep up with their mail-order business. For years I've been trying to get them to give me the recipe, but so far no luck.''

Another low laugh escaped his throat. Brooke loved the sound. In fact, she was loving the whole situation far too much. Evidently, so was Sarah who had started to nibble on her popcorn ball. The only thing she hadn't touched yet was the pear. Enough was enough.

''Why don't you start to open your presents, Sarah?'' Brooke suggested. Thank heavens she'd had the foresight to bring some gifts from the store a little girl might like.

Vance rolled off the bed and went over to their young houseguest. ''If you eat all your candy, you won't have room for breakfast. Remember that Brooke's going to make us pancakes with huckleberries.''

''Is that a fact?'' Brooke teased him. ''Did you know a little elf whispered that maybe we'd have scones instead?''

''That'd be even better,'' he quipped, and rewarded her with a wolfish grin that set her heart racing out of control.

''How about opening this present.'' He handed Sarah a package.

''What is it?''

''That's for you to find out. Go ahead. Take off the paper and see what's inside.''

With hands that appeared to tremble from too much excitement, Sarah did his bidding. Out came the cowboy hat. She studied it, then proceeded to put it on her head. Vance tightened the drawstring beneath her chin, then gave her another kiss on the cheek.

"You look like a real cowgirl now."

"What's a cowgirl?"

"A girl who can ride a horse."

"But I don't have a horse."

"*I* do." He hunkered down in front of her. "In fact, I have a little pony that's just about your size."

"Where?" she cried out with touching eagerness.

"At my dad's ranch."

She got up from the floor and stood inside the shelter of his arms with such trust, Brooke felt her eyes smart.

"What's his name?"

"*Her* name," he amended with a grin. "She's called Patchwork."

"Patch what?"

"Patchwork," Brooke broke in. "See that quilt over on the love seat?" Sarah looked where Brooke was pointing, then nodded. "It's made from different pieces of cloth. Each color is a patch. When you sew them together, it's called patchwork.''

Brooke could almost hear Sarah's brain computing everything. The little girl stared earnestly at Vance. "Does your pony have lots of colors?''

"Lots,'' he answered in kind.

Sarah's face lit up. "Will you let me ride on her?''

There was a long silence.

Brooke understood Vance's hesitation. Once you told a child something, you had to keep your promise. Sarah was so enchanted by everything, it was easy to get carried away. Brooke ought to know. She could already imagine Sarah as *their* child, hers and Vance's. The fantasies had to stop.

He must have thought the same thing because he slowly rose to his full height. "Maybe one day,'' he muttered. "For now, you can pretend you have a horse.''

"You don't even need to pretend,'' Brooke chimed in. "Stay right there.''

While the two of them stared after her, she ran from the living room to the utility closet off the kitchen and reached for the broom. After putting it between her legs, she pretended to gallop as she reentered the living room shouting giddyap.

Sarah broke into laughter and begged to ride

the broom. Vance flashed Brooke a message that said he was grateful for her help in lightening a rather tense moment.

When Sarah had made several trips around the room, Vance said, "Why don't you open this other present? All cowgirls need these."

At his suggestion, she put the broom on the floor and hurriedly tore the wrapping from the next package. "What are they?"

"Spurs. Run upstairs and bring down your new cowboy boots. I'll show you how to put them on. Cowgirls use them to make their horses go faster."

Brooke went to the staircase and turned on the lights for Sarah who raced up the stairs as fast as her thin legs would go. Vance approached Brooke. For the moment, the two of them were alone. His expression was all business now, exhibiting a remote demeanor that caused Brooke's spirits to plummet.

"I need to call headquarters." His grating voice reminded her that a killer was still on the loose, that they still had no idea of the true identity of their little Christmas guest.

Brooke shuddered. "As soon as she comes down, I'll ask her to help me fix breakfast."

His hand made a fist at his side. "The storm has abated. I'm going to have to leave."

"Of course." She avoided his eyes so he wouldn't be able to see the yearning in hers. "Actually I'm surprised you were able to stay the night. I'm sure it made all the difference to Sarah. When she woke up from that bad dream, you were there to comfort her."

"Don't forget you were there, too."

A palpable tension hovered between them. "Promise me you'll go over to Julia's," he urged. "Until that psycho is caught, I don't want you and Sarah to be alone."

"Then you're going after him?" she cried softly, forgetting that she shouldn't make eye contact with him.

"That's my job."

She struggled for breath. "I know." *But in twelve hours you've become so important to me, the thought of anything happening to you is killing me.*

"I've got my boots on," Sarah called out as she hurried down the stairs. She looked so cute in her hat, pajamas and boots, Brooke couldn't resist reaching for her and giving her a hug.

While she held her in her arms, Vance fastened

the toy spurs on the boots. Once that was accomplished, Brooke lowered her to the floor.

"Okay, cowgirl." Vance grinned. "Start walking around the place like you mean it."

Sarah took a few steps. Each time she moved, the spurs clinked. The noise amused her no end. She grabbed the broom and played horsey for a full five minutes while Brooke and Vance egged her on.

Finally Brooke said, "Come on, darling. Put your horse away. It's time to cook breakfast. I'll let you make the pancakes."

While they headed for the kitchen, Vance took advantage of the moment to slip out of sight. The sense of loss was staggering.

Brooke told Sarah to pull a chair up to the sink so she could stand on it to work. Within minutes, they had the batter ready and bacon sizzled on the grill. Vance walked in as Brooke put the huckleberry jam on the table along with milk and coffee. He carried Sarah and her chair to the table, then removed her hat.

One glimpse of his eyes told Brooke she'd better gear up for his departure. She would have to handle this carefully so Sarah's fragile sense of security wouldn't be traumatized any more than it already was. But as they all enjoyed their breakfast a few minutes later, she realized Vance was way ahead of her when it came to Sarah's needs.

"Sweetheart? Do you remember Julia and Kyle, my cousins who visited us last night and brought you the teddy bear?"

She nodded while she munched on her bacon.

"They want us to come over as soon as we finish eating and make snow angels."

Clever Vance. The more people to entertain Sarah, the less pain it would bring when Vance had to go. And a game in the snow was a perfect idea. During the night, the blizzard had blown itself out. It looked like they were going to have a clear blue sky for Christmas Day.

"What are those angel things?"

Laughter rumbled deep in Vance's throat. "We all lie down in the snow and move our arms and legs back and forth. When we stand up, it looks like angels have been playing in the snow."

"What are angels?"

"They're people who live in heaven with Jesus. They watch over us and protect us," Brooke offered.

Sarah's eyes grew huge. "Can we go?"

"Of course. As soon as you've drunk all your milk."

She swallowed it in one long gulp. "I'm ready."

"Except that you need to run upstairs and put on your clothes. Bring down your parka and gloves."

"Okay. I'll be right back. Don't go away."

CHAPTER SEVEN

"LORD," Brooke heard Vance murmur as Sarah dashed from the kitchen, her spurs clanking all the way through the house and up the stairs.

Brooke pushed herself from the table, dreading the idea that he had to leave them to go after a cold-blooded killer.

He brought the dishes to the sink. "We don't know yet if Sarah is the daughter of the woman who was murdered. For that matter, I don't know if the man I'm hunting is one of those convicts. He could be another wanted felon. Nevertheless, I won't rest until he's caught and made to pay for what he's done to Sarah."

"He's evil," she practically hissed.

"Amen. Under the circumstances, Kyle and Julia have promised to help you take care of Sarah until someone from the federal marshal's office contacts you. That ought to be sometime tomorrow. They'll take over from there." The grimace on his face led her to believe he was as disturbed by the prospect as Brooke.

She bit her lip. "Whatever family she has will be overjoyed to learn she's been found alive."

"Thanks to you," he said in a thick voice. "What I could have told Sarah is that not all angels are confined to heaven. Some of them live right here in West Yellowstone."

She shook her head, embarrassed. "I'm no angel. I just happened to come upon her first. Anyone would have done what I did."

"No. Not anyone," he said with a bitterness that was almost tangible. Something in his past still haunted him.

She heard him suck in his breath. "Sarah can thank God you were the person who found her in time. She needed a lot more than physical comfort. You sensed instinctively what to do. I stand in awe of you, Ms. Longley."

She braced her hands against the counter and turned her head to look at him. "As long as we're being truthful, then it's time you accepted a compliment yourself."

He frowned in self-deprecation. "All I did was commandeer your house, horn in on your Christmas and eat your food. The huckleberry jam was better than my mother's, by the way."

Brooke smiled. "Even if that's a lie, I'm flattered. But what I meant to tell you was that after

Sarah's experience with that lowlife, you would have thought she'd be terrified of any man. Instead, *you* were the one to bring her out of that closet last night. She clung to you. Your special brand of psychology was an absolute revelation to me. Whether you know it or not, you're a natural with children. W-with people," she stammered. "I happened to love that story, too."

He smiled, making mush of her insides. She wanted to tell him he should do it more often. It turned him into the most breathtaking male she'd ever met in her life.

"Everyone loves it, young and old," he said as they heard the distinct *clink-clank* of little footsteps. Their gazes fused for a moment. She felt breathless, light-headed. Another second and she was very much afraid she was going to kiss his compelling mouth.

"Brooke..." he said in a muffled voice just as Sarah entered the kitchen, all dressed for a winter outing.

To hide her flushed face, she knelt in front of Sarah who was holding her teddy bear. "We'd better remove these spurs or you'll have trouble trying to make an angel. I'll put them on the table for now. All right?"

"Yes. Can I take Jimmy with me?"

"Of course."

"Can he make an angel, too?"

"I don't think so. He's made of material, and if he gets too wet, he'll be ruined."

"Oh."

"Come on, my little cowgirl." Vance swept her up in his arms and put the cowboy hat on top of the hood covering her head. "While Brooke's getting dressed, you sit in the Blazer and watch me shovel snow. Otherwise we won't be able to get out of the driveway."

Brooke reached for her handbag on the counter. "Here are the keys."

He stared at her through narrowed eyes so she couldn't tell what he was thinking. "We'll have it all warmed up for you by the time you're ready."

Naturally he was in a hurry to track his quarry. She determined to get dressed as fast as she could in olive-green wool pants and a silky print blouse with a matching green sweater. Gathering her parka, gloves and boots, she hurried through the house, switched off the Christmas-tree lights and locked the front door.

When she turned around, the sun glinting off the newly fallen snow dazzled her eyes. She'd seen other beautiful winter days like this, but there was something infinitely different about this Christmas morning. The attractive dark-haired man who'd shoveled her out of her own driveway had everything to do with her euphoria.

Please, God. Don't let anything happen to him. Bring him back safely to Sarah and me. Her eyes closed. *Bring him back to Sarah and me? What am I saying? What am I thinking?*

When she opened her eyes again, she discovered that Vance had parked his Land Rover on the street overnight. There had to be at least twelve inches of new snow on its roof. Was he going to leave it here?

He seemed to read her mind. As she started for the Blazer, he said, "I'll drive us over to Julia's in your car, then come back here for the rest of my things and the Land Rover. Kyle will you bring you home later in his car. I'll leave your keys above the front-porch door."

Once again, he'd put Sarah's needs first. The last thing either of them wanted to do was alarm her by drawing her attention to his car, let alone his hat and gun. Fortunately Sarah didn't appear to notice his Land Rover as they backed out to the street and took off for the other side of town. In Sarah's mind, Vance was simply a good friend of

Brooke's, nothing more. They would keep her in the dark for as long as necessary.

When they arrived at Kyle and Julia's cabin, the couple was already outside building a snowman. They shouted for Sarah to join them in the fun. She needed no coaxing to scramble out of the Blazer behind Vance and run over to them.

Sarah asked Kyle to place Jimmy by the front door where he could watch without getting snow on him. This produced a chuckle from everyone as Kyle did her bidding.

Brooke gathered up the sack of presents for the other couple and started to get out of the Blazer. Vance seemed to have extrasensory radar where she was concerned. The next thing she knew, he'd reached for her and swung her to the ground. Somehow she lost her balance and fell against him. She felt like a fool until his arms tightened around her and other emotions took over.

Good heavens. To be this close to him was heaven.

Brooke wanted to wrap her arms around his neck and merge with him. Her intense attraction to him was nothing short of astounding. If he had any idea at all what his nearness was doing to her...

"Are you all right?" Concerned eyes probed hers relentlessly.

Heat scorched her cheeks. "Yes, of course. I was just my clumsy self. You can let me go now. I'll be fine." A few yards away, she could feel Julia's curious eyes observing the byplay with unfeigned interest.

"You know my cousin is loving this," he whispered in an aside. "Why don't we give her something she can really dig her teeth into. After all, it *is* Christmas. Where's the harm when we're two old friends?"

Before Brooke could beg him not to touch her, Vance lowered his head and extracted a kiss from her astonished mouth. Their lips were cold, but his mouth was warm like mulled wine. She knew he'd meant it to be playful and teasing, but once there was contact, the nature of the funning changed.

Like a bolt of lightning out of nowhere, desire shot through her body, causing her to tremble. Suddenly their kiss deepened, igniting her passion. Everything began to spin out of control. She could hear Sarah calling to them in the background, reminding Brooke they had an audience.

Shocked, humiliated by her own uninhibited response, she finally managed to break free of his embrace. To her mortification, she had to clutch his arm for a moment while she swayed on unsteady legs to regain her equilibrium. During that millisecond before his eyes shuttered against the brilliant sunlight, she thought she glimpsed fire in their impossibly blue depths.

Sarah ran up to them and tugged on Vance's hand. "Can we make snow angels next to the snowman now? Come on, Brooke."

"I'm coming, darling." She reached for the sack and trudged through the snow behind them, so shaken by their physical encounter she could hardly pull herself together.

He should never have touched her, kissed her. Now she would ache for things she could never have. Something told her she would go through the rest of her life aching for him.

Dear God. What had she done?

Julia and Kyle couldn't have helped but notice what had just happened, but to Brooke's relief, they had the decency to pretend nothing untoward had transpired. Later, when they were alone, Julia would demand a debriefing, but for the moment Brooke was spared any explanation.

A field of glistening white surrounded their cabin. At Sarah's urging, Kyle lay down in a pristine spot and made the first angel.

Julia followed suit. Sarah squealed in delight when she saw the shapes they made. Before

Brooke could prevent it, Sarah had grabbed both Brooke's and Vance's hands.

"You go here," she ordered Brooke. When she was satisfied that Brooke stood in the right spot, she dragged Vance a few feet away and said, "You lie down here."

Vance cocked his dark head. "Where's my cowgirl going to be?"

"Right *here*!" She plopped herself between them. "Okay—let's make angels."

As if it were her only mission in life, Sarah spread her arms and legs back and forth as fast as she could. Vance darted Brooke an amused glance over Sarah's moving form before they rested their heads in the snow and carried out her wishes beneath a blinding winter sun.

"Okay, stop!" Sarah shouted after another minute.

When they got to their feet again, Sarah inspected their angel impressions before jumping up and down with her infectious laughter.

"See, everybody? There's the mommy, and there's the daddy, and there's *me*!"

At that disturbing outburst of a child's wishful thinking, Brooke felt swamped by a myriad of staggering emotions—pain for this little girl's tragic history, fear for Vance's safety because he was going after the killer, fear that over the past fifteen hours both Vance and Sarah had become far too important to her. She had the undeniable conviction that if she were to lose them, she would never be able to reconcile the loss....

Kyle saved the day. He plucked Sarah from the snow. "Do you know what? We've been waiting to open Christmas presents until you got here. Santa Claus left something special for everyone under the tree."

"He did?" she cried with excitement. Her dark blue eyes shining, she fastened her attention on Brooke and Vance. "Come on. Santa Claus brought presents here, too!"

Vance strode up to her and gave her a kiss on the cheek. "I'd like to come in, but I have to go deliver a very special Christmas present to someone."

While Brooke trembled at the hidden meaning, Sarah's face crumpled in disappointment. "Are you going to take a long time?"

Brooke looked down at the snow. *I want an answer to that question myself, Sarah.*

"I'm not sure. This person doesn't live here in town."

"Do you *have* to go?"

Oh, Sarah. I know exactly how you feel.

"I'm afraid so, sweetheart. But I'll be back as soon as I can."

"Sure he will," Kyle assured her, plunking her cowgirl hat back on her head before he started for the cabin. After sending Brooke a commiserating glance, Julia gave her a cousin a peck on the cheek, then followed after her husband.

Thanks to Kyle who moved straight into the house, Sarah wasn't given the opportunity to extract a promise from Vance. As for Brooke, she didn't have the right.

Though she wanted to throw herself into his arms, she remained at a brief distance, knee-deep in snow. Beads of moisture still glinted in his rich, dark brown hair. She moaned inwardly because his masculine appeal reached out to her like a living thing.

In turn, his eyes made a thorough inspection of her face and figure, almost as if he were memorizing her, almost as if the past fifteen hours had meant something special to him, as well. Of course, that was probably wishful thinking on her part. All she knew was that saying goodbye to this man was the hardest thing she'd ever had to do in her life.

"Be careful," she whispered, hoping to disguise the ache in her voice.

There was a perceptible hardening of his handsome features.

"However long it takes, I'll find him. Sarah will never have to worry about him again." His eyes remained shuttered. "Merry Christmas, Ms. Longley. It's been a pleasure."

As he made swift strides toward the Blazer, it struck her that she'd fallen helplessly in love with him. There could be no other explanation for her precarious condition.

"Merry Christmas, Deputy."

CHAPTER EIGHT

"MAY I speak to Brooke Longley, please? This is Gwen Shertleff from Social Services in Great Falls calling."

To Brooke's bitter disappointment, the woman from the governmental agency was on the other end of the line.

It was ridiculous, but in her heart of hearts, Brooke had hoped it might be Vance phoning.

Of course it wouldn't be Vance, she mocked in self-denigration. He might be gone days, weeks, before he caught up with that criminal.

Brooke sank onto one of the kitchen chairs, thankful that Sarah had finished her bedtime snack and was now playing in the living room with the set of electric elves Kyle and Julia had given her for Christmas.

One at a time ten little elves lit up and played different musical instruments over and over again. It was the kind of gift you could look at for hours.

"This is she. Deputy McClain said you would call, but somehow I hadn't expected to hear from you on Christmas night."

"Unfortunately Christmas happens to be a time when too many children fall victim to domestic violence or worse. I've been assigned to this case. My job is to accompany the little girl you call Sarah back to Mississippi."

Brooke let out a quiet gasp. "Has a positive identification been made? Have her relatives been found?"

"Apparently so."

The knowledge that Sarah had extended family waiting for her tugged at Brooke's heartstrings.

"What I'm supposed to do is deliver her to Social Services in Jackson where she'll be turned over to temporary foster care until the legalities are settled. I understand you're the one who found her and has been taking care of her."

She swallowed hard. "Yes, I have."

"Is she in good enough shape to travel?"

Brooke struggled for breath. "Physically, yes."

"All right. Since there's a lucky break in the weather that's supposed to last another forty-eight hours, I'll fly into West Yellowstone in the morning on a government transport helicopter and we'll airlift her to Salt Lake for the flight to Mississippi."

Dear God. So soon?

"Can you have her waiting at the airport by nine in the morning?"

"Well, yes...b-but she's been so traumatized by her situation, I don't think she'll trust you enough to go with you."

"I understand. These situations are always difficult and heart wrenching. Nonetheless, because of the kidnapping charges, the law states she must be returned right away. The authorities will be anxious to talk to her.

"Naturally the sooner she's united with loved ones and gets into counseling, the better for her in terms of her adjustment and ability to heal emotionally."

"You're right," Brooke answered with tears in her voice. But deep inside, she reasoned that the authorities wouldn't treat Sarah with Vance's sensitivity and tenderness. As for her extended family, would they truly love Sarah the way she needed to be loved?

"As a representative of Social Services, I want to thank you for your help and generosity. From what I understand, the little girl might not have made it through the night if you hadn't found her."

Tears trickled down Brooke's cheeks. "It was a miracle."

"That's what Christmas is all about," the other

woman said in a kindly voice. "I'll see you at nine. If there is a problem, you can reach me at my home."

Brooke jotted down the woman's number, then hung up the receiver in abject despair.

Tomorrow Sarah would be gone.

Unable to fathom it, Brooke made the decision that she would say nothing to her little houseguest about travel plans until morning. Tonight was Christmas night, a special night. Brooke needed this time with Sarah. *It might be the only time I ever have.*

Resolute in her plan, she made sure the back door was locked, flipped off the light and went into the living room.

The glow from the Christmas-tree lights illuminated the enchanted smile on Sarah's sweet face as she lay on her stomach in her Rudolph pajamas and watched each elf perform its trick.

"If you can tear yourself away from your toy, I have a story I'll read to you that I think you'll love."

Sarah got up from the floor, her expression eager. "What story is it?"

"That's my surprise." She unplugged the toy, made sure the front door was securely locked, then transformed the couch into a bed once more.

Sarah scuttled under the covers while Brooke reached for the large, treasured storybook in question from the bookshelf. Once she had settled in, Sarah snuggled up to her and studied the picture on the cover for a long time without saying anything.

Finally her curiosity got the better of her. "Who is that? How come her dress has so many colors?"

Brooke grinned. "She's the patchwork girl of Oz."

Sarah sat straight up. "That's the name of Vance's pony."

"You're right. Remember what he said? It was born with a whole bunch of different colors."

Sarah clapped her hands in excitement before she fell back against Brooke's arm once more. "Why is her head so little?"

"Because she lives in the land of Oz where anything is possible."

"Ohh." The wheels were turning. "Where's Oz?"

"A happy place you can dream about when you fall asleep."

"Her eyes look like the buttons on my pajamas."

"Did you know the patchwork girl was made by an old woman who took scraps of material and buttons from her sewing basket? When the doll was ready, her husband used his magic to make the doll come alive so it would talk and dance around. Do you think the patchwork girl is pretty?''

A look of concentration formed on Sarah's face. "No. I think she looks funny."

Spoken with a child's honesty.

"I do, too, but the patchwork girl thinks she's the most beautiful creature in the land of Oz, and she tells everyone so."

They both laughed at the silly notion. Again Brooke was pierced by the knowledge that she loved this little child with a love that wasn't going to go away.

Opening to the first page, Brooke began reading to Sarah who was totally entranced and asked a hundred questions. She wanted to know why the cat in the story was made of glass, why its brains were pink and why the cat and the patchwork girl never had to eat.

Brooke didn't remember if she had asked her mother that many questions when she was a little girl hearing this story for the first time. But she bet her mother didn't feel any more pleasure and contentment than Brooke felt right now, pretending Sarah was her own little girl. *Hers and Vance's.*

After a long time, Sarah grew quiet and finally fell asleep. Brooke gave her a kiss but continued to read in silence. She needed the wonder and magic of this book so she wouldn't think about the trauma tomorrow's parting would bring.

Dream of Oz, Brooke. If you dream, then you won't think about Vance somewhere out there in the unforgiving elements, tracking down a killer who could turn on him and...

"Brooke? Can we have pancakes for breakfast again?"

Brooke lifted her head from the pillow. Her watch said 7:10 a.m. Evidently Sarah had been awake for some time and been waiting for Brooke to open her eyes.

"Of course, darling. Why don't you run upstairs and get dressed while I make the batter. I can tell there's a little girl in this house who is hungry!"

Sarah let out a happy cry and ran up the stairs.

Taking advantage of the time alone, Brooke flew into the kitchen to call Julia. She needed to discuss her strategy for saying goodbye to Sarah with her dear friend. Julia might also have some word on Vance.

While she prepared breakfast, they talked everything over. Julia admitted she didn't envy Brooke her task when there was no good way to send Sarah off without pain for all parties concerned. As for Vance, there'd been no news from headquarters about him or the progress of the statewide manhunt.

As Brooke replaced the receiver, Sarah rushed into the kitchen fully dressed and ready to eat.

She gobbled down her pancakes. "Can we make snow angels this morning out in front?"

Brooke groaned. "I have a better idea. How would you like to take a ride in a helicopter?"

"What's that?"

"It's kind of like an airplane."

"You mean I get to go in the sky?"

"Yes. All the way home to Mississippi."

"Missi *what*?"

Brooke didn't know whether to laugh or cry. "It's another town where you lived before those mean men took you away with them. You're going to ride on an airplane, too. And when you arrive in Mississippi, your family will be waiting there for you."

Please, God. Let them be good people who love Sarah and want her as much as I do.

"But Charlie said I don't have a mommy."

"But you have other family members just like

Ojo, the little boy in the book we read last night who had an uncle he loved.''

"Do I have an uncle, too?"

"Maybe. Maybe you have a grandma and a grandpa and cousins, too. A very nice lady named Gwen is going to take you to them. We'll be meeting her at the airport in a little while. First of all, though, we need to get your clothes and presents packed in a suitcase to take with you."

"Will Jimmy fit in the suitcase?"

Her question astonished Brooke who couldn't believe Sarah would capitulate this fast without problems. "Probably not. You can carry him with you. After you finish your milk, why don't you gather up everything while I hunt for a suitcase? We're going to have to hurry so we won't be late."

"Okay. Can I take my elves?"

"Of course."

"Can I take the *Patchwork Girl of Oz*?"

"Yes, darling. And your cowgirl hat and spurs, your slippers and your stocking with the rest of the candy you haven't eaten yet."

Before Sarah flew out of the kitchen, she ran straight for Brooke and hugged her tightly around the waist.

What an irony that at the very moment Brooke learned the true meaning of maternal love, Sarah was about to be snatched away from her. The debilitating pain worsened when they left for the airport in the Blazer a half hour later.

The day after Christmas had turned out to be as beautiful as Christmas itself. Gwen Shertleff was right to take advantage of this window of opportunity where the weather was concerned. But Brooke couldn't help wishing the blizzard that had blown Sarah into her life had lasted for at least a week so no one could go anywhere. Not Sarah, not Vance.

As Brooke turned onto the airport road, the distinctive sound of rotor blades whipping the frigid air set off alarm bells inside her body. It took every bit of willpower not to turn the Blazer around and head north where no one could find them.

With a sense of dread, she pulled close to the main hangar.

"There's the helicopter!" Sarah shouted with excitement.

"That's going to be fun to ride in, darling. Stay inside the car until I let you out. Okay?"

"Okay."

Larry, a father of five, and one of the mechanics talking to an auburn-haired woman, waved to Brooke. The pilot of the helicopter sat at the controls ready to take off.

Gwen Shertleff started to approach as Brooke climbed out of the Blazer.

"Good morning, Ms. Longley. Thank you for bringing Sarah here on time." She talked in a loud voice to counteract the noise from the blades.

"You're welcome." Brooke shook hands with the attractive, middle-aged social worker.

"Does Sarah know what's going to happen?"

"Yes."

"Has it been a struggle?"

She sucked in her breath. "Not at all."

The woman sounded sincere when she said, "Thank you again for being a Good Samaritan. Sarah is a lucky little girl."

Brooke's throat had swelled until she could hardly make a sound. After a battle with tears, she said, "I'm the lucky one."

The social worker's compassionate brown eyes seemed to understand. "I promise to see her home safely."

"I'm sure you will." Brooke brushed the moisture from her cheeks.

"Do you want to settle her inside the helicopter?"

"Please. Just so you know, I'm sending a suitcase and presents back with her."

Gwen smiled. "I suspected as much," she confided as they walked around to the passenger side of the Blazer where Sarah had already opened the door.

Brooke made the introductions, still amazed over Sarah's docile acceptance of her circumstances. The little girl reached obediently for her hand and started walking toward the helicopter, her eyes sparkling in anticipation of the adventure ahead.

Larry stowed everything on board while Sarah was shown where to sit. He strapped her in with a kiss on the cheek. Gwen took her place next to Sarah, sending Brooke a silent message to make the goodbye as brief as possible.

But before Brooke could formulate the words, Sarah said, "Where are you and Vance going to sit?"

With that one question, Brooke's worst nightmare was realized. Only now did she understand why Sarah had been so cooperative.

"We can't come with you, darling. That's why Gwen is here. She'll be taking you to your family who's waiting for you and loves you. Remember?"

The child's adorable little face crumpled in pain. *"I don't want to go! Don't let her take me away,*

Brooke! I want to stay with you and Vance! Don't leave me! Don't leave me!"

"You'd better go." Gwen mouthed the words to a horrified Brooke as Sarah struggled to get the seat belt undone.

Talk about your heart being ripped from your body.

Brooke had to force herself to turn her back on Sarah. With Larry's help, she jumped to the ground. The mechanic's expression reflected her torment as Sarah began screaming uncontrollably. Even with the door of the helicopter shut, Sarah's heart-wrenching sobs reached their ears. It reminded Brooke of the night she found Sarah banging on the storefront window. Brooke thought she might die on the spot. Larry caught her around the waist as the blades rotated full throttle and the helicopter rose in the air.

"That poor little tike," he murmured sadly.

"Dear God, Larry...what have I done?"

"No matter how painful, you had to do it."

"Are you certain about that? Because I'm not."

"Of course. Remember. Children are resilient. When she's with her family again, she'll forget about this. You saved her life. Let that be the thought to comfort you."

"Nothing could comfort me right now, but thank you for being so kind."

She stumbled her way toward the Blazer. Once inside, she collapsed over the steering wheel. There'd been too many painful losses. Her anguish had reached its zenith.

CHAPTER NINE

January 5

BROOKE stared at the calendar. Almost two weeks since Vance and Sarah had disappeared from her life.

Even with Julia working police dispatch, there'd been no news about either one of them. Brooke didn't think she could stand this limbo any longer.

"Brooke? Why don't you go on home? I'll close up tonight. You've stayed late every night since Christmas."

"I'd rather be here." *I can't bear being home alone with my thoughts.* "You have a family waiting for you."

Dave started to say something, then thought the better of it. She knew what he wanted to say. That she should have a family of her own to go home to.

He put on his parka and fur hat. Before he went out the door, he paused for a moment. "Pardon me for butting in, but with that English degree, have you ever considered letting someone manage the store so you could go to a big city and get a good teaching job? You'd meet a lot more people than you do here."

"Naturally I've thought about it."

"Then think about it some more. That's all I'm going to say."

"Thank you for caring, Dave. Good night."

He nodded before leaving the store.

The second he went out the door she put the Closed sign in the window, then broke down sobbing. All day she'd been forced to hold back the tears in front of customers. Now that she was alone, she could give in to her excruciating pain.

After the first paroxysm subsided, she slipped on her parka and locked up for the night. Snowflakes had been falling for some time. Another storm front was moving in. Before long, it would reach blizzard intensity. Was Vance still out in it?

The bad weather suited the blackness of her thoughts as she drove home and let herself inside the empty house. When the door closed, it echoed the emptiness in her own heart.

All the Christmas trappings had been removed so there'd be no reminders of the most magical Christmas she'd ever known.

Dave's right. This is no life.

She could easily turn over the management of

the store to him and rent the house. As for a teaching job, they weren't that easy to come by. However, with her credentials, she could always work in retail. She knew a variety of store owners in cities like Salt Lake, Los Angeles or Las Vegas who would hire her in a minute.

Finding work elsewhere wasn't the problem.

Finding her life—*that* was her spiritual dilemma.

Since the life she wanted with Vance and Sarah wasn't possible, she would have to create a new one. No one else was going to do it for her.

Mustering a resolve she didn't feel, she went into the kitchen with the intention of phoning Dave. She had a proposition for him.

As she reached for the receiver, the phone rang. Her heart thudded. Could it be Julia with some news of Vance?

"Hello?" she answered in a breathless voice.

"Brooke Longley?"

She recognized the social worker's voice. Her eyes closed tightly. "Gwen? How's Sarah?" she blurted. "I've been out of mind with worry."

"I'm doing something highly irregular by phoning you, but I thought you should know what has happened. We have positive proof that she's the little girl whose mother was murdered by those convicts. Her birth name is Myra Lyman. She's being put up for adoption."

Brooke gasped at the unexpected news. "You mean she doesn't have family who wants her?"

"Her only known relative is her Uncle Jimmy who's in the marines stationed overseas."

"*That's* why she named the bear Jimmy! Vance and I wondered why the name came so easily to her."

"Apparently this Jimmy Lyman made rare visits to his unmarried sister before she was murdered. Though he seemed glad his niece was found alive, he has no vested interest in her situation. He's single, unwilling to accommodate her. Since he has no desire now or in the future to be the custodial guardian, she'll be put up for adoption.

"At the moment, she's with a foster family in Jackson and utterly inconsolable. My contact at Social Services there tells me the little girl has bonded with you and Deputy McClain. She calls out your names over and over again in her sleep."

Brooke was so overjoyed by the news she had difficulty forming words. "Can I go see her?"

"I don't think that would be a good idea unless you're prepared to do something about the situation. You do love her?"

"With all my heart." Her voice shook. "Can I

become her foster parent until I can formally adopt her?''

"You mean you and the depu—''

"No,'' Brooke cut in. "He's single and intends to remain that way. But he was marvelous to Sarah while she was staying with me.''

A long pause. "I see. Normally a judge wants a child to go to a stable home with a loving mother and father. But Sarah's circumstances are highly unusual and the damage done has been acute. I would vouch for you in court, Ms. Longley. When the helicopter left the ground, there was no doubt in either the pilot's mind or mine that we were separating a little girl from the woman she wanted to be her mother.''

"Thank you for telling me that,'' Brooke murmured emotionally. "How soon can I go to her?''

"As soon as you can get a flight out, I'll arrange for you to meet with the social worker in Jackson. She'll take charge of things from there.''

Tears streamed down Brooke's cheeks. "Thank you, Gwen. Thank you from the bottom of my heart.''

"When a case turns out like this, I love my job. Like I said, little Sarah's lucky.'' She cleared her throat. "Now, if you've got pad and pencil handy, I'll give you all the particulars.''

*　　*　　*

"What's chili?"

"It's something yummy for your tummy," Brooke teased Sarah who was poised on the chair at the sink watching her. "I peel the tomatoes like this, and then we add them to the meat and beans."

"I want to do something."

"Okay. You can get me those onions and green peppers in the bottom of the refrigerator."

They worked in harmony until a big pot of chili was simmering on the stove.

"How come Vance hasn't come over?"

Sarah had asked that question twenty times since Brooke had brought her back from Mississippi last week. No one wanted the answer more than Brooke did. There'd been no word of him since Christmas Day.

"He's working."

"What kind of work?"

"He's a deputy marshal."

"What's that?"

"He helps people who are in trouble."

"Are *we* in trouble?"

Brooke smiled. "No, darling. We're not."

"I wish we were," Sarah asserted with her child's naiveté. "Then he would have to come over and help *us*."

Her faultless logic defied comment.

"If you're going to be my mommy, why can't he be my daddy?"

"Because of his job, he can't live in one place all the time. He has to travel all over the country helping people."

"But if I was his little girl, wouldn't he stay home to play with me?"

"I'm sure if you were his daughter, he would make lots of time to be with you."

"When he comes over, I'm going to ask him if I can be his daughter."

Panic set in. "Sweetie, you're going to be *my* daughter."

"But I want to be his daughter, too."

"He would have to marry me for that to happen."

"What's marry?"

Brooke heaved a troubled sigh. "When a man and a woman love each other very much, they decide to marry. That means they live together in the same house all the time. But as I told you before, Vance has to live in lots of different places."

"We could live in lots of different places with him, couldn't we?" she asked in all earnestness.

Oh, Sarah.

"I suppose we could. But we're not married."

"Then let's ask him to get married."

"Girls don't do that."

"Why not?"

"Because it's up to the man to ask the woman to marry him. He has to love her very much to do that."

"Does Vance love you very much?"

This conversation was tearing her apart. "I don't think so."

"I saw him kiss you."

She bit her lip. "I saw him kiss you, too. He was just having fun with us."

"I saw you kiss him. Do you love him very much?"

Very much. "I think he's a wonderful man. Now, young lady, while our dinner is cooking, I'm going to hop in the shower. While I'm gone, you stay in here and work at the table on printing your name with those crayons. I won't be long."

"Okay. Can I make a picture, too?"

"Of course."

She kissed the top of Sarah's head before leaving the kitchen on a run. The talk about Vance had gone on long enough. Just the mention of his name increased the worry and the ache growing inside her. When she felt her cheeks, she thought she might be running a temperature.

CHAPTER TEN

"HELLO?"

When Vance heard a little girl's voice answer on the other end, he almost dropped his cell phone. "*Sarah*?"

"Is this Vance?"

He chuckled in spite of his shock on learning that she was still living at Brooke's. "It sure is. How's my cowgirl?"

"I'm fine. When are you coming home?"

Home?

He shook his head in disbelief. "Whenever you say."

"Can you come over now?"

"Do you think that would be okay with Brooke?"

"Yes. Before she got in the shower, she said you were a wonderful man."

His heart raced faster. "Is that so?"

"Guess what? I'm going to be Brooke's daughter."

"You are?" He found himself responding exactly the way Sarah normally did.

"Yes. She came to Misisip to get me and now she's going to adopt me. My real name is Myra Lyman, but she's going to call me Sarah Longley."

A lump the size of a boulder lodged in his throat. "I'd say you're a very lucky girl to get a mother like Brooke."

"Don't you wish you had a daughter?"

His eyes misted over. *I do now.* "Of course."

"Would you like *me*?"

Lord. "I'd love to have a daughter like you."

"Okay. Then all you have to do is ask Brooke to marry you because she says girls can't ask guys."

He didn't know whether to laugh or cry. "What else did she say?"

"She says you're not married because you have to go all over the country helping people. But we could go with you, couldn't we?"

"Is that what you would like?"

"No. I'd like you to stay home with us all the time."

So would I, sweetheart. So would I. Now that the monster who stole two years of your life is behind bars, the life of a rancher sounds like heaven.

"Maybe that can be arranged."

"What does arrange mean?"

"It means I'll see what I can do to stay home all the time."

"Then we're going to get married?"

"If Brooke says it's okay."

"Wait! I'll run and ask her!"

"No, Sarah. Let me talk—"

But it was too late. He heard the receiver drop and knew the little girl had gone in search of Brooke.

While he waited for her to come back on the line, he drove through the streets of West Yellowstone with perspiration beading his brow because he feared this dream just might backfire on him.

But after the kiss he and Brooke had shared, it was all he'd been able to think about while he closed in on Charlie.

The snow, plus the vastness of the Park had made the hunt difficult, but Vance had finally caught up with him near Mammoth Falls. They'd exchanged gunfire until Charlie ran out of ammo. Vance had fired the final shot that caught him in the leg and snagged him.

Thank God it was over. Thank God he'd be seeing Brooke and Sarah within the next few minutes.

"Vance?" Sarah cried out.

By now, his heart was hammering out of control. "What is it, sweetheart? What did Brooke say?"

"She thinks you're teasing because you're a bachelor."

His smile deepened into a grin. "I used to be a bachelor, but not anymore."

"How come?"

"Because I fell in love with Brooke."

"Oh...then that's okay. She says a man has to love a woman very much to ask her to get married."

"She was right."

"When are we going to get married?"

He laughed out loud. "That's up to Brooke."

"Just a minute."

The phone banged down so hard it hurt his ears. He didn't have to wait long before she came back on the line.

"She says that maybe we should all be friends first."

"We already are," he murmured, "but I think she's right. What's for dinner?"

"Chili."

"Set me a place at the table, Sarah sweetheart. I'll be there in a minute and I'm hungry."

Close to 11:00 p.m., Sarah fell asleep on the couch. A nervous Brooke followed Vance as he carried her upstairs to Brooke's bed and settled her under the covers.

Because Sarah had answered the phone while Brooke was in the shower, the subject of marriage, which should never have been broached, was out in the open. Thank goodness Sarah had finally drifted off. Now the two of them could have a serious discussion.

When they'd gone downstairs, Brooke whirled around to face Vance. But his blue gaze wandered over her face and figure with such intensity she could hardly concentrate.

He was alive! Nothing bad had happened to him. The reality of his physical presence, his handsome features and vitality took her breath away.

"Vance..." she began awkwardly. "I hardly know what to say, where to begin. Please don't think I mentioned marriage to Sarah out of some devious plot to catch myself a husband.

"She wants so much to belong to a family, she asks for things she can't possibly have. Don't assume I took any part of the earlier conversation seriously."

The light in his eyes dimmed. "Are you saying that the idea of marrying a crusty old bachelor who doesn't call any place home is repugnant to you?"

"Of course not!" she cried too vehemently. When she realized how that sounded, she blushed and averted her head. "But you don't decide to marry someone on the strength of a child's wishes. You certainly don't make a decision like that based on one night's acquaintance."

"Under normal circumstances, I would agree with you. But the fifteen hours we spent together were illuminating for me. I think they were for you, too, if that kiss you gave me in Julia's front yard was anything to judge by. That's why I'm here. I've been dreaming about it and the way it made me feel. Make me feel like that again, Brooke," he urged in a husky voice.

"I—I think—"

"Don't think," he whispered as he pulled her into his arms. His mouth closed feverishly over hers. "Give me some of that love you've been showering on Sarah. I need it badly, just like she does."

How many times over the past few weeks had Brooke imagined him begging her to love him like this?

Later, when sanity returned, she would be shocked by her response. Right now, such powerful feelings were driving her to express her need of this man that she lost track of time and place.

The storm growing in intensity outside could never hope to match the burgeoning desire his hands and mouth aroused. She thought she'd known love with Mark, but Vance carried her into another realm where souls as well as bodies communed.

Slowly, without realizing how it had happened, she found herself lying in his arms in front of the fire. Each time the wind made moaning sounds around the corners of the house, he held her a little tighter, kissed her a little deeper.

Trying to exercise some semblance of control, she reluctantly tore her lips from his and molded a palm to the side of his rugged face. He needed a shave. She relished the raspy, masculine sensation against her fingers.

"I'm so thankful you're not out there still searching for that horrible excuse for a human being."

"Amen," he murmured into her tender neck.

"Tell me what happened. I have to know."

With a resigned sigh, he pulled her closer. For the next while, he related the details of the capture.

"After he was handcuffed, I heard from headquarters that the other convict's body, and the body of a dog, had been found in a barn in Santaquin. Both had been shot twice."

She stirred in his arms. "I hope you don't think I'm horrible for saying this, but I'm glad he's dead. Now we can tell Sarah she doesn't have to worry about the other man coming after her."

"I feel just as relieved," he muttered a trifle fiercely. "No doubt when the forensics experts finish their work, they'll have linked the bullets to Charlie's gun. The department doesn't know where the dog came from. When I heard it was white with brown spots, I suddenly realized why Sarah had mistaken the cow for a dog in your Christmas ornament."

Brooke clung to him. "She's going to need counseling."

"There was a time when I didn't believe in it, but there are certain experiences in life that require outside help."

His admission caused her to pull far enough away from him to look into his eyes. "Do you want to talk about it?" she whispered.

Slowly he nodded. "When I was on the police force, an emergency cropped up that required all officers, even those off duty, to respond. I couldn't reach my partner who had probably unplugged his phone to get some sleep. So I drove over to his apartment and let myself in the back door to wake him up. When I entered the bedroom, I discovered my fiancée in bed with him.''

Brooke cringed. What he'd just told her was far worse than anything Mark had done to her. She buried her face in his shoulder.

''A couple of my buddies had been through the same experience and suggested it wouldn't hurt to talk to a professional. They were right. When you lose your trust, you're so irrational it's almost impossible to get it back.''

''I know.''

''Julia told me about your experience,'' he confided. ''Obviously we've both come a long way since our experiences. I recognize now that I chose a shallow person to love. But I never realized just how shallow she was until I met you.

''Lord, Brooke...'' His eyes glowed like hot blue coals. ''You're a beautiful-looking woman, but the way you took Sarah in without any question or thought for yourself, I understood what a beautiful person you are on the inside. That's what I've been looking for. An inner beauty that will last forever. When Sarah answered the phone tonight and told me you were going to adopt her, I knew you were the woman I wanted to be my wife.''

Brooke heard the throb in his voice and couldn't

resist kissing him once more. "I knew I wanted you for my husband when you asked me what I thought would be the best way to gain Sarah's confidence. Your sensitivity is so rare, something inside told me I'd found the man I'd been looking for all my life. I realize it's too soon to say this—" her voice caught "—but I can't help it. I've fallen in love with you, Vance."

"I'm in love with you, too," his voice grated before his mouth covered hers once more. "I told Sarah as much over the phone. What I feel for you isn't going to go away. Love happened without my even realizing it, otherwise I wouldn't have made the decision to sleep over here on Christmas Eve."

"But you did that to keep us safe."

"That was part of it, but certainly not all. Do you honestly think I make a habit of spending the night with anyone who happens to be associated with my case load, particularly a single woman? If the marshal's office ever knew I'd done that, they'd strip me of my badge."

His words thrilled her. "That night, I was secretly hoping that maybe you didn't want to leave me."

"Now you know the truth," he murmured before he kissed her again. Several minutes later he said, "I want to stay with you forever. I want to marry you, but first I want you to meet my family. I want Sarah to get to know all the nieces and nephews she'll inherit. We have life-changing decisions to make. Sarah let me know she wants me around *all* the time."

"So do I!" Brooke cried softly.

"How do you feel about moving to Great Falls where I can do full-time ranching? That pony is just waiting for Sarah."

"I think you know how I feel." Her voice trembled. "As for Sarah, she'll be ecstatic."

His expression sobered. "If we do that, it means tearing you away from your home here, your family business."

"After you and Sarah went away," she began quietly, "I was so heartsick I decided I'd let Dave manage the store or buy me out so I could move someplace else and start a new life."

He inhaled sharply. "I like the new-life part as long as I'm included in that scenario."

"What's that scenario thing?" a young female voice broke in on them unexpectedly.

Both their heads turned toward the stairs and they cried her name at the same time. Vance held out his arms. "Come here, my little cowgirl, and I'll explain."

Sarah ran toward them as fast as her slippered

feet would go. "Are we getting married?" she demanded once she was wrapped safely in Vance's strong arms.

Brooke's face broke out in a radiant smile. "We are, darling. We are."

"Goody."

The next thing they knew she was on her feet again.

"Where are you going?" Vance wanted to know.

"I have to tell Julia! She made me promise to call the minute it was *ofishal*!" Sarah called over her shoulder.

Upon that pronouncement, the two of them collapsed with laughter in each other's arms. This was only the beginning....

An emotional new trilogy by
bestselling author

Rebecca Winters

Three dedicated bachelors meet thrills and danger
when they each fall captive to an innocent baby—
and clash mightily with three exciting women
who conquer thier restless hearts!

Look out for:

THE BILLIONAIRE AND THE BABY
(HR #3632) in December 2000

HIS VERY OWN BABY
(HR #3635) in January 2001

THE BABY DISCOVERY
(HR #3639) in February 2001

*Available in December, January and February
wherever Harlequin books are sold.*

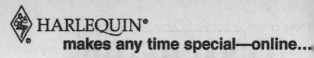

HARLEQUIN®

makes any time special—online...

eHARLEQUIN.com

shop eHarlequin

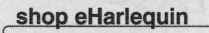

- ❤ Find all the new Harlequin releases at everyday great discounts.
- ❤ Try before you buy! Read an excerpt from the latest Harlequin novels.
- ❤ Write an online review and share your thoughts with others.

reading room

- ❤ Read our Internet exclusive daily and weekly online serials, or vote in our interactive novel.
- ❤ Talk to other readers about your favorite novels in our Reading Groups.
- ❤ Take our Choose-a-Book quiz to find the series that matches you!

authors' alcove

- ❤ Find out interesting tidbits and details about your favorite authors' lives, interests and writing habits.
- ❤ Ever dreamed of being an author? Enter our Writing Round Robin. The Winning Chapter will be published online! Or review our writing guidelines for submitting your novel.

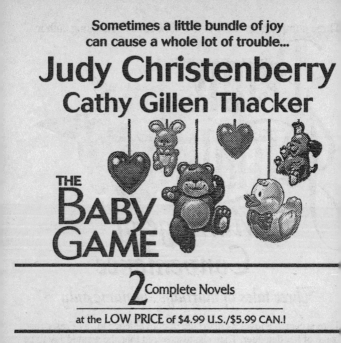